Jo Watson is an award-winning writer, whose romantic comedies were originally published on Wattpad. *Burning Moon* won a 2014 Watty Award for being one of the site's most downloaded titles and it has now had over 6 million reads. Jo is an Adidas addict and a Depeche Mode devotee. She lives in South Africa with her family.

Follow her on Twitter @JoWatsonWrites and find her on Facebook at www.facebook.com/jowatsonwrites.

Praise for Jo Watson's hilarious romantic comedies:

'Witty, enjoyable and unique' *Harlequin Junkie*

'A treat of a book' *Smut Book Junkie Book Reviews*

'Well written and lovable . . . a bundle of laughs' *The Mo Times*

'Heart-warming and raw . . . I urge you to go on this journey with Lily' *Four Chicks Flipping Pages*

By Jo Watson

Burning Moon
Almost A Bride

Burning Moon

Jo Watson

HEADLINE
ETERNAL

Published by arrangement with Forever,
an imprint of Grand Central Publishing.

First published in Great Britain in 2016

First published in paperback in Great Britain in 2017
by HEADLINE ETERNAL
An imprint of HEADLINE PUBLISHING GROUP

2

Cataloguing in Publication Data is available from the British Library

ISBN 978 1 4722 3792 7

Printed and bound in Great Britain by CPI Group (UK) Ltd, Croydon, CR0 4YY

Headline's policy is to use papers that are natural, renewable and recyclable
products and made from wood grown in well-managed forests and other
controlled sources. The logging and manufacturing processes are expected
to conform to the environmental regulations of the country of origin.

HEADLINE PUBLISHING GROUP
An Hachette UK Company
Carmelite House
50 Victoria Embankment
London EC4Y 0DZ

www.headlineeternal.com
www.headline.co.uk
www.hachette.co.uk

This book is dedicated to Wattpad
and all my amazing readers.

To Depeche Mode – many long nights,
much need for loud music.

And most importantly, to my brother James. I wrote you
into this book so you will live on in these pages.

Burning
Moon

PROLOGUE

⌒

I'm sorry, I can't.

I'm sorry, I can't.

I'm sorry, I can't.

No matter how long I stared at the scribbled note, the meaning stayed the same. I held it up hoping, praying that the sunlight would illuminate the other words that had been written in magic invisible ink.

But nothing appeared.

Just those four tiny little words…and yet they had the power to bring my whole world crashing down around me in an instant. Splintering and exploding into a million little pieces.

I finally managed to pry my eyes from the note and found myself staring into the terrified faces of my stepsister and two best friends. They were looking at me as if I was about to have a celebrity meltdown, shave my head, and then poke someone's eye out with an umbrella. They looked very concerned. Like I was a ticking time bomb waiting to explode.

And they were right.

I was.

Tick. Tick.

I was teetering on the brink of insanity. I could feel it trying to suck me in like an all-consuming black hole. The tug was almost too hard to fight.

Did I even want to fight it?

But what would happen if I let go? I knew I was in shock right now, drenched in a sort of numb, detached feeling. But I could feel the other hostile emotions bubbling their way to the surface and fighting to take control.

I blinked. My eyes were stinging.

I tried to open my mouth and speak.

It was dry and nothing came out.

I looked at my best friends Jane and Val, my rocks, the two people I could always rely on for help…But they said nothing. Not a word. Just terror plastered across their faces.

I shifted my gaze to my stepsister Stormy-Rain. Unlike her name, she was a ray of tie-dye-wearing sunshine. She had the ability to turn even the most terrible situation into a positive. *Again…nothing.* Just stupefied horror plastered across her now-ashen face.

I looked down at my shaking hands; they were crunching the corners of the note. My heart felt like it was going to break through the safe confines of my rib cage, taking my stomach and lungs with it.

Rage combined with shock and gut-wrenching sorrow, and I snapped. It overwhelmed me, rising up from the most primitive part of my soul where logic, rules, and intellect wielded no power. This was a place of red, raw, uninhibited emotion.

And so I screamed at the top of my lungs until my voice went hoarse and my throat was raspy.

"Get me out of this dress. Get me out of it. Get it off!"

My desperate fingers frantically ripped at my wedding dress, a dress that had taken my two friends ten minutes to get me into, thanks to the intricate crisscross ribbons of the bodice. But I was trapped.

Jane and Val sprang into action, simultaneously grabbing at the stubborn ribbons, but it was taking too long. The air around me became too thick to breathe, and I felt like I was drowning.

"I can't breathe. I can't breathe. It's too tight."

Val made a move for the knife that had arrived earlier with the room service, and, without hesitation, she sliced through the intricate satin ribbons. The sound of the serrated knife eviscerating them was like fingernails down a blackboard; it made my skin crawl. But I could feel the bodice getting looser and looser, until it finally slipped down my aching body and pooled lifelessly on the floor.

I was finally free.

And then the tears came. Hot, wet tears streaming down my cheeks and streaking my flushed skin with angry black mascara lines. The tears turned to sobbing.

I looked at my dress, reduced to a pathetic puddle of ribbons, satin, and beads at my feet. But I still felt trapped. *My hair!* The perfect updo, held together with delicate pearl clips. Suddenly, it felt like every strand of hair was tightening around my head, like a boa constrictor going in for the kill. My fingers ripped, desperately trying to free it from its pearly captives.

I wanted to get the pearl clips removed. Gone. Off. Out. I wanted to rub every single trace of the wedding away.

I pulled out my earrings and grabbed the nearest tissue, rubbing my red lipstick off until my lips hurt. It smeared across my face like an ugly rash.

If someone were standing outside the window looking in, they would have pegged me for a crazy person. And I wouldn't have blamed them. Because somewhere in the back of my now-estranged rational brain, I knew I looked like a lunatic escaped from a mental asylum in desperate need of a straitjacket and drastic electroshock therapy. But how the hell else should I be . . .

Because he . . .

Michael Edwards—fiancé of one year, perfect boyfriend of two—had left me, Lilly Swanson, just ten minutes before I was scheduled to walk down the aisle. The bottle of perfume that he'd wanted me to wear today, insisted I wear, because "it was his favorite," mocked me from the dressing table. So I picked it up and threw it against the wall, watching it shatter into a million pieces, just like my life. I was hit by the sweet smell of jasmine and felt sick to my stomach.

What was I going to tell the five hundred guests who were sitting in the church waiting for me? Some had even flown here to South Africa all the way from Australia.

"Hi, everyone. Thanks for coming. Guess what? SURPRISE! No wedding!"

A wedding that my father had spent a small fortune on.

A wedding that was going to be perfect.

Perfect, dammit. Perfect!

I'd made sure of that. I had painstakingly handled every single tiny detail. It had taken months and months of meticulous planning to create this day, and now what?

Things went very blurry all of a sudden. I vaguely remember my brother James bursting into the room, screaming insults and then vowing to kill him. He even punched the best man when he claimed to have no knowledge of Michael's whereabouts. My rational, logical father tried to find a legitimate motive for Michael's behavior, insisting we speak to him before jumping to any rash conclusions. Hundreds of phone calls followed: Where was he? Who had seen him? Where did he go?

At some stage the guests were told, and the rumor mill went into full swing...

He'd had an affair.

He'd eloped with someone else.

He was a criminal on the run.

He was gay.

He'd been beamed up by aliens and was being experimented on. (Hopefully it was painful.)

People threw around bad words like *bastard*, *asshole*, and *liar*. They also threw around words like *shame*, *sorry*, and *pity*. They wondered whether they should take their wedding gifts back or leave them. What was the correct protocol in a situation like this?

While the world around me was going mad, I felt a strange calm descend. Nothing seemed real anymore, and I began to feel like a voyeur looking at my life from a distance. I didn't care that I was sitting on the floor in my bra and panties. I didn't care that my mascara and lipstick were so smudged I looked like Batman's Joker. I just didn't care.

Some minutes later my other brother Adam, the doctor, burst in and insisted I drink a Coke and swallow the little white pill he was forcing down my throat. It would calm me, he said.

Shortly after that, my overly dramatic, theater-actress mother rushed in to give the performance of her life.

"Why, why, why?" She placed her hand across her heart.

"What is this, a madness most discreet? A stench most foul?" She held her head and cried out, "Whyyy?!"

"For heaven's sake, Ida, this isn't some Shakespearean bloody play." I could hear the anger in my father's voice. Even after eighteen years of divorce, they still couldn't be civil to each other.

"Lest I remind you that all the world is a stage," my mother shouted back, the deep timbre in her voice quivering for added dramatic tension as she tilted her head upward and clenched her jaw.

"There you go again with your crap! Clearly you still haven't learned to separate fantasy from reality!"

"Well, I managed to do that with our marriage!"

Adam jumped between them. "Stop it. This isn't the time!"

And then all pandemonium broke out.

The priest came around to offer some kind of spiritual guidance but exited quickly, and very red-faced, when he saw my state of undress. Some inquisitive relatives stuck their heads through the door, painted with sad, sorry puppy-dog looks, but they, too, left when they saw me spread-eagled on the floor.

An enormous ruckus ensued when the photographer burst in and started taking photos of me—no one had told him. The ruckus became a total freak show when my favorite cousin, Annie, who had designed my dress for free as a wedding gift, saw the state of her "best creation" lying crumpled and torn on the floor. She looked like she was about to cry.

Then the room went very blurry and the noises around me combined into one strange drone.

I closed my eyes and everything went black.

CHAPTER ONE

I woke up with a big happy yawn, pulling the crisp white linen of my duvet down and stretching my sleepy legs. The sun was rushing into my apartment and the birds were chirping in the newly blossoming trees. I could just make out the soft, sweet smell of flowers on the warm morning breeze. *Wow, this is the perfect spring morning. This is the perfect day to get married.* I skipped out of bed, excited for the day ahead, and then I saw it…

My wedding dress. Draped over the chair like a dead, decapitated duck.

Like a sledgehammer to my stomach, those four little words came slamming back. The words that he'd scribbled in messy cursive on a crappy piece of torn paper and slipped under the door like a coward. I scrambled for my cell phone. My frantic fingers slid across the touch screen, running through the twenty-two messages that were lighting it up. They were from my friends, my family, my coworkers, my pedicurist, and even my mother's psychic (who was clearly going to get fired!).

But nothing from Michael.

I logged on to Facebook, heart racing with anticipation, and went straight to his page. No new activity. I went to Twitter, also nothing. I checked to see if he was still following me. He was. I checked Instagram, but again, there was no recent sign of life. It was as if he'd dropped off the face of the social media planet, which was completely unlike him. Michael couldn't sharpen a pencil without tweeting about it. He couldn't buy a pair of shoelaces without Instagramming a picture of them, and he couldn't scratch his head without sharing his thoughts on Facebook. It had been one of the *only* things I disliked about him. *Past tense.* Now there were many.

My mind went into overdrive as a series of disgusting thoughts battered their way in.

Where the flaming fuck was he? Was he holed up in a sketchy pay-by-the-hour hotel with some slutty thigh-high-boot-wearing stripper with tassels and an STD? Was he partying up a storm, celebrating the fact that he'd missed the wedding and dodged a bullet?

I was grateful when the rich smell of coffee and fatty sausages being cooked yanked me back to reality and gave me something physical to focus on. Because I suddenly realized that I was starving. More hungry than I'd ever been in my entire life. I followed my growling stomach into the kitchen, where I found my friends and family keeping vigil around the table. A chorus of caring hellos rang out. The only response I could muster was a halfhearted nod.

But it wasn't long before they flocked. They'd always been over-protective that way. Adam rushed to my side with a glass of orange juice, a capsule for my headache, and a prescription for those little white pills. I'm sure he would've taken my temperature and blood pressure and set up an IV if I'd let him. Val and Jane ushered me to a seat, Stormy-Rain waved some incense around and brought me a cup of herbal tea with what looked like dead, drowned flowers floating in it, and even Buttons, my usually unaffectionate cat, rubbed herself at my ankles. It felt like a hundred pairs of eyes were staring at me. They all looked expectant, as if I was meant to say something. A sickening, awkward silence filled the room. Finally someone spoke.

"How did you sleep?" Annie asked.

I nodded. "Fine. Sorry about the dress…"

"Oh God. No! Please. Don't worry about it." She jumped up. "Besides, perhaps it will start a whole new trend…derelict wedding wear." She smiled at me and I was so touched at her attempt at a joke that a small tear oozed out of my eye.

Then the loud *click-clack* of expensive heels marched past me. "I swear, don't push me on this. I might just advise my client to seek damages on the grounds of emotional injury. Not to mention damages for the money spent on the wedding."

My sister-in-law, Sara, feisty lawyer and wearer of impossibly high heels, was shouting threats down her phone. She'd been trying to track Michael down all morning, speaking to every single one of his relatives, no matter how distant and thrice removed. But no luck. Michael was nowhere to be found and now she was threatening to call in her private investigator, Lizzy Brown. My stomach growled again, angry that I'd ignored it, and I pulled the plate of sausages toward me. I'd been dieting for months, trying to squeeze my naturally voluptuous figure into that dress, especially after Michael had pointed out a few extra creeping pounds.

In fact, I was sure I deserved a gold medal or some other accolade for the amount of time I'd spent fat-cell busting on the treadmill. I hadn't eaten saturated fat or been in the same room as a carbohydrate for at least three months, and now…I was going to make up for it.

I grabbed the sausage and shoveled it into my gaping beak, washing it down with the glass of orange juice and a butter-laden bagel. Everyone stared at me, but no one dared to speak.

"Val." The sausage almost fell out of my mouth as I tried to talk. "Val, I need you to go down to the shops and buy me two, no, *five* Mars Bar chocolates, six bags of Jelly Babies, and bread—I *need* bread."

Right now, I needed bread like a junkie needed their early morning fix. Before I'd even finished giving Val these instructions, I'd already started killing a crumpet, dragging it through syrup and practically inhaling it. No one ventured to argue or suggest that I shouldn't mainline with pure sugar. Val jumped into action and scuttled out the door.

She returned ten minutes later with my bounty. But the food could push the emotions away only for so long. I looked up at the clock. The minute hand seemed to be ticking in slow motion, and I felt like I was trapped in a surreal dream, where the landscape was tilting and the clock face was melting down the kitchen wall like a Salvador Dalí painting. It was hard to walk; my brain was struggling to send messages to my sluggish legs, which were now encased in psychosomatic concrete.

I crawled to the living room and poured myself onto the couch, clutching a bag of newly acquired Jelly Babies. Friends and family took turns sticking their heads through the door. I suspect they didn't want to let me out of their sights. I needed a distraction. *Badly.* I flipped to a reality show, confident that I would find solace there. Someone always had it worse—like the guy with four arms and wayward warts, or the person trapped in their house under the piles of magazines and toothbrushes that they'd been hoarding since 1966, or, better still, the woman who went into labor while trapped on a steep cliff face in the Himalayas, or someone equally morbidly fascinating. But the current show was about a guy who baked cakes, and unless his arm got trapped in the electric mixer and he was forced to gnaw it free with his teeth, I wasn't interested.

I was happy when the overwhelming crowd finally left and Jane, Val, Annie, and Stormy-Rain joined me in the lounge. The fearsome fivesome. That's what we'd called ourselves as teenagers, and we'd always been there for one another, no matter what.

"So now what?" The tears welled up again. "What do I do next?"

"I don't know." Jane took me by the hand. "But we're all here for you, whatever you need."

"Whatever!" The others all echoed the sentiment.

I felt mildly better knowing that they were there for me. I thought back to the time that we'd all rallied around Jane when she'd found herself in a very embarrassing public scene with her then-boyfriend and his secret mistress. It had not been pretty, and at the time, she didn't think she would survive the pain and humiliation, but she'd come through it fine.

Maybe I would be okay, too? *One day.*

But right now, the future looked pretty damn bleak.

"Why did he do this?" I angrily bit the head off a Jelly Baby and obliterated it between my molars. What the hell had I done to deserve this? Was Karma trying to punish me for something?

But none of them could supply an answer. My mind replayed our last interaction over and over again. We'd eaten breakfast together two mornings ago before I'd checked into the hotel. We'd drunk espresso. We'd chatted about the wedding and what to do if my mother got drunk and started singing show tunes—a common occurrence at all family gatherings.

He'd kissed me good-bye.

He'd told me he loved me.

He'd said he couldn't wait to see me walking down the aisle.

So what the hell had happened?

Maybe he *was* having an affair? But how? We practically lived together. Maybe it was something more benign; perhaps he was just scared? Or maybe he was worried about marrying a woman he'd barely taken out for a test-drive. We'd had sex only a few times. I wasn't exactly the most sexual person around. Twenty-four and basically an almost-virgin! It all seemed so stupid and pathetic now in the face of so many maybes.

I dismembered another Jelly Baby, legs first this time, and that's when I noticed my engagement ring. The perfect princess-cut two-carat diamond made my stomach churn, and I ripped it off my finger, leaving a red mark behind. We all stared at it for a moment in absolute silence, and then Val spoke.

"Pawn it. Sell it and buy yourself something awesome. Like a Porsche sports car." Michael was pretty flashy with money, and my ring was no exception.

"No!" Stormy jumped in excitedly. "Let's burn it in a sacrificial fire. We'll dance and chant the bad vibes away."

"Yes!" Annie cried. "In fact, let's burn everything of his, starting with those revolting corduroy pants he always insisted on wearing!"

"I could give him a root canal without anesthetic if you'd like?" Jane piped up. She was studying to be a dentist.

I inspected my ring. It was so beautiful. And I hated it.

It reminded me of him and the empty promises he'd made. In fact, everything reminded me of him. His presence was rudely painted across everything I owned. The couch I was lying on, the TV that he'd hung on the wall, the carpet he used to trip on, and the happy photos of our beach vacation on the coffee table.

Oh my God, the honeymoon!

We were meant to be leaving for Thailand this afternoon! We had very expensive, paid-for-in-full reservations for the honeymoon suite at the White Sands Hotel and Spa. I cringed at the thought.

"I can't take this anymore. I have to phone him." I pulled my phone out and started dialing the number that felt ingrained in my DNA. But before I could finish, Annie snatched it away.

"Wait. Just think about this for a second. What are you going to say to him?"

"I don't know."

"Won't talking to him just make it worse?" Jane offered. "And what if he doesn't answer? No one's been able to get ahold of him."

"Or…" Val spoke. Her tone was sensitive. "What if he tells you something you're not strong enough to hear right now?"

"Like what?" I felt my stomach tighten into sickening knots. "Do you think there's someone else?"

Annie hugged me. "I don't know, sweetie. But I do know it's a bad idea to phone him now. Give yourself a little time to calm down."

I glanced around at my friends and something dawned on me. "I love you guys, but you are the worst people in the world to be giving relationship advice." A look of mutual acknowledgment swept over their faces.

"Stormy," I started, "you date guys for three weeks tops before you break up with them and the last guy was a fire breather."

"Juggler. Fire juggler," she corrected.

"I rest my case. Val, you've been secretly in love with your neighbor for years and haven't told him."

Val nodded. "I can't deny it."

"Jane, the last guy you dated spoke Klingon to you…in bed."

The others burst out laughing. This had been the subject of much amusement lately.

"I wouldn't laugh, Annie." I waggled a finger at her. "Remember Xavier?"

Annie lowered her eyes self-consciously.

"The 'avant-garde' fashion designer who is definitely gay and really named Jeff."

"Fair enough," Annie conceded.

I sighed loudly. Despite their sketchy track record with relationships, my friends were right. Calling Michael was a bad idea. "Fine. I won't call him, but I need a drink."

"Negative. Contraindicated with those pills you're taking, as they are both central nervous system depressants," Jane spoke.

I looked at her blankly.

"I think what she means is it will probably make you go as mad as a capper," Stormy, the serial idiom-mixer, clarified in her own special way.

"Fine. Then bring me another chocolate!"

***

There are moments in a person's life that change everything. Shake things up. Steer you in a different direction and push you onto another course, toward different people, places, and things. These moments don't come around often, but when they do, they rip through the very fabric of your world.

I knew that this was one of those moments. I knew this because I'd had one of them before when I was twelve.

Ever since that age, I'd known exactly what I wanted from life. I had planned it down to a T, to the second, to the minutest detail imaginable. The reason for this, I guess, was that I'd been shown a very good example of how *not* to live—thanks to my dramatic mother. She was a theater actress of some fame and status, which was something she liked to remind everyone of...*constantly*. After she divorced my dad when I was six, I endured what could only be described as hell. We moved around frequently, from one play to the next, one rehearsal to the next, one man to the next. The musician, the actor, the director, the yoga teacher, the voice coach, and even some magician who turned out to be a criminal. When they locked him up, he vowed to escape, as "no handcuff could hold him." To my knowledge he's still there.

My mother had terrible taste in men. She was drawn to bad men like a hippie was drawn to tie-dyed T-shirts and world peace. She also had some rather terrible hobbies: drunken, scantily clad parties laced with cocaine were a regular occurrence. On many occasions, while on my way to school, I'd have to navigate my way through a sea of unconscious bodies lying limp and littered across our living room floor. My dad finally won the custody battle when I was twelve, and that's when everything changed for the better.

I moved into an ordered world of perfect symmetry and seamlessly structured routine. A beautiful, neat home with a stepmom who drove me to school and cheered me on at hockey practice and two older brothers who adored me. We took holidays twice a year to the same place, our beach cottage on the beautiful Natal Coast of South Africa, and ate the same meals on the same days of the week. My new life was predictable and I loved it. My "new" family took me under their wing as if I were a damaged little bird, which at the time I was.

I loved my new life so much that I vowed mine would be exactly the same. Everything would have its place and everything would fall in line with my plan.

Michael had been part of that plan:

Graduate top of my class, go to college, earn my degree, work at my dad's auditing firm. Married by twenty-five (at the latest). First child by twenty-six. Two boys and two girls. Live in a double-story house in a leafy suburb not too far away from my family. Vacations at the cottage. Roast chicken on Sundays.

But in less than twenty-four hours, my entire plan had gone up in a puff of stinking smoke. I wasn't just not getting married; I was losing everything that I'd meticulously planned for since the age of twelve. And then another thought hit me. A memory that made my body ache.

"Won't it be romantic if we conceived our baby on our honeymoon?" Michael had said one night.

I rubbed my throat. The lump that was forming made it hard to swallow.

I started to cry again. I grabbed the remote and randomly pressed buttons until I got to the nature channel…

Swirling, turquoise waters. White sands made luminescent by a low-hanging tropical sun. Massive palms, swaying seductively in the cool sea breeze and gentle waves lapping on the shore. It all looked so peaceful. So beautiful and, most importantly, *so remote*.

So, so far away from the farce that had just become my life.

And then a thought hit me. It was so decisive, and it slammed into me with such force that I almost fell off the couch in shock. It was also, by far, the craziest thought I'd ever had in all my twenty-four years on this planet. A part of me couldn't believe it was even mine.

I was going to go on my honeymoon! Alone.

I leapt off the couch, suddenly imbued with purpose. I ran into my bedroom and rummaged through the drawers for my passport and ticket. *Crap!* The flight was leaving in a few hours and I hadn't packed yet. My brain went into hyperdrive trying to upload the list of things I needed to take with me as I tore around my apartment tossing whatever I could find into a bag. I grabbed Buttons and dropped her off with my neighbor, a lonely old woman with a purple rinse who loved nothing more than painting my cat's claws and knitting her little jerseys.

I thought about my friends and family. I knew they'd be worried and wouldn't want me to go. So I decided it would be better to send them a text from the plane, when it would be too late to talk me out of it. I typed the message so it would be ready to send.

Guys, I'm going on my honeymoon by myself. Don't worry about me. I'm going to be fine. Love you all and thanks for the support. XoXo

An hour and fifteen minutes later I was sprinting through O. R. Tambo International Airport. People gaped and stared at me like I was a woman possessed, but I pressed on. The gates were about to close and I was officially the last person to board. I could even hear them calling my name over the booming intercom. I finally boarded the plane in such a flustered state that it took me a minute or two to notice the stares being thrown my direction. Clearly the other passengers weren't pleased I'd kept them waiting. But quite frankly, I didn't care.

Heart pounding like a racehorse and out of breath, I collapsed into my chair, pressed send, fastened my seat belt, sat back, and tried to relax.

But I couldn't.

I felt unnerved. I had an eerie feeling that I was being watched. And I was. I turned to investigate and was met by a pair of dark, piercing eyes. The eyes belonged to a guy sitting two rows away. Pitch-black hair framed angular, unusual features, which came together in the most dangerous face I'd ever seen. He was dressed in black. Black sneakers, black pants, and an old, faded black shirt that gave off a distinctly *I don't give a flying fuck* attitude. I could see the hard geometric lines of a tattoo peeping out of his sleeve. He was clearly a drug addict, or a drummer in a goth band, and he was definitely depressed and into vampire movies! His face was cold and serious, but then...

Then...

The corners of his mouth curved into the slightest crooked smile as he glanced from my feet to my face and back again. I felt the lick of his eyes on my skin as he gave me the once-, twice-over. And although I was fully clothed, I'd never felt more naked in my entire life. I turned away as quickly as possible, but even with my back to him, I could still feel his probing, dark eyes.

And then indignation rose up inside me. *Who the hell did he think he was, looking at me like that?* I decided the best way to deal with this situation was to turn around and face him with all the defiance I could muster. So I swung around with bravado, my accusing eyes met his, and I surprised myself when a word came tumbling out.

"What?" I glared at him.

His smile grew bigger, and a twinkle illuminated his black eyes as he looked down at my feet. My eyes followed his and that's when I came face-to-face with two pairs of goggly eyes. They were attached to two pink, fluffy bunnies, with cute pink noses and big floppy ears.

I'm wearing my slippers!

I could feel my face going red-hot with embarrassment. My eyes looked from my slippers to my pants and then up to my top. And I realized that I wasn't just wearing my slippers…

I'm wearing my pajamas!

CHAPTER TWO

*Have you ever tried to relax when you're so embarrassed that all you want to do is climb under a bush or, in my case, into the overhead storage compartment and into someone's hand luggage? Have you ever tried to relax when you know there are dozens of curious eyes watching you? Dozens of lips curled into smirks, brows raised in query. The sound of whispers all around.

"Oh my God, Tony, look at what that poor girl's wearing."

"She must be mad."

"She's probably sick."

"Shame, maybe she's depressed or schizophrenic or something sad like that."

Yep, at this stage telling me to "sit back, relax, and enjoy the flight," like the overly enthusiastic stewardess was doing, was just not going work. It was like telling a patient at the gynecologist's office, with her legs up in stirrups, *"Relax...you won't feel a thing."*

At least I was able to dispose of the slippers under the seat. Unfortunately, what I wasn't able to dispose of were my bright-pink, practically luminous pajamas with the picture of the smiling fork and spoon holding hands plastered across the front, with the slogan that read SPOONING LEADS TO FORKING.

Annie had given them to me at my bachelorette party. And, oh, how we'd laughed! Ha-ha-ha-ha…

I certainly wasn't laughing now. Even if everyone else was.

But it was the inevitable toilet run that I was dreading the most. I'd been holding it in for as long as humanly possible, but with each passing moment, and each pass of the drinks cart, it was becoming harder. I'd even rejected the free alcohol that had been offered to me in an attempt to keep it at bay. But finally, seven hours into the flight, I realized that my camel-like bladder was failing. And I knew it was time to make the walk of shame.

I glanced in the direction of the restroom; my seat couldn't be farther away from it if I'd been sitting on the wing of another airplane. There were at least thirty rows of people between me and my destination. I took a deep breath, trying to psych myself up—it wouldn't be that bad. I'd already suffered the worst humiliation in the world; this would be a piece of cake in comparison. So what if a hundred people were about to see me in my pj's. It wouldn't be that bad, surely?

I got up, my legs shaking and my mouth dry. I started shuffling down the aisle and decided I would smile at people as I went. Perhaps if I looked friendly, they wouldn't notice the blindingly pink pajamas. But I think the smiling only made it worse.

I carried on walking; a mother put her hand over her son's eyes when she saw him starting to figure out what my pajamas meant. Another mother pulled her child close…She looked frightened. At one point a man gave me a little *meow* and another one winked. A few seats up a group of giggly teenage girls turned their selfie stick on me and took a photo. Wasn't that a bit excessive? I threw my head back and tried to look dignified, but inside I was dying.

I was so happy and overcome with relief when I finally reached the toilet that I flung open the door and practically hurled myself inside…

Whack! Thump!

I bumped into something. Very hard. When I finally oriented myself, I came face-to-face with Goth Guy—that's what I'd named him as I'd mentally cursed him for several minutes after our initial contact—and he was rubbing his head.

"What happened?" I asked. I could see he was clearly in pain.

"I just got beaten up by a girl, that's what happened."

I gasped. "I'm so sorry, I didn't know anyone was in here."

"Don't worry, it's my fault. I was just washing my hands so didn't bother locking the door." He was still rubbing his head and when he took his hand away, I could see a small red mark.

"Oh my God! You're hurt." I was so embarrassed.

"It's okay. I'll get you back when you least expect it," he said, and shot me a wicked smile.

I felt a shiver shoot up my spine. What was he saying? That when I was sleeping, he was going to creep up behind me and whack me over the head? I eyed him up and down. If this comment had come from anyone else, I would've been able to dismiss it as a joke. But coming from him, I wasn't sure.

He must have sensed my concern, because suddenly he extended his hand.

"Hi there." He had a normal South African accent like mine,

which surprised me. I was expecting something darker, and more vampirical-sounding.

"We haven't officially met yet. I'm Damian."

Aha! Now that was more like it. Wasn't there a horror movie where Satan's child was named Damian? This I could work with. I'd expected a Lucifer or a Xavier or Beelzebub or something equally evil-sounding.

"I'm Lilly," I said dismissively. The last thing I wanted was to encourage interaction with him. Especially when I noticed a leather cuff on his wrist and a tattoo on his forearm that read *Depeche Mode*. My suspicions about him were definitely confirmed.

He smiled that crooked smile at me again. "Well it was nice to kind of meet you, Lilly." And then he walked away. I stared after him, reflecting on the two interactions we'd had.

Bizarre!

Truly bizarre.

He was the weirdest person I'd ever met.

My bladder gurgled at me, if that's even possible, and I jumped inside. I'd never been happier to see a toilet in my life and the relief was instant. But when I got up and caught my reflection in the mirror, I came face-to-face with what could only be described as a monster.

I stared.

Tilted my head up. Tilted it down.

I turned profile—hoping that the apparition had a better side.

It didn't.

Black mascara lines crisscrossed my face like a zebra's stripes, the smeared red lipstick made me look like I had some kind of contagious rash, and my hair was so large and bushy that a flock of seagulls could've easily moved into it. At the back of my head I could see one poor pearl clip desperately clinging on for life.

I grabbed some toilet paper and tried to wipe the mess off my face. It didn't budge and I cursed the fact that I'd chosen to wear that ColorStay lipstick that promised seventy-two hours of kissable color. At least the stuff worked, not like some of the other products I've been conned into buying.

"Apply daily for lashes that appear two hundred times thicker, stronger, and longer..."

Why exactly? So you can go bungee jumping on them.

I sighed. This world was so full of empty promises.

* * *

Two hours and *only* one glass of wine later, I started feeling woozy.

Very, very woozy. I looked around and the aisle was undulating. The plane was tilting and the chair I was sitting on had turned to jelly. Very disturbing. Suddenly I heard a *pssst*.

"Hey, pssst! Pssst!"

The noise was coming from the direction of the floor, so I glanced down and that's when the two pairs of goggly eyes winked at me. *Really, truly, my slippers winked at me!* One even turned to the other and said something.

"She doesn't look very well, does she?"

"No, no," the other bunny said in a British accent. *"Pale. Very pale."*

I looked around to see if anyone else had heard them, but everyone's faces had started melting. I began to panic—my heart started pounding and my palms became very sweaty. What was happening to me? And then I remembered…my brother's little white pills! I'd taken one earlier. *Crap!* Jane had warned me not to drink alcohol.

I was struck by a sudden wave of intense nausea. My head started spinning, my arms felt like they were floating, and the bunnies began laughing. The waves of nausea were becoming more and more intense, and I didn't think I could fight it any longer. I turned to look at the restroom; it was so, so far away.

I had just suffered through the worst twenty-four hours of my entire life, and now it was going to get worse? The injustice of it stung me as I angrily grabbed the sick bag.

Please, please, please, please, please no…

If this had been a movie, this is when the director would have cut away to show the reactions on the other passengers' faces.

The woman next to me recoiled.

The man in the row behind me gagged.

The kid to my left started laughing and pointing.

The elderly couple to my right clutched each other and whispered something.

I looked down at my slippers; they weren't moving anymore and I realized I felt instantly better—physically, that is. Emotionally, I was a total wreck and beyond embarrassment. I started to wonder if I'd been cast in some kind of elaborate reality show where everyone was in on it, except me. A show where the producers were plotting against me, making sure I was having the worst time of my life. Or was it that bitch Karma again?

I felt so alone and put my head in my hands, wishing that the plane would just crash. Or at least that the roof would rip off and I'd be sucked out. Of course, I didn't want to end up like those people in the Andes who were forced to eat one another just to survive, but still I wanted out.

And I wanted Michael.

I wanted him so badly it hurt. I wanted to be going on my honeymoon right now, to be married, to be happy and holding hands and—

"Lilly, are you okay?" Goth Guy had gotten out of his seat and was crouching in the aisle next to me. He looked genuinely concerned.

Why did he care? And then in a move that completely surprised me, he placed a gentle hand on my shoulder.

"I feel a bit better now," I offered timidly.

"Can I get you a Coke? It's good for nausea…" But before I'd even replied, Goth Guy was already up and getting one. I was taken aback by the unexpected act of kindness from the strange stranger. Surely he was the least likely person on this plane to care? If you'd asked me a few minutes ago, I would have said that he was probably most likely to steal your handbag and dance naked around a fire in the woods.

He returned with the Coke and cracked it open. I sipped the cool liquid, and he was right, I did feel better.

"Thanks." He was quite close to me now, and I used the opportunity to inspect him further. Although he wasn't my type, *at all*, there was something attractive about him in a dirty-rock-star-Pirates-of-the-Caribbean type of way. I noticed another tattoo on the underside of his noncuffed wrist; it was a small pink heart, and it looked so out of place next to the strong geometric lines of the others. It was almost cute. Something he was definitely *not*.

"What's that?" I was intrigued by it.

Goth Guy glanced down. "It's for my little sister. She died."

And with that, he was gone.

Clearly I'd offended him, and I felt terrible. I'd offended the only person on the entire plane who had been nice to me.

I watched him sit down, and I was hoping he'd turn around so I could try to communicate a silent apology. But he didn't. Instead he put on his headphones and closed his eyes.

CHAPTER THREE

ᴄ

I don't love flying.

There's nothing normal about being forty thousand feet above sea level in a glorified sardine can.

I have two main fears, really. Firstly, that we'll simply fall out of the sky and plummet to our grisly deaths, and secondly, that when we land the brakes will fail and we'll go thundering into a building, burst into flames, and blow up—of course, it doesn't help that I've seen the exact same thing unfold on a TV show about plane crashes.

But this never happens. *(Knock on wood.)*

But what *does* always happen is that the split second the plane comes into contact with the ground, people jump up, practically leap, and throw themselves at the storage compartments for the start of the great bag jostle.

I've never understood the urgency. I didn't feel physically strong enough to fight for my bag or stand in line for ten minutes while I waited for the doors to open, so I just sat there. Goth Guy was already up, and I wanted to say something to him, but he was too far away.

The interior of the Phuket airport was bustling, and all the sudden noise and movement made me feel sick again. I leaned against a pillar and took a deep breath, hoping it would quell the sick feeling, lest I embarrass myself again in front of an entirely new audience.

After a few breaths the feeling dissipated and I was finally able to look around and orient myself. I glanced at the clock on the wall and reset my watch to local time. A hotel shuttle was fetching me in an hour and a half, so I had plenty of time to get my bags, go through customs, and maybe even squeeze in some duty-free shopping. Perhaps things were looking up after all—but then I got to the luggage carousel.

What is it about airports that make people lose all sense of propriety, politeness, patience, and anything else that resembles manners? People shoved. They pushed. They elbowed one another and acted as if getting their bag one second before the next guy was more important than finding a cure for cancer.

I saw Damian through the marauding crowd and knew that this would be my last chance to say something to him.

I tapped him on the shoulder. "Hey." I smiled apologetically. "I never got a chance to thank you for helping me earlier." I was trying to find an indirect way of saying it without causing more offense.

"No prob." He looked at me again with those black eyes; they really were startling. "I'm sorry for walking away like that. I just…didn't expect that."

I jumped in. "No, I'm sorry. That was out of line, I shouldn't have asked."

"It's okay. You just caught me off guard. It's not something I usually talk to people about."

His candor surprised me, and I was about to say something about his right to privacy when five security guards interrupted us. I smiled at them, but they didn't look friendly. In fact, they circled like vultures around a carcass. I had a very bad feeling about this.

"Can I see your passports?" the guy with a face like a bulldog asked.

I pulled mine out immediately and handed it over, but Damian objected.

"This is so typical. It's discrimination. I'm not giving it to you."

What was he talking about? Was I missing something? I looked from him to Bulldog and back again.

Bulldog growled. "Give me your passport." His eyes blazed with aggression.

Damian stared back at him indignantly. "No."

The tension was building and the other vultures stepped forward, pecking at us with their evil eyeballs.

"What's going on?" I was suddenly very nervous.

Damian turned to me. "What's going on here is a clear case of ignorance and discrimination."

"But they're just asking for our passports," I offered.

"No, they're not!" Damian was adamant.

Now I was really confused and the vultures came even closer.

And then it happened. And it happened so damn fast. They swooped, they grabbed, they handcuffed and then dragged us across the room.

"Hey," I was screaming. "What are you doing?"

There was a lot of loud angry shouting in Thai, and several more vulture guards came lunging over. And then, for the third time that day, people gawked at me. Accusatory looks, and looks of horror and disgust, were thrown in my direction. I recognized some of the faces from the plane; many of them were nodding at one another with knowing looks. Their suspicions about me had been confirmed.

"I told you, Tony. She's a total criminal."

"Please, the hotel shuttle will be here any minute to pick me up. I have to get my bags and get to my hotel. Just tell me what's happening?" No response. They didn't even look at me. At least if I knew what was going on, I could have defended myself and proved to them that I was innocent of whatever crime they thought I'd committed. No such luck. They dragged us into a small, miserable-looking room. The type of room that hardened criminals are kept in.

"I know my rights!" I screeched. "My sister-in-law is a very powerful lawyer, and if I phone her and tell them what's going on, she'll be on the next flight over here and you'll all be in trouble." I was over being nice.

I took out my phone but before I could press a single button, it was whipped away from me and taken out of the room. I heard a loud click and swung around to see my suitcase being pried open and rummaged through.

"Hey, what are you doing? Those are my clothes!" I glanced at Damian, who looked totally unperturbed as someone started tearing his backpack apart.

"Damian!" My voice was demanding. "What's going on?"

"They think we're drug smugglers."

"What!" I shrieked. "That's ridiculous. Why?"

"I told you, discrimination. It's happened to me before. They see someone with a tattoo and black clothes and assume."

Something red flew past my face. It was my honeymoon underwear. A little lacy risqué number that was *so* not me! I went crimson with embarrassment as the tiny swath of see-through fabric went flying through the air and landed on the table just inches from Damian. I shot up, practically slid across the table, and grabbed them, which only ended up drawing more attention to the itty-bitty red things.

He looked up at me and smiled, which made my blood boil.

"This is all your fault." I was furious.

"How is this my fault?"

"Well, obviously, I'm only guilty by association. I was talking to you and you're the one who looks like a drug smuggler."

I could see this statement hit a nerve. "I hate to break this to you, Lilly, but you're the one who looks like she's smuggling drugs. In fact, you look like a junkie on a very bad comedown in those pajamas, with your black eyes and red face. I'm the one who's probably guilty by association."

My heart dropped. I was so offended. But I also knew he was right. I slunk back into my seat, devastated, and watched them pull my suitcase to pieces. But when it became clear they weren't going to find anything, they left. I was happy they'd gone, but I wasn't happy to be alone in a room with Damian.

And so we sat in silence and waited. And waited. And waited.

It was awkward.

I was embarrassed.

And I was angry.

I could feel him looking at me from time to time, but I refused to shift my gaze. I also refused to cry, which was difficult, because the tears were close to the surface now. At some stage I glanced at my watch and realized we'd been there for two hours—so much for my hotel transfer.

After what seemed like another hour, the door finally opened and two new vulture guards walked in: one male, one female. The guy grabbed Damian and dragged him out, while the female approached me looking very suspicious and wearing a latex glove.

Not a chance! *Not a chance in hell!* I jumped out of my seat and ran to the other end of the room, but when the glove followed me, I flipped.

And for the second time in two days, I lost it.

I screamed and flapped my arms. "Please, I am *not* a drug addict or smuggler and any resemblance to one is because I have had the shittiest two days of my life. I mean total S-H-I-T." I spelled it out for added drama. "Crap. The worst, crappiest, crap day you can ever crapping imagine."

Like I said, I lost it.

"Yesterday was supposed to be my wedding and my fiancé decided it would be fun to leave me at the altar in front of five hundred guests. Fun, right? Yay, for me. Woo-hoo!" Yes, I definitely lost it. "The only reason I look like this is because I've been feeling like a mad cow for the past twenty-four hours, barely able to move off the couch or stop eating sugar! I've probably put on ten pounds in the past day. And guess what? This trip is supposed to be my honeymoon, and do you see a husband anywhere? *NO!* That guy's not my husband. I don't even know him."

I slumped against the wall feeling utterly defeated. "This was the worst decision of my life coming here. Clearly I'm off my rocker and need to be locked up somewhere. So please, *please* I beg you, don't stick that thing up my…!"

And then I started to cry. I couldn't hold back, and I hated myself for showing that kind of vulnerability to a total stranger with a latex glove. The woman studied me curiously and then called out to someone else in Thai.

Another woman rushed into the room and looked at me with horror. She shook her head violently and spoke.

"Bastard," she said in her thick Thai accent.

"I beg your pardon?" Was she talking about Damian?

"He left you on the wedding." Her English was broken. "You were in dress?"

I nodded. The women said something to each other and shook their heads again.

"This happen to my friend. We say he was bad man. She not listen. But better you know what bad man he is before wedding." She was right. I nodded.

And then another woman joined them; clearly I was speaking some kind of universal language here. Suddenly we were sisters, bonded together in our collective disgust and disapproval of men's actions.

"You must find someone else. He not worth time! You very pretty," said the new woman who'd joined in. One of them handed me a tissue and then a lot of tutting and oohing and head shaking took place.

I smiled; it was the first time that day. One of the women even brought me a chocolate—clearly chocolate is the universal currency for the brokenhearted. I discovered that their names were Ang, Piti, and Ginjan, and they were only too happy to listen as I regaled my woeful story.

I was more than happy to throw the words *bastard* and *lying* and *asshole* around a few times; it made me feel better and my attentive audience lapped it up. They nodded, shook their heads, and said some loud things in Thai. After a few much-needed minutes of female bonding and a lot of expletives, the ladies said I could go free.

We all hugged one another and threw a few more bad words around for the hell of it.

I was relieved to be free, and even more relieved that I could finally get out of my pajamas and slippers. I collected my scattered clothes from the floor and started packing them back into my bag. I chose a pair of jeans and a white T-shirt and glanced around for a place to change. But there was nowhere. I'd have to do it quickly and hope no one walked in. As fast as humanly possible, I pulled off my offensive pajamas.

"Take that, you little bastards," I said as I tossed them and the slippers into the nearby dustbin. I then bent down to pull up my jeans...and that's when I noticed it.

The wall behind me was nothing more than two partitions pushed together. There was a large gap between them, and I approached it. I pressed my eye to the gap and there sat Damian, looking at me.

Shit! Three questions ran through my mind:

One, had he seen me get undressed? *Two*, was I wearing a G-string? And *three*, had he heard everything I'd said?

Since I certainly wasn't going to wait around for him to answer any of those, I quickly grabbed my bag and left.

I was hit by a wall of humidity when I walked out of the airport. The air was hot and sticky and I wished I'd had the foresight to wear something other than my jeans. I examined the place. Everything around me was so foreign. I mean, I knew I was in a foreign country, but really, it was extremely foreign. And then it suddenly dawned on me.

I was really here.

In Thailand.

On my honeymoon.

Alone.

I'd never done anything on my own before. I felt very out of my depth and comfort zone. To make matters worse, I'd also missed my hotel transfer. Across the street stood a row of yellow cars with yellow lights; I assumed they were taxis. But I certainly wasn't going to take a taxi alone. You just never know who'll be behind that wheel—they could be an axe murderer or a pervert, and you might just find yourself the subject matter of a program on the crime channel.

I dug in my handbag for the hotel details, found the number, and called. But the next available shuttle wasn't until ten p.m. I looked at my watch and it was only seven p.m. What was I going to do here for three hours? All I wanted to do was bathe, wash my hair, soak my face, and brush my teeth.

"Hi."

A voice from behind made me jump, and I was surprised to find Damian standing there with a strange look on his face. God, I hoped that look didn't mean *I've heard your sob story and I've seen you in your underwear, lady*. I gave him a halfhearted nod, but all I could think about was what direction I'd been facing when I'd bent down to pull my jeans up.

"I need to apologize. It was wrong of me to say that stuff about you looking like an addict. I heard what you said in there, and I'm very sorry. If I'd known I would never have—"

I cut him off abruptly. I didn't want to talk about it. "It's okay. Let's leave it. I insulted you and you insulted me. Now we're even."

Our eyes met and I held his gaze.

"Deal," he said, extending a hand for me to shake. I took it and was surprised to find it was pleasantly soft, not that I was expecting him to have scales and horns and warts...*or maybe I was.*

"So where're you going?" Damian asked.

"Nowhere right now. My hotel shuttle can't pick me up for another three hours."

"Why don't you just take a taxi?" He'd pulled out a bottle of water and started slugging it down. Some of it missed his mouth and spilled onto his shirt. He poured water into his hand and ran it over his face and hair, obviously in an attempt to cool down. His wet hair was now slicked back, and for the first time I could actually see his whole face. He was...he was...*gorgeous?* (Insert multiple question marks here.)

WTF?

I didn't like guys like this. *At all!*

I liked big, tall, muscular, blond jocks who wore polo shirts, Lacoste shoes, and pastels. Guys who played tennis and wore Calvin Klein underwear. I liked guys with tans, neat hair, perfect teeth, shoes without holes, shirts without holes, body parts without holes, and no tattoos. I hated tattoos.

Damian was clearly none of these things. He had a small build, he was pale, his hair desperately needed a trim, and his clothes looked like they came from a thrift store.

I forced my brain to snap back to reality.

"I...I don't trust taxis."

He smiled at this.

"And where are you going?" I asked.

Damian shrugged. "Don't know. I think I'm pretty stranded."

"What do you mean?"

"I had to give that guy all my money to avoid the…um, intimate search he was about to perform."

"You could probably get some more at your hotel."

"I don't have a hotel."

"So where're you sleeping?"

"I was going to go to a backpackers lodge, but now I guess I'm sleeping on the beach until I can get more cash."

He was making absolutely no sense.

"Why don't you just go to an ATM?" It seemed so obvious to me.

"I don't have a card."

"What?" I looked at this guy with the clothes and the backpack and I wondered what on earth his story was. Who the hell didn't have a bank card? That was like not having a Facebook profile or Twitter account. It was madness.

"I'm backpacking. I just did Europe and moved around from place to place earning bits of cash from odd jobs, and now I'm going to explore the East."

This guy was completely nuts.

"Anyway," he said, "I hope you don't have to wait too long for your shuttle, Lilly." He gave me one last smile and then turned.

I watched him walk away and a thought started bashing about in my brain. I didn't like the thought. I didn't like it one little bit.

No, no, no, no, no! Don't say it, Lilly! No. Don't you dare bloody say it!

"You can stay with me." The words came tumbling out of my mouth, and I regretted them immediately.

Damian turned around with a shocked look on his face.

"I mean, just for one night, while you figure out what you're going to do for money. I have this big suite." I rolled my eyes and scoffed. "Deluxe honeymoon suite. And it's got a separate lounge area, so…"

Damian stepped forward and his eyes met mine with such intensity that I felt unnerved.

"You sure?"

"No, I'm not sure, but…what the hell, I guess. When in Thailand, *or whatever*." I shrugged and looked around. "Besides, you'd be doing me a favor. I really want to get to the hotel, and I don't want to take a taxi alone, so…"

He smiled that crooked smile at me again. He smiled a lot for someone who listened to Depeche Mode.

"Well, if I'd be helping you…" He strode out into the street and called a taxi with brazen confidence.

God, this was a bad idea. The worst idea. Ever. But it was too late!

CHAPTER FOUR

There's awkward:

Like your dad catching you making out with your boyfriend when you're fifteen (and it's not just first base).

Or stalking your boyfriend's ex on Facebook and accidentally "liking" her profile picture (and she's thinner than you).

Or enthusiastically going in for a hug when the other person was only going for a handshake (and your boob accidentally grazes their outstretched hand).

Or buying a box of condoms at the drugstore and bumping into your mother's friend (and they are ribbed and chocolate-flavored).

I could keep going, but I think you get the message.

And then, there's *Awkward* (with a capital *A*).

Like sitting in the back of a taxi with a total—and slightly weird—stranger, who you inadvertently bashed in the head while wearing your pj's and then threw up in front of. Who heard you pour your guts out and then cry like a baby. Who you suspect might have seen you bending over in your G-string, and who you've accidentally invited on your so-called honeymoon.

If I'd thought the plane ride was painful, well, this was definitely worse. We were squashed together in Thailand's answer to a taxi, called a tuk-tuk: a tiny little creature that looked more like an enlarged tricycle with a box attached to it. We were so squashed, in fact, that whenever the tuk-tuk went over a bump (which was pretty often) our bodies would press together in ways I'd really rather they didn't. There was a lot of…

"*Oops, sorry!*" (That was my boob.)

"*Sorry!*" (Elbow dangerously close to crotch.)

"*Excuse me!*" (Boob again.)

To say I was relieved when the ride came to a stop was an understatement. The tuk-tuk pulled up (chugged up) to a somewhat palatial-looking hotel, and I was momentarily caught up in the romance of it all—the luxurious five-star-ness of it; the turquoise sea in the postcard background; the fragrance-filled, colorful flowers floating in bowls of water; and the warm glow of atmospheric lighting. But my bubble was rudely burst when I remembered I was missing the most important ingredient for a successful honeymoon—*the groom!*

"Impressive." I'd almost forgotten Damian was there when he came up behind me and spoke.

"Yes my fiancé…" I corrected myself. "My *ex-fiancé* always said the more expensive something is, the better."

"Yeah, my parents are like that," Damian said casually. "They always fly business class and refuse to stay in anything less than a five-star-plus hotel."

This revelation shocked me.

I'd built up a mental image of Damian, and this little tidbit of information about wealthy parents certainly wasn't part of it. I'd imagined something a little more—*how shall I say this?*—dirty! In my mind his dad was a Hell's Angel or some such leather-clad thing. He probably had his own motorcycle repair shop and his mother was a tattoo artist, with body piercings and blue stripes in her hair. And they lived in a house with cigarette burns on the carpets and cat hair on the couch, because his mother was also a cat hoarder. Terribly judgmental of me, I know.

My curiosity had *definitely* been piqued, and I decided to pry, as subtly as possible.

"Um…" I was trying to sound casual, so I threw in another one. "Um, so where do your parents live…um?" (Okay, maybe that hadn't worked as well as I'd imagined, but he didn't seem to notice.)

"They live in Clifton, Cape Town." He said this phrase as casually as someone might when they say "pass the salt." But there was nothing casual about this statement at all.

And now I was downright floored.

Let me try to explain Clifton, although I doubt I could do it the slightest bit of justice. For starters, it's the most expensive place to live in the whole of South Africa—perhaps even in the whole of Africa. Not to mention that it has to be one of the most beautiful places in the world. All the massive houses are perched on cliffs overlooking the Atlantic Ocean. They're the kind of homes that have their own helipads and butlers named Giles or Hamilton, and where women have walk-in closets the size of small African countries. Now, my parents are what I would call wealthy, but this was on a whole other level.

I eyed him up and down as he walked in front of me carrying my suitcase, which was very gentlemanly of him, I must say. Damian was definitely a curiosity. Son of possibly billionaire parents dressed in a crappy T-shirt, walking around without a bank card, and in possession of a dirty backpack and terrible split ends.

How could such a curious creature actually exist?

I followed him into a rather spectacular entrance hall, up to the reception desk where an exotic beauty greeted us.

"Welcome to the White Sands Hotel and Spa." She flashed us a perfect smile. I was struck by how absolutely stunning and graceful Thai women were. She was ever so petite, with perfect, delicate features and the tiniest waist in the world. (I hated her!)

"Hi, I'm checking in. The reservation is under the name…" I hesitated again. "The name Edwards." Some buttons were pressed at lightning speed and then she nodded.

"Mr. and Mrs. Edwards. Congratulations on your wedding."

I jumped in to correct her. "No, no we're not—"

But before I could finish, Damian cut me off, putting his arm around my shoulders and pulling me closer. "Not able to keep our hands off each other." And then he turned to me with a goofy smile. "Isn't that right, honey-bunny-sweet-cheeks?" He was really milking it.

The woman smiled at us.

"What the hell are you doing?" I hissed at him.

"Shhh, go with it. In places like this they bring you all sorts of free stuff like champagne, especially when you're on a honeymoon."

Now this guy could probably buy the whole province of Champagne in France and he was getting excited over a free bottle of bubbly. Like I said, a curiosity.

"Come with me, please, I'll show you to your room," the friendly petite woman said, stepping out from behind the desk in an exquisite traditional Thai dress. It was made of brilliant purple silk and covered in the most intricate gold embroidery I'd ever seen. Annie would love it. Perhaps I should buy her one to apologize for ripping all her hard work to shreds?

When we walked all the way through the hotel and out the other end into a beautiful lush garden, I realized that the honeymoon suite must be separate from the rest of the hotel. The evening air smelled sweet and sticky, and I looked around. The moon was almost full and hung so low, it felt like I could reach out and touch it. The sea was only a short distance away now, and it had been turned into a silver liquid under the moon's glow. The sand, too, had been transformed into something that shimmered. It was all very magical and this should have pleased me, but it didn't. Because a movie started playing in my head.

Roll romantic music and in three, two, one. Action!

Michael, big, beefy, beautiful, and strapping strides onto the beach in his swimwear. He turns, his oiled chest glistens in the moonlight, and he smiles. He holds out his hand and Lilly runs. Lilly runs and jumps into his arms. He swings her around, and they go tumbling onto the soft, cool sand. His big body rolls over her. He strokes her face.

MICHAEL: (*Looking intently into Lilly's eyes*) I love you, Lilly.

LILLY: I love you, too.

MICHAEL: I'm so happy you're my wife.

He kisses her forehead. He kisses her cheek. He kisses her on the lips, and she kisses him back. It's slow and passionate and then everything goes soft-focus and the director pans to a palm tree swaying in the breeze. The romantic music swells.

Cut! Cut, cut, cut!

Suddenly there was a searing pain in my chest, as though someone had plunged a knife into my solar plexus. My heart was beating fast, but it was fighting against the strong grip of an invisible fist tightening around it, trying to squeeze the life and blood out of it.

This was the pain of my heart breaking.

"Are you okay, Lilly?" Damian was right next to me. "You look pale."

"I'm fine. I'm fine." But I wasn't.

We finally arrived at the suite. It was situated behind a neat perimeter of palm trees for maximum privacy, I guess, giving honeymooners the opportunity to do what honeymooners do best. It was also close to the beach. We walked up four small stairs and onto a wooden deck, where an inviting plunge pool greeted us—again, probably there for the purpose of "aqua aerobics." The receptionist stopped and handed Damian the keys, which made me very uncomfortable.

"I hope you'll be happy here. I'll get someone to bring your bags and some complimentary champagne and snacks." The elegant woman turned and glided away, and I felt Damian elbow me in the ribs.

"Told you. Free stuff." Despite myself, I smiled. A real one. "I hope you don't mind if I don't carry you over the threshold?" he said in a joking tone.

"Not at all. I'm probably too heavy anyway, considering the amount of food I've sucked down in the past twenty-four hours."

Damian flicked his eyes at me quickly before putting the key in the lock and opening the door.

"Nonsense. You look great."

Did I hear that correctly? Were my ears deceiving me? Okay... rewind!

I implied I was fat, and he told me I "looked great." Not good, not nice, not okay. But great! I was speechless, for several reasons really. First, it's a bit of a weird thing to say to a stranger. Second, it's a *really* weird thing to say to a stranger. Third, it's even weirder to say to a stranger whose nonhoneymoon you're on. And last, I clearly wasn't his type.

I didn't have any tattoos or piercings in strange places. Nor did I listen to depressing music and write angst-filled poetry about my inner child and pharmaceuticals. And I'd never worn a pair of skinny black jeans in my life! (My thighs were too big.)

I mean, I had a "Caribbean Caramel" spray tan; long, shiny (and may I add protein-enriched) blond hair with no split ends; and a French manicure. I listened to Taylor Swift and didn't take antidepressants.

Perhaps he felt obliged to be polite since I was putting him up for the night?

The honeymoon suite was, quite frankly, the most beautiful hotel room I'd ever been in. I briefly wondered if Damian had seen better on the numerous expensive holidays he'd no doubt enjoyed with his rich family.

It was spacious, equipped with sleek, modern finishes—and beyond comfortable. It was, however, far more open-plan than I'd initially imagined. It *did* have a living room, but one that wasn't very separate from the bedroom…something that would surely prove to be Awkward (again, with a capital *A*), since I'd offered Damian the couch.

More awkward, though, was the totally open-plan bathroom, complete with outdoor shower and sunken Jacuzzi bath. Someone had already filled the bath and sprinkled it with rose petals. A feeling crawled up from my gut again as I watched the delicate petals glide on the surface of the water. My bouquet had been made of roses, as were the centerpieces on the beautifully appointed tables. I thought about Michael again, and this time we weren't rolling in beach sand.

No, this time I had taken a photograph of us, cut his face out of it, and stuck it on a voodoo doll, and I was stabbing him in the crotch with a pin! (Maybe I did need antidepressants.)

I was angry. Very fucking angry! Where the hell was he? What was he doing right now? He probably didn't even know that I was on our honeymoon, and he certainly didn't know that a strange man was with me. Suddenly I hoped he would find out and die from the excruciating pain of jealousy. Or didn't he care enough? Did he still love me?

My face must have betrayed my feelings, because Damian slid up beside me and looked at the bath.

"I hate those bloody things, they always get stuck in the drain," he said, bending down and scooping the petals out.

Although I would never have guessed it, or even predicted it, this was one of the kindest things anyone had ever done for me.

"I'll just chuck them outside," he said, exiting with an armful of wet petals. He stopped at the door and turned. "I'll go and have a dip in the sea while you bathe. I know you said you wanted one." He paused. "You're going to be fine, Lilly." And then he was gone.

This guy didn't know me from a bar of soap, and yet he had this uncanny ability to say, and do, the right things at exactly the right time.

Michael had known me for years, but I guarantee you he would never have worked out that staring at floating red petals was making me feel homicidal. But Damian had.

CHAPTER FIVE

⌒

I met my fiancé, Michael, *ex-fiancé* I mean, when I was still in college. I was bright-eyed and bushy-tailed, full of youthful optimism and my half-full glass runneth over.

Michael and I met at a very pretentious play, which might as well have been written in Greek, because I wasn't able to extrapolate a single syllable of sense out of it. The play had been written, directed, and acted in by my stepsister—my mother briefly married a theater director when I was five.

The marriage had lasted only eight months, but I still remain best of friends with my stepsister, Stormy-Rain. (The story goes that Stormy was literally born in the rain. I'm not sure how true this is, but I always loved to tell everyone that.)

People are surprised that Stormy and I are so close, because she is the complete antithesis of me; for starters, she wears a lot of knitted scarves and crushed velvet (even in summer). She lives hand to mouth as a theater actress, director, astrologer, and tarot card reader. She has also been known to fire juggle on occasion.

Personally, I think we were forced to bond during those terrible eight months, when our parents were either violently fighting or drunk, high, and partying.

But as much as I love Stormy—and I really do—I'd been dreading her play all week. I'd never enjoyed or understood any of them, and the evening always ended with the inevitable "So what did you think?"

I reflected on some of the answers I'd lavished on her over the years. You see, I'd had the foresight to kidnap one of my mother's theater books, *Acting for Theater: The Joy of the Fourth Wall* and used it as a reference. This had furnished me with the following answers:

"Mmmmm, wow, you really took that character off the paper and reassembled her with a profound* three-dimensional depth."

or

"Mmmmm, wow, I thought the use of kitchen sink staging techniques really highlighted the fullness of your character and her profound* complexities."

Note: I use the word profound *a lot, because it is the word du jour with the theater ilk.*

As usual, Stormy's play confounded me. She rolled on the stage, cried out for her mother, and bathed in a tub of green water. But what was different about that night was that I happened to be sitting next to the most gorgeous man I'd ever seen.

Michael was good-looking, no doubt about it. He was tall, muscular, and blond with blue eyes and an incredible smile, which was something I'd been looking forward to seeing while walking down the aisle. He ticked all my requisite aesthetic requirements and then some. Although right now, I wished Michael looked more like a short, fat, hairy hobbit with leprosy and a limp so he'd never be able to find another girlfriend again and would die a sad, lonely, and pathetic death in a damp sewer somewhere.

The attraction between us had been instant and mutual, and we'd found ourselves stealing glances at each other throughout the play. During the second half, when he turned to me and whispered, "What the hell is going on?" I knew I wanted to get to know him better.

We went for coffee after the play and worked out that his brother was the graphic designer who'd made the poster for *A Mother's Jealous Tears*—obviously the reason for the green water—and that he'd been given a free ticket and felt obliged to go. During our initial conversation, we established that he was a computer systems analyst (very professional), his family belonged to a country club (very respectable), he owned his own house (very upwardly mobile), and we enjoyed several of the same hobbies, TV shows, music, and movies. We also seemed to have the same ideals: He also wanted marriage and kids and dogs and a big house.

He was perfect. He crossed all my t's and dotted the i's. It was even better when everyone said they liked him. So when he'd started playing golf with my dad and my brothers, I knew I was in love.

And Michael said he felt the same way, too.

The funny thing, though, the thing I can't wrap my head around, is that our relationship had been perfect. We never fought, conversation was always easy, and we fell into a predictable, comfortable daily routine. *So what had happened?*

I'd played our entire relationship over in my mind, looking for the telltale signs of dissatisfaction. But I couldn't find any. Unless I was missing something? Stormy-Rain had said something to me once that was suddenly reverberating in my ears. *"You know, if a guy's not getting it regularly, he's going to go looking for it somewhere else!"*

My blood ran cold. He was a red-blooded male after all, and one who could probably get sex a million times a day with a million different women. Hot, thin women. God, my mind was spinning. My thoughts were going haywire, and once again I was overcome with an urge to phone him. I needed to speak to him.

I reached for my phone and realized it was off. I suspected that my friends and family were panicking by now and had probably sent out search and rescue helicopters and sniffer dogs, so I dropped them all a reassuring message.

And then I logged on to Facebook, went straight to his page, and scanned. Nothing.

Twitter. Nothing.

Instagram. Nothing.

I dialed his number and it immediately went to voice mail, and hearing his voice made me feel sick.

My heart started pounding and I broke into a cold sweat. Panic washed over me in waves.

I dialed again. Voice mail.

I dialed again. Voice mail.

Again. Voice mail.

Should I leave a message? But what would I say?

"Hey Michael, it's me, Lilly. I was just calling to ask why the fuck you left me at the altar, you bastard asshole jerk-face. Anyway, chat soon, bye."

I was relieved when I heard a knock at the door, and I decided to take it as a sign that I should leave well enough alone. I was still wet from my bath and opened the door in my towel, just as Damian was coming up the stairs.

"Good evening." A man in a black suit greeted us both. "Your dinner is ready."

"What dinner?"

"The romantic dinner on the beach that Mr. Edwards"—he turned and looked at Damian now—"that Mr. Edwards organized for your wedding night."

"That sounds great, I'm starving," Damian said.

"No, I don't think so!" My tone was fierce, and the man in the suit looked surprised.

"But it's all arranged, and it's very beautiful."

"No thanks," I quickly said.

Damian jumped in; he was making a habit of that. "Would you mind giving us five minutes?"

The man in the suit left and Damian stepped forward.

"But aren't you hungry?" he asked.

"I am but…" The very mention of the word *food* made my stomach growl and my mouth water.

"It's not like I'm going to play footsie with you under the table or anything, if that's what you're worried about."

God, I was torn! I was starving, but the idea of a romantic dinner with Damian on the beach, well, that was just weird. I started mentally making a list of pros and cons, but my stomach wasn't having it. It needed food. *Oh, what the hell, I guess.* Besides, maybe I could get someone to take a picture of us and post it on Instagram with a soft-focus romantic filter and make Michael jealous.

"Okay, give me a minute to get ready."

***

There've been a few moments in my life when I've been overwhelmed by something so beautiful that it literally took my breath away. Like when I tried on my wedding dress for the first time or met my baby niece for the first time. And right now was one of those moments. Looking around, I could see that this location had been carefully planned, manipulated, and manufactured for optimal romance.

"One hundred percent romance guaranteed or your money back."

The actual setting was magnificent: The dinner was laid out on a table for two on a sandy embankment. You had to walk through warm, ankle-deep water to get there. In the middle of the embankment, in the middle of a heart made of candles placed on the sand, was a tentlike structure. It was open on all sides and draped with thin white curtains that were waving rhythmically in the warm breeze. The small table was scattered with pink flowers and more candles and was flanked by two chairs also draped in white fabric. All in all, it was the most romantic thing I'd ever seen.

It was stunning, and the feelings that it evoked in me were very overpowering; it simultaneously stole my breath away and reached deep inside and tickled every one of my senses. It really was…it was…well, it's really hard to describe, I don't even think I have the adjectives to do it justice. In fact, feel free to insert them yourself.

It looked like a _____ *(insert noun).*

It made me feel _____ *(insert adjective).*

Etc.

I hope I've painted this picture accurately enough, because it's important for you to visualize it correctly in order to understand why my next reaction was so surprising. Because despite its manifold beauty described by the endless bounty of adjectives, all I could do was look at it all and laugh.

And, oh, how I laughed. I laughed like a cackle of hyenas.

My shoulders shuddered as I struggled to get enough air into my lungs, gasping in between the shrieks. This was not a normal laughter, either—this was hysteria. And I wasn't able to stop it. In fact, the more I tried to control it, the worse it got. The laughter escalated until I had tears rolling down my face and was whimpering—at some stage, I think I heard myself snort. My ribs hurt, my stomach and my mouth hurt. I looked up at Damian—expecting him to be backing away from me with a look of terror on his face, clutching a fork in case he needed to stab and subdue me—but he wasn't. He was smiling at me.

"It's so, so, *so* romantic," I spluttered in between the crazed laughter. "It's the most romantic thing I've even seen and this has officially been the most unromantic day of my entire life. The irony." I grabbed my stomach—it was hurting so badly.

Someone behind us cleared his throat and Damian and I turned to find the waiter staring at us. He looked frightened. This set Damian off, and soon we were both laughing.

There's that corny saying about laughter being the best medicine. But it really is, because when our laughter had finally tapered off, I felt better than I'd felt in days! A momentary lightness settled in, providing me with some much-needed relief.

We sat down at our little table for two, and I pulled the menu toward me, excited by the prospect of *real* food and the decision I'd made to no longer watch what I ate. Getting fat was the least of my worries. But after reading the menu several times, it soon became clear to me that I had absolutely *no* idea what they were trying to serve us.

The menu claimed the dishes were "an adventure in molecular gastronomy," and the kinds of foods listed included seared scallop ravioli on a bed of deconstructed salad with balsamic pearls sprinkled with truffle ashes. Ashes? I kept reading and the word *deconstructed* appeared three more times, along with other confusing phrases such as *sweet and sour pineapple veal*, *ginger bubbles*, and *edible sea stones*.

"Um…" I looked up at Damian, hoping he was feeling the same way and that I wasn't just some uncultured slob with no appreciation for the art of modern cuisine.

"Is it me or is this a little…" I was searching for the words.

"Disdainfully avant-garde, a pretentious wank!"

"Wow, you don't pull any punches."

"Well, I have very strong feelings about this type of food." His face was totally serious when he said this.

"Pray tell." I was intrigued again.

"Well, my parents *love* this kind of cooking. It's expensive and denotes good taste and culture, you see." He said this last part in a very posh-sounding accent, which made me laugh. "We once went to this restaurant in France where they actually served crab ice cream."

"No they didn't."

"It's true, you can Google it," he challenged.

I pulled my phone out and typed the words into the search bar. The signal was slow, but I finally found what I was looking for. I read a few lines and recoiled. "Not just that, but I see it also serves bacon-and-egg ice cream." What did we do before we had the ability to access information instantly?

"It was disgusting," he added. "But it was very, *very* expensive."

I looked up and we smiled at each other and our eyes locked for a few seconds. The strangest feeling rushed through me; I couldn't quite put my finger on it, and as I was trying to, Damian broke eye contact.

"Hi." He waved his arm in the direction of the waiter. "Hi, please can we have your other menu?"

"I beg your pardon." The confused waiter looked at him blankly.

"You know, the one with the normal food on it."

I tried to hide my snicker. I certainly didn't want to offend anyone.

But still the waiter gave him a blank look.

So he tried again. "Let me put it this way. Can I get a hamburger with fries and, Lilly, what do you want?"

"The same, thanks."

The waiter, although thrown, smiled cordially and walked off, splashing through the water as he went and finally disappearing over the beach and into the hotel.

And then I realized we were totally, I mean *totally*, alone.

In the most romantic place in the world.

Oh, did I mention we were *totally* alone and that it was ridiculously *romantic*?

I shuffled in my seat a bit. We exchanged a few awkward smiles, drank a bit of champagne, and moved our napkins around on the table a lot. At one stage I picked up a flower and smelled it...

And then...

Something terrible happened...

CHAPTER SIX

I've only ever regretted wearing two outfits in my entire life, but I have legitimate excuses for both.

Like most, my teenage years were a confusing time. Made even more confusing by the fashion choices of the day. The mid-2000s boasted two very conflicting looks, making confused teenagers, with confused self-identities, confused hormones, and low self-esteems, even more confused.

It was all very traumatic for us. We just didn't know where we fit in.

So one night, we experimented with our darker, emo-esque sides; we put so much makeup on that we transformed our eyes into black pits of hell. We donned our Converse sneakers, worn in of course to look old, and some baggy camo shorts held up with studded belts. We hadn't washed or brushed our hair for at least five days to give us that *I just don't care* tussled look, and for the most important touch, I borrowed some of my dad's ties to hang around our necks for absolutely no reason whatsoever. We put on our most angry rebellion faces and all went to Jessica's party.

There'd been a lot of head banging that night, as well as bumping into one another on the dance floor (i.e., Jessica's parents' living room). We all acted very angry and pretended we knew how to skateboard and smoked cigarettes so the boys would think we were cool. But the next day we woke up with bruises from the bashing, sore necks from the banging, and dry throats from the smoking. We concluded that this was not a good look for us.

A couple of weeks later it was Phillip's party, and Annie made us some bright, color-coded outfits. We wore the biggest fake diamanté hoop earrings we could find, oversized shades—even though it was dark—and lip gloss that shined so much it could be seen from space.

But after a night of too many energy drinks and a *doof*, *doof*, *doof*, *doof*, *doof* hip-hop base that reverberated so hard it made Phillip's mother's ornaments vibrate on the shelves, we decided that we would leave that look for Destiny's Child and J. Lo.

But that regret was *nothing* compared to this one...

There was nothing aesthetically wrong with the outfit I was wearing tonight; rather, it was more of a practical issue. It was a stunning white vintage, knee-length dress with delicate lace detailing. The neckline tied together with beautiful cream ribbons that hung just below my bust.

And who could have predicted what happened next?

A warm gust of wind suddenly came out of nowhere, knocking several candles over. One went flying into my lap, instantly burning a little hole in the fabric. But that wasn't the problem. The real problem was that the beautiful cream ribbons around the neckline caught fire. Who knew ribbons were so damn flammable?

I was on fire!

I jumped up and started swatting myself frantically. The look on Damian's face was pure horror, and I've never seen anyone get out of his seat so quickly.

"Oh my God, Lilly, you've burst into flames!" Damian rushed at me with a napkin and started slapping.

"Ow!" I shrieked. "That hurts!"

"Would you rather I left you to burn?" Damian shouted back at me. The whole scene was very dramatic.

The little flames were getting higher and higher and heading directly for my face.

"Take it off! Take it off!" Damian shouted.

"What? My dress? Are you kidding?"

"Jesus, Lilly, this is no time to be prudish, just take it off. It's not like I haven't seen it before."

I flushed hotter than the creeping flames.

"I knew it. You watched me get undressed at the airport, didn't you?"

"It was an accident. I didn't mean to."

I was mortified and put my face in my hands, temporarily forgetting about the impending incineration. "I'm so embarrassed."

"It's getting worse." He pointed at the dress as the other ribbon went up in flames. I could feel the heat now. It wasn't burning me yet, because the ribbons weren't attached directly to the dress, but it was only a matter of time.

And then I felt two strong hands on my back and...

Splash.

Everything went wet.

Wet and sandy.

Damian had pushed me face-first into the water.

I emerged spluttering, my face and mouth full of sand.

"What the hell?" The initial shock at being thrown into the water quickly turned to anger. "I can't believe you did that!" I was seething at the nerve of it!

"Hey, I might have just saved your life, Lilly, and this is the thanks I get?"

I paused and thought about it. What would I have done if I'd been in his shoes?

Yup, I would have done the same thing.

"Look, if it makes you feel any better, I'll do it, too."

And then there was another huge splash as Damian threw himself into the water right next to me.

"You're crazy, you know that?"

"I've heard that one before," he said, flashing me yet another one of those wicked smiles that gave him his dangerous-looking edge. I looked straight back at him this time and got that same strange feeling I'd had before.

What the hell was it?

It's not like I liked this guy or was even attracted to him.

So why on earth did I suddenly have butterflies?

It was my turn to break eye contact.

The warm, shallow water felt amazing, and neither of us got up; instead, we just sat there together in the moonlight, looking up at the night sky, our shoulders almost touching.

"You see that bright light over there?" Damian pointed and my eyes followed his finger.

"Yes."

"It's a galaxy called Andromeda, and there are one trillion stars in it. Can you imagine that? The sheer scale of it? Kind of makes you feel insignificant, really."

I turned and looked at Damian; he was engrossed in the night sky, with a look on his face that could only be described as awe, and for the first time ever, he seemed vulnerable.

The moonlight was illuminating his face, and I took the opportunity to study him through this new lens. Strands of dark wet hair fell into his face. His features definitely didn't belong to that of a pretty boy, but they worked. He had a certain intensity to him; it was present in the way he spoke, the way he moved around with such confidence, and the way his smile lit up his dark eyes.

"How do you know so much about this stuff? Space?" I asked.

"I studied physics at university," he said, without the slightest hint of playfulness in his voice. He sounded serious.

"No! You're kidding, right?" He had to be joking—only mathematical geniuses like Einstein studied physics.

"Nope, I'm a big old nerd," he said casually. "My main area of interest is Hawking radiation. "

"Wow! Sounds impressive, although I have no idea what the hell that even means." I looked at the tattoos running up and down his arms, the old sneakers, the T-shirt with a biohazard symbol on it, and the very wrinkled button-down shirt that was hanging open in the front. Damian was definitely a complicated puzzle that I was nowhere near solving. And if I ever did solve it, there would probably be a missing piece, anyway.

"So, genius physicist, with really rich parents, backpacking the world with no bank card. How did that happen?"

He shrugged. "I decided I couldn't work in a career studying what lies beyond our planet when I knew so little about it."

"That's so deep!" I said in my best stoned-hippie accent.

He smiled his sideways smile at me. "I can be deep from time to time."

A silence settled in; only the sounds of the tiny waves gently lapping around us could be heard.

"And you? What's Lilly's big story?"

Oh God, I hate questions like this. They're so open-ended that I never know where to start.

"Ask me something. What do you want to know?" I said, secretly hoping he wouldn't.

"Okeydokey…" Damian said, folding his legs and turning to face me.

The movement caught me off guard, and apart from that taxi ride, this was the closest we'd ever been. I felt very awkward and quickly busied myself by running my hand through the warm waters, picking up the sand and letting it gently fall through my fingers. Suddenly, Damian took off his button-down shirt, attempted to squeeze out the water, and passed it to me.

"Here," he said, averting his eyes.

"What's this for?"

"It's to cover… well, your dress is a bit see-through."

"Oh God." I gasped and looked down. To say it was see-through was an understatement. I put the shirt on and buttoned it up quickly. "Thanks."

"Pleasure."

Another strange, awkward silence moved between us again until Damian finally broke it.

"So I know your sister-in-law is a lawyer." He stifled a small chuckle. "I think everyone in the airport knows that. What do you do?"

I was relieved he'd spoken and even more relieved he'd chosen an easy question and not something existential and profound about the meaning of life or something.

"Well it's nothing as fancy as physics, but I love it! I'm an auditor. I work at my dad's auditing firm."

"You love it?" Damian echoed, sounding surprised. People were often surprised that I could enjoy a job like that.

"Yes. I like the way it all works out perfectly in the end. You reconcile the value of the assets. You check all the costs, see if they match the values in the books, and make sure everything balances out perfectly. It's simple. I like that about it. It's either right or wrong. Black or white. Like life."

Damian looked at me curiously. "You really believe that? That life has no gray areas? Don't you think the world is a little more complex than that, Lilly?" he said in a voice that seemed to challenge me.

"No, I think that everything can be boiled down to one or the other. Black or white. Right or wrong. Left or right," I replied, confident that I was right.

Damian turned away. His eyes glazed over and he suddenly looked very distant.

"My sister died when she was five," he said in a hushed tone that was almost inaudible. "She was beautiful. She had this pitch-black hair, with pale skin and the bluest eyes you ever saw. We all called her Snow White. She was so curious and full of energy; she never stopped, like a little Energizer Bunny. One day, ten years ago, she was riding her bike on the street. We lived on a quiet suburban road at the time, so it wasn't dangerous; we used to do it all the time. This guy, Brian, was driving down the street, driving under the speed limit, even, when his car hit a jagged rock and his tire burst. He lost control momentarily and hit her. And even though he was going slowly, she died instantly. The doctors said that had she been older, she would've survived. But she was so tiny." Damian's voice quivered, and I could feel his pain.

"Brian jumped out of the car and tried to resuscitate her. Eventually he picked her up in his arms and started running to the hospital. He must have run a mile before someone helped him. He took her to the emergency room but...like I said, she was already dead." He paused and looked down at the heart-shaped tattoo on his wrist. "It was a freak accident. The wrong place at the wrong time. There's no one to blame, no right or wrong, no justice. And I've wanted to blame someone so badly, but the fact is, I feel sorry for Brian. I feel sorry for the guy who killed my sister. We've even become friends over the years, if you can believe that. Talk about a gray area. He still calls and sends us a card and flowers every year on the anniversary. He's a good guy, and it was a terrible thing that happened, for him, too. He struggled with the guilt, he still does, and eventually fell into a deep depression and his girlfriend left him. So you tell me...Right? Wrong? Simple? Life is far, *far* from simple and sometimes things are very gray."

I was stunned. At a loss for words. It felt like I'd had the wind knocked out of my sails. What could I say in response to that? He'd been so honest and open with me that I couldn't imagine any reply in the world would do it justice. And in that moment, I felt so close to this stranger.

We sat in silence for a few moments before I finally spoke. "My parents got divorced when I was very young and I lived with my mother. She's a theater actress." I rolled my eyes and saw Damian give a faint smile. "She's an alcoholic and an addict, too, and we moved around constantly. I think we lived in about twenty different places in the span of four years. She didn't even care if I went to school or not, all she cared about was getting drunk or high and being adored on stage. She once disappeared for seven days when I was eight. My dad fought for custody for years, and every time it looked like he was going to win, she swore blindly she'd clean up, and the courts would give her another chance. She would be fine for a couple of months, but then something would happen and she'd drink or use again. But when I was twelve, she had a car accident with me in the car. I broke my arm and my wrist. She was obviously drunk and that was the last straw, my dad got custody. But…"

I felt sad just thinking about it. "Those first twelve years of my life were really tough and I was pretty messed up when I finally moved in with my dad. I guess that's why my family is so protective over me." I could feel the tears building, but I took a deep breath and fought them back down.

And then I flinched as a tiny fish swam to my foot and past me. Soon, another fish went by and another and another until a small school of brightly colored fish swam between us. Damian put his hand into the water, and we both watched as the tiny fish darted through his open fingers.

"Try it!" But without waiting for a reply he took my hand and plunged it into the water next to his. I watched in wonder as the silver-and-blue fish wove their way through our fingers. They tickled, and we both laughed out loud.

"So, I guess we're both damaged souls then, Lilly." Damian looked at me and I could see that his mood had lifted, and so had mine.

"I guess we are," I said, as I watched the last of the fish disappear.

I heard a loud swishing sound and turned to see that Damian was standing up.

"How 'bout we find out where those hamburgers are?" he said, trying to shake some of the water off.

"Sounds like a plan. I'm actually starved."

I'd just started getting up onto my knees when a hand reached down to help me up, and without thinking, I took it. In one swift movement Damian pulled me up out of the water and we came face-to-face. The two of us stood dead still, inches away from each other, holding hands, and for some bizarre reason I don't understand, neither of us let go.

We just stood there.

Staring.

Holding.

I could hear him breathing.

I could hear my heart beating in my ears.

He smiled at me.

I smiled at him.

And then he reached up and touched my cheek. It was so gentle and soft, my whole body responded with a shiver. I felt his finger trace the surface of my cheek and then he held up a single eyelash in front of my face.

He took a small step toward me. "Make a wish, Lilly."

CHAPTER SEVEN

⸺

*A*nd so I blew.

And blew.

And blew.

And blew.

But the lash clung on for dear life.

And so I blew some more.

Harder.

Maybe a bit too hard.

I winced as I caught the glimmer of a tiny fleck of spittle tumbling through the air with a trajectory that put it on a collision course with his finger.

But no matter how hard…

Or how much…

That lash wasn't going anywhere.

So much for my much-needed wish.

"Oh my God, *I can't believe this*!" I jumped up and flung my arms in the air.

"What?" Damian was clearly taken aback by my sudden and rather dramatic outburst.

"I don't know whether to laugh or cry or scream or shoot myself."

He looked puzzled. "What do you mean?"

"Nothing is going right in my life at the bloody moment and I keep making a complete idiot of myself. I mean, I set myself on fire—*fire, for heaven's sake*—and now I can't even blow an eyelash off a finger, and, and, and…"

Damian's eyes followed me as I started to pace up and down the embankment waving my arms in the air like a rag doll in a tumble dryer.

"This has got to be some kind of elaborate plot against me! My life cannot be going this badly, surely?"

"Lilly…" His tone was soft and soothing, which made me want to slap him. "That stuff could have happened to anyone."

"Name one person that it's happened to. One person."

Damian rubbed his forehead thoughtfully. "This girl at university once wore mismatching shoes to class," he offered pleadingly.

I swung around and looked him directly in the eye. "That's hardly the same. Besides, did her fiancé leave her at the altar the day before and did she embarrassingly throw up on everyone in class? *No!*"

I kicked some sand into the water, hoping it would serve as a good exclamation point for the end of that sentence. "You know what these past few days have felt like? They've felt like someone, or something, has been conspiring against me, turning my whole life into some kind of sick joke. I'm almost expecting Ashton Kutcher to rise up out of the water disguised as a merman and shout, 'Surprise. You've been *Punk'd*.'"

I kicked some more sand into the water, trying to make the

mother of all exclamation marks. It was all very dramatic. But I didn't care, because that eyelash was the straw that broke this camel's back. It wasn't about the lash. This was about the fact that I felt victimized by the world. That I felt like somewhere, out there, was a cinema full of people with popcorn and Coke laughing at me.

"He-he-he-he. Look, she's gonna get sick, she's gonna get sick." *Hides behind a tub of popcorn*

"Ha-ha, look, she's wearing pajamas on the plane." *Laughs so hard, Coke shoots out of nose*

"Wa-ha-ha, she's on fire! She's on fire!" *Slaps knee and sprays popcorn everywhere*

I was angry, and kicking the sand into the water wasn't generating the kind of punctuation marks that could even remotely emphasize my current state of distress; in fact, my toe was sore. I think I hit a shell or, knowing my luck, a giant, rusty metal anchor, and now I was bound to get tetanus.

"I guess I'm just tired of crappy stuff happening to me." I walked over to the table, sat down, and hoped that we were close enough to the Bermuda Triangle for it to magically suck me in.

"Guess what my wish was?" I said.

"What?"

"That bad shit would stop happening to me."

Damian walked over to the table and sat down. He looked genuinely concerned.

"I've been trying so hard not to think about it, but do you know what it felt like when he didn't show up, in front of five hundred guests?"

"I can't even imagine, Lilly." Damian reached across the table, and for a moment I thought he was going to hold my hand, but at the last second he picked up the bottle of water and poured us both a glass.

I mentally sighed; my life was a complete disaster zone.

We sat there in silence, sipping our sparkling water and listening to the bubbles pop and fizz. For some reason I thought about my wedding invitations—I'd put so much effort into them.

I'd spent hours at the paper shop choosing just the right color, texture, and thickness. Hours spent with the designer finding the right layout and design elements to make it perfect. The invites were an off-white color—Romantic Eggshell Dream was the name of the paper. They were embossed in the corners with a delicate flower design and all handwritten in calligraphy—some old lady sat there for days doing them all—and then folded them in half and tied them together with pale lavender ribbons. What a waste!

And then another thought hit me. This scandal was going to be spoken about by my family for the next millennium, *at least*. In fact, it would probably be passed down from generation to generation in the great African tradition of oral storytelling. Some great-great-great-niece of mine living in the year 2104, where robots feed you breakfast and everyone lives in hydroponic bubble suits, would still be hearing the legendary story of poor Aunt Lilly who was left at the altar in front of all her friends and family. So for the rest of my life, at every family function I would probably hear…

"Shame, shame poor Lilly. You must be heartbroken."

"Oh shame. You must be so embarrassed. I don't know how you cope."

"Poor, poor Lilly, maybe you should just go live out the rest of your sad, pathetic, lonely life under a rock in the middle of the desert with only lizards to keep you company."

I was grateful when a loud voice suddenly broke through my terribly unhappy thoughts.

"Your hamburgers," said the man in the black suit, who seemed to have appeared out of nowhere. He started moving things around the table to make space for our food. He glanced at me with a displeased look as he bent down and picked up all the candles and flowers that had fallen over. I mentally kicked him in the groin and smiled politely.

I looked at my plate. My burger might as well have been hanging from the roof of the Sistine Chapel. It was a work of art and I almost felt bad for eating it...*almost*. But at this point, I was famished. I grabbed the burger, took an enormous bite, and started wolfing it down. It dawned on me that I didn't care that I probably looked like a hungry scavenger, frantically gnawing on the last remains of a carcass. Because the one good thing about having your life declared as a disaster zone is that things that bothered you before seemed so insignificant now.

Take eating in front of a guy, for example. Why is it that when a waiter arrives, whilst in the company of a male we're trying to impress, we become panic-stricken and in anxious trembling little voices say, "I'll have the salad, please. No dressing, no croutons, no feta, just leaves."

We have these strict woman rules about what to eat and what not to eat on a date—no spinach or any other kind of green that clings to your teeth, no ribs or spaghetti, and definitely no soup. So we order a bunch of leaves and spend the night moving a lonely piece of lettuce around our plate, as if eating something with the calorific equivalent of air would impress him. And you know the hotter the guy, the less you're gonna eat!

But since I didn't like Damian in that way, and this wasn't a date, I didn't care if he looked at me like I was a yeti that had just emerged from hibernation and was eating the arse end off a low-flying crow.

I continued to ravage the burger, and I got so lost in the process that at some stage I caught myself making loud *mmm* sounds. I don't think I looked up once, either. I was just so focused on the task of consuming as much fat as possible. I swallowed the last mouthful and finally looked up and straight into the face of a smiling Damian.

"What?" I snapped at him, a fleck of something flying onto the table.

"Have you ever considered a career as a professional eater?" he said, putting a chip into his mouth.

Although I'd just claimed not to care, I was terribly offended by this suggestion, and he could see that.

"I mean that in the nicest way possible," he said, pointing to the corner of his mouth in a *You've got something on your face* kind of gesture.

I grabbed my napkin and rubbed my mouth, then looked at him for confirmation that it was gone. He shook his head and pointed to the other side, and I repeated the process again, looking up for confirmation once more. But Damian shook his head again, got his phone out, and then took a photo of me. He turned it around so I could see.

How I'd managed to get tomato ketchup on my forehead was beyond me.

"Oops" was all I could manage. But before I could do anything about the splotches of wayward sauce, Damian leaned across the table and wiped my face with his napkin. He had such a look of concentration on his face as he poured a little bit of water onto it and went to work on my forehead. Then my cheek, and then the corner of my mouth. My lips tingled as the cool fabric touched them. Suddenly all I could feel were my lips and all I could see was him.

I pulled away quickly and sat back in my chair.

"Thanks."

"Pleasure."

This whole situation was just so, *so* bizarre. Here I was, on my honeymoon, in the most romantic place in the world, with a stranger who had just been gently, and very familiarly, wiping my face clean with his napkin. Who the hell had seen this coming?

Not even my mother's psychic Esmeralda (real name Mary) had predicted this, not that I placed much confidence in her psychic abilities, but surely something this big would have come through somewhere, considering she "read me" the day before my wedding! My mother had insisted on it. My mother didn't do anything without consulting her; she barely went to the toilet without a phone call to find out whether her bowel did in fact want to move. I'd never held psychics in very high esteem, especially not this one, who my mother met in rehab. I do placate my stepsister Stormy in the nicest way possible, though. She too professes to get "vibey vibes and the feels" about things. They're usually along the lines of, "Lilly, you must wear pink today. Or red. Maybe both. Actually, I think it's green I'm seeing, and watch out for the number 794."

When Michael and I had first gotten together, my mother was adamant that I get our cards read to make sure we were compatible. Of course I'd said no, but then she pulled one of her famous guilt trips.

"It's fine, don't go, it's your choice. But what am I going to do now? I've already paid. Maybe I can get a refund? But it's fine if it's not for you,

sweetie. Oh my God, but she canceled that other appointment for you! But I'm sure she won't mind. Like I said, no worries."

So half an hour later I was sitting in Esmeralda's "reading room," a dark and very dingy cottage at the back of her property. As I walked in, I was instantly deafened by the cacophony of wind chimes. Chimes made of shells, feathers, crystals, and the skulls of little woodland creatures hung like bats from her roof. The next thing to assault my senses was the incense that practically choked me, followed by the near heart attack her pet monitor lizard, Sid, gave me as his scaly tail brushed past my ankle.

And there she was, in full chiffon-draped glory, the star, Esmeralda, sitting at her little table covered in black velvet. And you know what it's like—even if you don't believe in the powers of the woman sitting across from you fingering a pack of dirty cards, you want to. My mother had obviously told her about Michael, and even though I knew that, I still soaked it all in.

"I see a man. A blond man." She had a very fake mystical-sounding accent.

Of course, my heart did cartwheels at this point.

"Yes, I see him very clearly now." She fanned her cards out and moved her fingers around in little circles. "I see your future with him. I see you walking down the aisle. I see he will be very rich one day and you will live in a big house." I hung on her words like they were a magical rope that would pull me toward a happy future. "Yes, I see three children. I see blond children with blue eyes, and one is a boy and the other two are girls. And you will be very happy and in love forever."

And of course you want to believe it all, and I did, right up until the second I held that note in my hand. Perhaps I'd wanted the fairy tale so badly that I'd missed something real?

CHAPTER EIGHT

*T*he wind had picked up, creating little ripples on the water. I was still wet, and although the breeze was warm, I suddenly felt very cold. I folded my arms across my chest to shield myself from the intensifying wind.

"Cold?" Damian asked.

"Freezing." I started to shiver.

The man in the black suit returned to inform us that they were expecting a storm and we should get inside as soon as possible. I was surprised by how fast and furiously the storm escalated, beating the sky into a frenzy of raging wind and rolling black clouds. By the time we'd reached our room, the rain was pelting down, soaking our already-wet clothes and hair. We rushed inside and I watched Damian get pulled into a wrestling match with the wind, until he finally managed to slam the door shut.

Thailand was a place of extremes—no doubt about it. Ten minutes ago we were enjoying a warm tropical evening, and now we were watching violent lightning severing a stormy sky. It was breath-taking.

I shivered, colder now than I'd been before, and all I wanted to do was slip into a warm bath, but then I remembered that slightly inconvenient problem—the open-plan layout of the room. I walked over to the bath and Damian must have noticed.

"I'm pretty sure I can resist the urge to look if you want to have another bath," he said with that devilish, slightly skewed smile again. "In fact, I'd love to have one, too, so I'll promise not to peep, if you promise not to peep?"

"Why would I peep?" I felt a little uncomfortable with this conversation and its subject matter—casually devising a strategy to get naked in the same room as if we were talking about something as casual as making a cup of coffee. And then, because we were talking about it, I suddenly started to imagine Damian naked. I couldn't help it, okay? It was human nature, or something. I banished the thought quickly, hoping that my shocked blush wasn't as visible as it felt.

"Um…" I scanned the room. "Okay, you have to sit on that couch over there with your back to me. And don't you dare look, not like you did at the airport."

"Hey, I turned around at the wrong time. It was an accident. Besides, it's not like I stared."

"Well, let's try and not have any accidents happen this time," I said, turning on the taps.

The bath was enormous, manufactured for optimal romance and relaxation, and stretching out in the warm water was exactly what my body needed. Of course, I made sure that my back was turned away from Damian at all times, and for added security, I'd dimmed the lights. This time, if there were any "accidents," he still wouldn't see anything.

We sat in complete silence, and I tried not to make any sudden movements that would draw additional attention to me. "How's the bath?" he finally said, which I was glad about, because it was all starting to feel pretty damn capital *A*.

"Good." Monosyllabic answer. I didn't want to encourage too much interaction in my current state of total and utter nakedness.

"Good." A monosyllabic answer back.

Then more silence.

Is there some foolproof method for defusing an awkward situation? Are there no self-help books about this common subject? *The Complete Idiot's Guide to Awkward Situations.*

I could really use a few tips right now. A joke, maybe? I was terrible at telling them. And what kind of joke; I didn't see "Knock, Knock. Who's there?" doing the trick. Perhaps if we listened to music? But I didn't have any on my phone and my iPod was at home, and I certainly didn't want to listen to Depeche Mode in case I felt an uncontrollable urge to slit my wrists. Perhaps I could steer the conversation in another direction. *"So what about South Africa's current turbulent political climate and the upcoming general elections? Death penalty perhaps?"* I was fast running out of ideas when...

CRASH!

"Holy fuck." I instinctually screamed and leapt out of the bath as it felt like an enormous bolt of lightning hit our room. The thunder was deafening and everything went very bright. Luckily, in that moment, I'd remembered something from my science class about water and lightning not being the best of friends—and it was this thought that had sent me scrambling for dry land. Everything then went very black as all the lights flickered and died.

"Are you okay, Lilly?"

"Um..." My heart was pounding. "Well, I didn't get hit or anything."

"It felt like it hit the room," Damian said, clearly sounding unnerved.

"Where are you?"

I looked into the darkness—my eyes had not yet adjusted and it was pitch black. "I don't know." And then I suddenly realized that I was completely naked. I gasped. "Oh my God!"

"What?" The concern in his voice was clearly audible.

"Nothing, nothing," I replied as quickly as I could. The last thing I wanted to do was remind him of my nakedness.

But...oh my God, what if the lights suddenly went on?

Terror took hold of me, and I strained my eyes against the darkness trying to see something, *anything*. But everything was so black and I was completely disoriented. There was a towel on the bed, that much I was sure of—but I had no idea in which direction the bed was, or even where the bath was. I decided to guess and started crab walking to my left very, very slowly. Shuffling one foot in front of the other and waving my arms around in the air in front of me. I inched my way forward, until I felt a pain in my leg. I'd walked into the corner of the coffee table, and hard.

"Ow!" I cried out loudly, wincing in pain.

"What happened?"

"I walked into something." My leg was throbbing now.

"Just stay where you are, I'm sure the lights will come on soon."

That's exactly what I was afraid of.

And then I heard it, the upward lilting inflection in his voice that made me realize he knew what was going on. "Oh, I see," he said.

God, I was embarrassed. The last thing I wanted was for him to start thinking about me naked. And I didn't want to wonder whether or not he was and have him wondering if I thought he was being a pervy naked thinker or—*crap!* This was awkward.

"I was looking for a towel," I said authoritatively.

"I've got one here," he said, and I heard a bit of shuffling.

"Why have you got a towel?" My tone sounded accusatory because for a split second I imagined him taking mine on purpose.

"I was going to bathe, so I took one."

"Oh. Right." Another silence, and I could practically hear the cogs in his brain turning.

"I could bring it to you?"

"Why don't you just throw it to me?" There was no way I wanted him anywhere near my nakedness.

"And how do you plan on finding it?"

He had a good point.

"Why don't you just wait until the lights come on. I'll keep my eyes shut."

"No way!" My tone was forceful. "I'm not standing here naked."

"Well, then let me bring it to you."

I was hesitant to accept his offer, but I didn't see an alternative.

"Fine, but—"

He cut me off. "No groping," he said, and laughed.

"And keep your eyes shut, in case the lights come back on."

"Sure."

Damian started to move toward me, and I could hear him as he bumped into things along the way.

"Say something to me, Lilly."

"Hello, I'm here."

I could hear Damian changing direction, and he was definitely getting closer.

"Again," he said. He was very close now.

"Hi."

"Right. I'm going to hold out the towel now. I think you're close enough."

I hoped he didn't touch me. I covered my boobs with my free arm and tentatively stuck my other arm out. I waved it about, expecting to bump into him at some point—but I didn't.

"Where are you?" My arm was moving from side to side.

"Here!"

He was close, but clearly not close enough. I cautiously took a tiny step forward, not knowing that he'd done the same, and suddenly jumped as I felt something hit my stomach.

Damian responded instantly. "Sorry, I didn't mean to. Sorry. I…I didn't hit you anywhere…um…?" His tone was hesitant and I knew what he was trying to say.

"No! No! It was just my…*never mind.*"

"Okay," Damian said. "I'm going to hold my arm out very still and you can find it."

Yes, this was clearly a better plan, and a few seconds later I had safely retrieved the towel and wrapped it around myself. I sighed with relief. And thought I heard him do the same.

"So now what?" I felt so much better with the towel around me, but I couldn't just stand there waiting for the lights to come back on.

"If you give me your hand, I can lead us back to the sitting area."

Damian didn't even give me the chance to respond, because a second later I felt his arm bump into mine, and our hands meet.

I remember the first time I held hands with a guy. At the time, it was the most thrilling and sexually charged thing that had ever happened to me. It was with a pimply boy called Charlie Lieberman, who sat behind me in math. One day I felt a tap on my shoulder and a little note suddenly appeared in my lap.

Lilly,
Do you like me, or like me, like me? Tick the box.
Like me ☐
Like me, like me ☐
Charlie

I ticked the second box and suddenly we were boyfriend and girlfriend. Which basically meant nothing. But after a few months, we went on our first real date. And when I say *date*, I mean that we went to a movie with a big group of friends—*and* we were chaperoned by my brother and future sister-in-law, who sat two rows behind us.

Charlie and I sat next to each other, and the atmosphere was electric. We had both strategically placed our hands on the armrest just a few inches away from each other—our little fingers almost touching. We must have then spent the next ten minutes moving our hands toward each other at a snail's pace until they finally touched. From that point, I think it took us about half an hour to finally do something that resembled holding hands. And even though I was only thirteen at the time, it was the most physically intense moment of my little life.

We sat there in silence holding hands, our eyes glued to the screen, not daring to look at each other. I can't tell you what that film was about because all I could feel was Charlie's hand. That was also the first and last time I felt it because soon after that he dumped me for Melanie Andrew. (Bitch.)

That day at the movies, with Charlie's hand in mine, I had felt something *real*. Something extremely potent. Because there's holding hands, and then there's Holding Hands (with a capital *H*). And you can instantly feel the difference.

Well, *I* instantly felt the difference…

Damian intertwined his fingers with mine. His thumb, instead of going straight to the top of my hand, slipped itself, oh so slowly, across my sensitive palm. I felt my breath quicken. I loosened my fingers so that they could gently slide down the length of his, until our fingertips brushed each other. We both moved our fingers simultaneously, letting them slip up and down, curl around, and stroke.

We finally reached the couch, and I sat down. Our fingers untwined themselves and I suddenly felt a rush of intense guilt. As if I was cheating on Michael. Not that I should care, but I did. My fingers were still tingling and I wanted to see the look on Damian's face. I was very glad that the darkness was concealing mine: my blush, my smile. I wondered if he was smiling, too. Under the shroud of darkness, everything felt so much more intense. The silence was deafening, until he spoke. His voice was soft, low and gravelly. It sounded different.

"Lilly?"

"Yes, Damian?" I whispered.

More silence.

The anticipation was killing me. What was he going to say?

"Yes, Damian?" My voice was even softer this time.

The silence throbbed in my ears.

But he said nothing.

I waited for what seemed like forever. And then I heard him.

"How's your leg?"

Huh?

"My what?"

"Didn't you bump your leg?" At first I didn't know what he was talking about, and then it clicked.

"It's fine." I snapped at him as anger bubbled up inside me.

I was angry. Furious even. But it wasn't at Damian. I was angry with myself for letting my thoughts go somewhere they shouldn't have. I was being such a moron…what was I expecting him to say to me? That he liked me? We didn't even know each other, and I had a fiancé. Well, at least I *had* one…

Clearly I was suffering from some kind of post-traumatic stress disorder. I was obviously still in a state of shock and it was seriously impeding my judgment and turning me into an utter idiot. *What the hell was I doing with this guy?* This was the second time tonight we'd held hands, and it was entirely inappropriate and weird and wrong and strange and all those kinds of words.

I heard a buzz and the lights flickered back on. I blinked several times as my eyes adjusted to the brightness. Damian sat opposite me, looking in my direction, and I quickly averted my eyes, furious for what I was letting myself feel.

"What's wrong? You look angry?" Damn, I hated that he was so observant. This was something completely new to me. Michael was as observant as a doorstop. In fact, I was always having to spell things out for him.

"Nothing." I spat the word out quickly but I didn't really mean it.

"Everything's wrong, okay? It's all gone so, so wrong. How has it all gone so bloody wrong?" I paused. I felt angry and victimized by the world.

Out of the corner of my eye I could see he was looking at me curiously.

"Can I make an observation, Lilly?"

This statement made me nervous, but I agreed.

"You're not actually as powerless as you think you are."

"What?" I snapped at him yet again. I didn't know where he was going with this, but I had a very strong feeling I wasn't going to like it.

"Well, you keep saying how you feel everything is going wrong, how the world is conspiring against you. I think you have the power to change that."

He was making no sense. "What do you mean?"

"I mean, you're stronger than you think. You made the decision to come on your honeymoon alone, that's a pretty brave move—I don't think there're many women who could have done that. And maybe what's happened to you is a good thing—"

I cut him off. "How the hell can any of this be a good thing?"

"Perhaps all the 'bad stuff'"—he gestured air quotes, which I hated—"that keeps happening is actually, well, good. Maybe it's steering you in a different, a better direction? Perhaps you weren't supposed to get married."

"What?" I flew out of my seat clutching my towel for dear life. "Of course I was supposed to get married. What the hell are you talking about? Do you know how much work I put into that wedding? How many hours of planning went into it? It was going to be perfect!"

"Work?" The word came out loudly. "Shouldn't you care more about the marriage than the work that went into the wedding?"

That sentence stung me. It stung me so hard I took a step backward and almost fell over another table.

"What are you trying to say? That I don't love...I don't love..." I was stammering. "Michael?"

"Do you?" His tone was strange and almost challenging.

"Of course I love him." I didn't even need to think about that. I did love him after all, *didn't I*? "Who do you think you are judging me anyway? What right do you have?"

The rain started pelting down again, and we had to raise our voices to be heard.

"How old are you, Lilly?" Damian stood up now; he looked fired up.

"What's that got to do with the price of eggs?"

"Twenty-three?"

"Twenty-four," I shouted at him over the rain.

"Don't you think you're a bit too young to be getting married?"

Oh wow! Now that was the last straw. I pointed my finger at him; it was inches away from his face, and I screamed.

"Who the hell do you think you are, Damian? Because you don't know me! You don't know the first thing about me! So if I were you I would just"—the rain softened, but I was still screaming—"shut the hell up!"

The volume of those last words shocked us both, and I think we could sense that there was absolutely no salvaging this situation. Whatever Damian and I had had, it was dead and buried. I turned and walked to the bedroom, climbed into bed with my towel still on, and pulled the duvet over my head. I was seething.

I don't know how much time elapsed, but at some stage, I started to feel better. Calmer. I closed my eyes and could feel that sleep would soon claim me.

I started to replay the fight in my head. Why had I gotten so angry with him? I thought about what he'd said. He'd tried to put a positive spin on my situation, tried to make me feel better, but I'd just kicked him in the teeth. He shouldn't have said that stuff about my not loving Michael and not getting married, but prior to that, he'd actually been nice.

Suddenly it occurred to me that *I'd* started the fight. I'd started it for my own reasons; I'd been feeling awkward, vulnerable, and extremely guilty for feeling something for him. I'd pushed him away. Punished him for something that wasn't his fault. I was also angry with Michael and Damian had just been a convenient punching bag. When it was Michael I really wanted to punch.

Sleep was creeping faster now and I knew I was about to succumb. I had one last thought…

I need to apologize to Damian in the morning.

CHAPTER NINE

I had a strange dream that night. I dreamed that I was at Esmeralda's having my cards read. At first glance everything seemed normal, but then Esmeralda walked in wearing my wedding dress, which looked terrible on her. (I was secretly very happy about this.) Annie was also there. She was shaking her head in horror and trying to cut the dress off with a giant pair of scissors while singing "Here Comes the Bride."

I was wearing my pajamas. I looked down and noticed that the floor was covered in soft, white beach sand. Her monitor lizard was sitting on the floor next to my foot eating a hamburger, which was very disturbing, because he was doing it with a knife and fork. Esmeralda began turning the cards over, but every one was the same. The jack of hearts.

I asked her if she still saw the blond male and she said no. She saw a man with dark hair. I told her she was most definitely wrong, because he was supposed to be blond. Then she got angry and told me her cards never lied. He was dark-haired and had dark eyes and was holding the moon in his hand. I don't really know why, but this made me very angry, and so I grabbed a glass of water and threw it at her. Then all her candles went out and I woke up.

I sat up in bed as if it had shocked me; the towel was still wrapped around me, and as soon as my eyes had adjusted to the bright light, I looked around the room. My first thought was yesterday's last thought: I must apologize to Damian.

I glanced in the direction of the sitting area, but he wasn't there. I called out his name, no answer. I assumed he was outside; the sun was streaming through the huge windows and the day looked glorious, with no sign of last night's storm. I started climbing out of bed but stopped dead when I felt something crunch under my hand.

I didn't need to look down; I knew exactly what it was.

A note on my pillow.

My recent experience with notes had not been a very positive one, and I had a sneaking suspicion this was just going to reinforce that sentiment. I called out for Damian one more time, hoping...*still no answer*. I had a feeling I knew what the note was going to say. In fact, I was positive I knew.

He was gone. And I would never see him again.

There was absolutely no need to read the note, so I got out of bed and tossed it on the floor. Why did I even care if he was gone?

I didn't. Damian was just some stranger that I'd met and felt sorry for. I stomped over to the coffee machine and turned it on aggressively, as if that would somehow make me feel better. The kettle started to bubble and I began making myself a strong cup of coffee, but all the while I could feel the note staring at me. Staring at me with its beady little paper eyes. I ignored it and walked over to the couch for my morning caffeine hit. But the note began to peck at the back of my head with its sharp folded paper corners.

Oh, who was I kidding? Of course I wanted to read it…

I'm really sorry, Lilly.
X D

Irony had clearly come back for seconds…just four little words once more. But there was something very different about this note. Something so seemingly insignificant, but to me, it was huge. A tiny letter, that when I looked at it, made my heart race.

X.

A kiss.

I stared at the *X* on the paper for ages.

Why would he have put one there? Did he want to kiss me? Was he just being polite? What does it all mean, or am I reading too much into it and this is just the way he signs off all his letters? Why is this even bothering me? Why am I analyzing a single letter on a note from a stranger?

And…why won't this incessant narration in my head turn itself off and give me a chance to breathe and wake up?

I turned the note over hoping he'd left me his number, or an email address or something. He hadn't. I suddenly realized that I didn't even know his surname, so I couldn't find him on Facebook. Or could I?

I went straight for my phone. The second it was in my hand I logged on to Facebook and typed in D-A-M-I-A-N. The reception was slower than a dead sloth and the anticipation was killing me as I watched that irritating thingy going round and round and round. Finally, it connected and about fifty pages came up. *Too many!* I tried to narrow the search and put South Africa in as a search parameter, and now there were only thirty pages. And so began my hunt.

There were a few promising-looking profile pics; a skull and a plain red block jumped out immediately. But neither one was him. I kept going until my eyes began to sting, but he was nowhere to be found. My heart dropped into my toes, and I was gripped by this terrible realization—I would never see him again. It also dawned on me that this was the first time I'd logged on to Facebook and *not* gone straight to Michael's page. So I quickly did, not that I was expecting to find anything new.

But I did. He'd updated his status…

Life works in mysterious ways.

Was I hallucinating? I read it again just to be sure.

Life works in mysterious ways.

What the hell did that mean? I'd never known Michael to say anything deep and vaguely meaningful in all the years we'd been together, and now he was speaking like the Dalai Lama. Like some guru-swami-sage person, spouting out pseudo wisdom like a bleeding fountain. *Bastard.* He'd probably downloaded some app that delivered meaningful quotes to his phone every morning. I desperately felt like commenting, but what would I say?

Let me take some of the mystery out of it for you; next time I see you, I'm going to kick you in the nuts.

What "mysterious ways" was he referring to? I skulked over to the window angrily; it really was a beautiful day, and I had absolutely no idea what to do with it. I reached for the hotel guide and read through the list of available activities. I wasn't outdoorsy, so no to all the tennis, water activities, and anything involving being lifted into the air—I was scared of heights.

There was a spa, which sounded more doable.

So I slipped into my bathing suit, grabbed a towel and a sarong, and went out into the sunny world even though I was feeling anything but sunny.

* * *

Four hours and thirty-five torturously painful minutes later, I decided that this was officially the most pointless day of my entire pitiful life and everything that I'd done so far just made me feel depressed, lonely, miserable, and pathetic. It was sunny, but I was walking around with a big, thick black cloud above my head.

1. *Breakfast*—initially I was excited; the large buffet had practically called my name, especially the waffles, the pancakes, and the bacon. But three cappuccinos and three thousand calories later, I looked around the room and saw that I was the only party of one.

2. *The beach*—every minute and a half some cute, giggling, cooing couple walked past me holding hands and drooling on each other. They wallowed in the water, latching onto each other like codependent koala bears. They cuddled in the sun and whispered sweet nothings. They made me sick.

3. *The spa*—same thing. Couples, couples, couples all clinging on to each other like they would die if several of their body parts weren't attached at all times.

4. *The pool*—same as the beach, but without the waves and sand.

Eventually I prowled up to the reception desk and demanded to know what else there was to do in this Godforsaken bloody excuse for a hotel—okay, I didn't say that last part out loud, but I was thinking it, so that counts for something, doesn't it?

After a few curious stares, the kind of stares that seemed to say, *Shame, I wonder where her husband has gone,* I was handed a large pile of flyers.

Botanical gardens—too many flowers. Flowers reminded me of weddings.

Elephant rides—too large and smelly.

Sightseeing bus tour—too much looking.

Tour of jungle ruins—too jungle-y.

Shopping at the market—*mmm,* now that was more like it.

In fact, that was exactly what I needed: some retail therapy. And everyone knows that the shopping in Thailand is supposed to be awesome. Let's face it, there's nothing like the smell of new clothes to make you feel better about your sad life.

With this in mind, I jumped into one of those tricycle boxes and headed for the market—the holy grail of all my future happiness. And when I arrived, it didn't disappoint.

I'm not sure there's an adequate way of describing the market that fully encapsulates its atmosphere. Certainly, I had never seen anything like it before.

Hundreds of stalls were packed together tightly, full of bright colors, exotic smells of cooking hanging in the warm air, and sounds—music blaring and people shouting over it, trying to sell their wares. Scooters buzzed past, and in the distance, someone was ringing a bell. My senses were assaulted around every corner, either by the never-ending sea of multicolored sarongs, or the smell from a stand selling pineapples and perfume. The atmosphere was electric and alive, and it hummed with the possibility of bargains and purchases aplenty. I almost didn't know where to begin...almost.

I immediately gravitated toward a large collection of colorful beach bags. Like someone under the influence of a hypnotic spell, I drifted toward them in a trancelike state, eyes wide, mouth open and salivating. My eye was immediately drawn to a large beach bag made from bright-pink, purple, and gold traditional Thai fabric. It was exquisite. But as I was about to reach up and claim the precious thing, a tiny little woman appeared out of nowhere. Without asking she grabbed me by the hand and started pulling me toward the back of the stall.

"Come, come, I take you to back room."

"I beg your pardon." What the hell did she mean?

"Nice bags, nice bags there."

With those magic words, my fears were forgotten. The little old lady pulled back a curtain, glanced around quickly, and dragged me inside. I had officially found the buried treasure. I was standing in a tiny room I could barely move my arms in, but it was covered from floor to the ceiling with some of my best—and usually very unaffordable—friends: Prada, Gucci, Louis, Salvatore, Fendi, Chanel, Chloé, and Dior. I didn't know where to look, where to turn, what to touch. It was all so dazzling and beautiful. Now, I'm not usually an advocate of fake anything, but after scrutinizing them all, there was simply no visible difference, and they were all so pretty and colorful and more importantly *cheap*.

Ten minutes later, and after much deliberation, I walked out with two handbags of happiness and a new understanding of how it all worked here. From then onward, every stall I went to, I asked for the back room (and they all had them).

Hours later and a Christian Dior watch, a pair of Gucci glasses, another three bags, a Fendi purse, a Louis Vuitton bracelet, a few shirts, skirts, bikinis, and sarongs, and two pairs of Manolos later, I was finally done. I was buzzing. High from adrenaline, endorphins, and handbags, Damian, Michael, and that wedding "thing" were distant memories. The only thing on my mind right now was my growling stomach. I needed to replenish my depleted reserves, and fast.

But I'm naturally suspicious of things like salmonella, food poisoning, and necrotizing fasciitis. (That's the flesh-eating bacteria. I once watched a show on the reality channel where a guy's leg was literally eaten by his own body, and since then I've been paranoid every time I get a scratch.) I chose my restaurant very carefully.

I decided on criteria: no plastic chairs, no plastic tablecloths, no sweaty-looking waiters in shorts, and definitely no pet meat, and it had to have air-conditioning. Sadly, nothing was meeting the criteria. So I jumped into another tuk-tuk and in my best Thai (Google Translate was officially my new best friend), I asked to go to the best restaurant around.

And what he took me to was beyond my wildest expectations. The restaurant was located on a small cliff overlooking a deserted beach. The building looked more like a traditional home than a restaurant, and it was surrounded by lush greenery. Walking into it, you got the feeling of being lost in paradise. I was led to a table on the balcony overlooking the pale white rocks that fell into the calm turquoise sea below. It was perfect.

co•in•ci•dence *(noun)* a remarkable concurrence of events or circumstances without apparent causal connection

Stormy-Rain is always telling me that there are no such things as coincidences, only fate pushing you toward a predetermined destination. Orchestrating your life in such a way that everything works out just the way it should.

Out of all the restaurants. Out of all the hours in the day. Out of all the people in the world. With all of those variables and many more that needed to combine in perfect synchronicity and unison to create this very moment, despite all of that...

Damian walked past me.

CHAPTER TEN

ou know those 3-D optical illusions? Those pictures made up of seemingly random patterns or dots that, when stared at for long enough, with just the right intensity and at the right angle, a 3-D image emerges out of the chaos? It's usually a galloping horse, a biting shark, or a bird flying toward you, or some other dramatic animal in motion. But once you've seen it, you can always see it, and the random patterns never look the same again.

That's what happened with Damian.

He looked completely different today. Or was I seeing him differently?

He was still dressed in his signature black, but he looked much more casual and relaxed. The sleeves of his shirt were shorter this time, and I noted that the tattoos on one of his arms crept all the way up to his shoulder. I'd never liked tattoos. I'd always seen them as a sign of heroin dependency, excessive moodiness, and a tendency to throw TVs into hotel swimming pools. But on Damian they were—dare I say it—sexy. As he turned around, I saw his T-shirt said READ BOOKS, NOT T-SHIRTS. I smiled to myself; that was so Damian.

His hair was different, though; it looked like a small child had taken a pair of scissors to it and created a strange lopsided Mohawk. It was weird and irreverent and wouldn't have suited anyone else but him. By this stage his facial hair was more than just a five-o'clock shadow, which only added to his dark mystery. His thick black eyebrows accentuated his big, wide-set black eyes, and I stared at him trying to figure out who he looked like.

But there was no one; his look was completely unique. It was gawky yet confident, definitely weird and naughty, sexy and sweet all at the same time. And right at that very moment, he looked dark and broody and dangerous.

Oh my God. He suddenly turned and looked straight at me, and I knew I had an embarrassing look plastered across my face. He waved tentatively, and I waved back. A moment later he was standing at my table.

"Hey…so…um…yeah, nice hair." What a stupid thing to say. But it was all that had come to mind.

Damian smiled and ran his fingers through it playfully, twisting it and creating a kind of spike that stuck straight up for a moment or two and then flopped back down. Why did I find that so cute? "The guy in the kitchen insisted."

"Huh?"

"I've been washing dishes here, and he said it was too long. So he attacked me with scissors and a razor."

"Why are you washing dishes?"

"Need cash."

"Oh, of course. I forgot about that."

"I can't. Trust me. The image of that guy coming toward me with a plastic glove will be burned into my brain forever."

We laughed, and when it tapered off, I knew I had to say it.

"Look…I'm really sorry about last night. I shouldn't have screamed at you like that. I'm really sorry." Our eyes met.

"Me too. I shouldn't have said that stuff about not getting married. I had no right to."

We smiled in mutual acceptance of the apologies.

"Well…" He started turning away from me. "Enjoy your meal and the rest of your vacation." And then he walked away. Just like that, he was heading for the door.

Anxiety gripped me; I'd lost him once today and now that I had seen him, I was overcome by this feeling that I didn't want to lose him again.

"Wait!" The word flew out at a volume that was entirely inappropriate for a public place; fellow diners turned and stared at me.

"Where're you going?"

"I'm going back to town to get something to eat and then I have a thing tonight."

A *thing*? That sounded very mysterious and my mind was conjuring up all sorts of images. Frankly, I was afraid to even ask.

"Why don't you have lunch with me?"

"I'm afraid I can't afford a meal like this on a mere dishwasher's salary. But thanks for the offer." He started walking away again.

Stop walking away. Stop walking away. I wished I was telekinetic now, and I could make him turn around with the mere power of my thoughts, instead of having to open my mouth again.

"I'll pay." The volume and the pitch were all over the place once more, and he turned back to me. "You can pay me back sometime.

I know you're good for the money." I'm sure I must have looked at him with pleading desperation in my eyes, and I mentally kicked myself for this, too.

"Sure," he said quickly, like he really hadn't needed that much convincing. He sat down with a smile.

Up until now our relationship (or whatever you call it) had been characterized by awkward moments. Awkward silences, strange smiles and looks (or a lack of looks). But from the moment he sat down at the table, the conversation just flowed. We ate, we drank, we laughed, and I found myself telling him the strangest things. Things I hadn't told anyone about.

I told him about the first and only time I'd smoked weed and thought that Buttons, my cat, was trying to tell me something in Russian. About the embarrassing time my mother did a live radio interview for one of her plays and was so drunk that she fell off her chair, hit her head, and had to be rushed to hospital midshow. I told him about the day I got braces, how I was so embarrassed that I stopped talking at school for two weeks so no one could see. How I got stuck in a glass revolving door at a shopping center and had to stay there for two hours while they tried to repair it and a crowd of people gathered to watch.

I gave him the low down on my friends, my absolute obsession with reality TV and any program that involved a crazed bride, teens giving birth, or housewives in various states of desperation and divorce. I even went into details about my favorite colors and clothes, my preference for baths, and that I favored sweets over savories.

I basically told him everything and anything that popped into my head in the moment. All the while, Damian held my gaze intently, and I could see he was listening to every single word I said. And he clearly found me funny, because he would laugh loudly at almost everything I said. It occurred to me that no guy had ever found me this funny. Michael certainly hadn't. Damian never took his eyes off me, not for a second. In that moment I felt like I was the center of his universe and he was hanging on my every word.

"And you?" I finally asked when I'd finished telling him my entire life story.

"What do you want to know?"

"Everything." I hadn't meant for that word to come out of my mouth the way it did. With that strange whispery tone that made it drip with a certain subtext that now hung in the air between us.

I blushed. I couldn't help it. And when I looked up at Damian, he was looking down at the table and smiling.

"Well," he finally said. "I've always been a bit obsessed with space, and I wanted to be an astronaut. I even tried to make a space suit out of my mom's tinfoil…didn't work. Um…my friend and I started a rock band when we were twelve and called ourselves The Worm Holes, but neither of us could play an instrument. And when I was sixteen, and had very bad taste, I got my first tattoo—the worst tattoo in existence."

He stuck his leg out and I noticed a small tattoo on his ankle of a butterfly with skulls on its wings and daggers for feelers.

"Oh my God. It's hideous."

"Yup." He smiled at me with a knowing look. It felt familiar, as if we were lifelong friends sharing a joke. It was slightly strange but good at the same time.

"I thought I was very hardcore and cool." He gave me a rather lame *Rock on* hand gesture and we both burst out laughing, and it went on and on like that for hours. We even figured out that his father—who happened to be the CEO of a billion companies—once used my dad's firm to do an audit.

At some stage I looked around and noticed that the restaurant had almost cleared out. The waiter had that desperate look on his face, like it was the end of his shift and he wanted to give us the check. The sun outside had started to dip below the horizon, filling the sky with a pale pink glow.

"How long have we been here?" I asked, gesturing at Damian's watch.

Damian looked at it and suddenly shot out of his chair. "I need to be somewhere and I'm running late. Thanks so much for lunch, Lilly." He took a pen out of his bag, grabbed my arm, and started writing his number across it. "I'm leaving soon, but call me. Please."

And then he leaned down and kissed me on the cheek. Although he was in a hurry, the kiss was not. It was slow, and he let his lips linger for a moment too long. I slowly turned my head toward his and our lips brushed past each other. I looked at him and his eyes were closed. He opened them and looked straight into mine. We were so close I could feel and taste his warm breath; it was sweet with a hint of red wine on it.

"Good-bye, Lilly. Thanks for lunch," he whispered, before turning and running out of the door. That same anxious feeling rose up again, and I jumped up and ran over to our waiter.

"How much is the check?" I practically shouted in the poor guy's face.

He told me and I quickly dug in my bag, grateful that I had almost the exact amount in cash. I shoved it in his hand and then ran outside as fast as I could under the weight of all my shopping. Damian was only a little way up the road and I called after him as loudly as I could.

"Wait up!" He turned, and although he was far away, I could tell he was smiling.

"I'm coming with you," I said, finally catching up to him. "Unless this 'thing' you're doing is illegal...*is it?*"

Damian burst out laughing. "Like what?"

I shrugged. "I don't know. You're pretty weird after all." I smiled at him teasingly.

His smile grew, his eyes locked onto mine, and he extended his hand. "I would love you to come with me, Lilly."

* * *

Twenty minutes later, we were back in busy Patong. Although it was night now, it was even busier than before. It was humming with people and lit up like Las Vegas. The market that I'd been to earlier was bursting at the seams with tourists and partygoers. I was so busy looking around in awe of the transformation that when I looked back, Damian was gone.

I tried looking for him, but there were so many people that I had to physically push them out of the way. I stepped off the sidewalk into the less crowded street hoping for a better vantage point, but I was suddenly very nearly knocked over by a man on a bicycle. I tried to jump out of the way, but it looked like the collision was inevitable, until I felt someone grab me by the arm and yank me back onto the sidewalk. It was Damian. He gripped my arm tightly and shook his head at me with a smile.

"Someone as clumsy as you shouldn't be left unattended in a place like this. Who knows what could happen?"

And then we were off again. He dragged me through the streets, past restaurants and karaoke bars with badly sung ABBA blaring out of them. I was struck by just how many there were; it seemed that every second restaurant had some kind of karaoke happening. Drunk students swayed together singing, while hot Thai girls dressed in heels and short skirts dropped it like it was hot. Old men with beers cheered them on.

But Damian was pulling me farther and farther into the bowels of the city.

The hordes of people started to dissipate and began to be replaced by small groups of the sexiest women I'd ever seen. They all had long, black shiny hair and the most incredible figures, with legs that went on for miles. Some of them were wearing garish outfits, complete with diamanté bikini tops and feather headdresses, and others were wearing almost nothing at all.

The atmosphere had suddenly changed from the happy-go-lucky energy of the night market to something that was much darker and sexually charged. The light around me became very red, and colorful neon signs lit up all the puddles in the road. I knew where we were. And I didn't like it. One little bit.

I stopped walking and let go of Damian's hand.

"Where are we going?" I looked up at the neon sign of a naked woman with ginormous breasts flashing at me. It was not subtle.

Damian flashed me a reassuring smile. "Come. I promise it's not illegal."

I heard a buzzing and looked behind me—the word *sexy* was

blinking at me angrily, and it was enough to give anyone an epileptic seizure.

"Why are we here?"

"Well…" Damian paused for a moment. "I kind of need to make some quick cash."

I gasped. "You're a male prostitute!"

Damian looked at me for a moment and then burst out laughing. "Is that what you think of me?" He was laughing even harder now.

"It's not quite like that, I promise." And he continued walking even though my feet were glued to the pavement. He turned to me and threw his arms in the air. "To come or not to come, Lilly, that is the question."

His corny words seemed to taunt me, as if he knew that I was the kind of girl who'd *never* been to a place like this. Ever. I looked around nervously; drunken men were stumbling into clubs with women draped over them. Women on street corners were hiking up their skirts and whistling loudly. Well, I certainly wasn't going to wait here alone, that's for sure.

"Wait for me!"

After walking up yet another two or three bright-red alleys, we finally stopped outside a club. It looked exactly like the other five hundred we'd just seen, complete with bright, flashing neon lights and a constant buzzing sound coming from the wattage of a thousand light bulbs.

"Here we are," Damian said.

I turned to survey the outside of the club, and then I saw the sign.

MALE STRIPPERS NEEDED. TOTAL NUDITY NOT REQUIRED.

WE PAY CASH. 2,500 BAHT.

It took me a few seconds to make the necessary mental links; they were offering money for men to take off their clothes, and Damian was a man and he needed money, and now we were here, which meant that…

And in five, four, three, two…*Oh my God, I got it!* And I couldn't believe it.

I swung around to confront Damian and voice my vehement disapproval, but he was already walking inside. I folded my arms angrily. There was no way I was going into an establishment like this. No way.

But then I looked around me; I was alone, in a dimly lit and excessively red alley, surrounded by scantily clad women who oozed sex and desperation, and drunken men who were thinking with their dicks.

I'd never been to a strip club before, so I had no way of knowing what lascivious things lurked around the corner. But now a disgusting-looking old, fat man was licking his thin lips and making a beeline for me at great speed.

Now what?

CHAPTER ELEVEN

⌒

𝒯he man outside had crossed the street and was winking at me with his one eye—okay, I'm making that last part up, but he really was awful. I clutched my shopping bags tightly, as if they were about to be stolen, and with great fear and trepidation, shuffled inside.

I've never been into a strip club before, so I wasn't entirely sure what I would see. It would definitely be dirty, though. G-strings and discarded nipple caps probably lay strewn across the floor. No doubt the rats used them to build their little nests. My skin felt sticky and itchy at the mere thought.

But the interior was nothing like I'd imagined. Not at all. It was clean, shiny, and well decorated, and there were no rodents or discarded tassels in sight. It was also gay, which I hadn't expected, either, but was very happy about. I'd always felt comfortable around gay men.

I scanned my surroundings; there was a lot of pink. The tables were full of older men with large sunglasses perched on top of fashionable haircuts—even though it was night and we were inside. There were many tight vests, a lot of unnaturally white porcelain veneers—Jane would have had a laugh about that—and spray tans aplenty. The tables were all full, which left me with nowhere to sit. To be honest, I felt slightly grateful for this as it allowed me to slink into the shadows undetected. I was hoping to somehow blend in, maybe disappear into the wall. I didn't want to be there and had no idea what to expect next, and that made me very, very nervous.

"Oh em gee, sweetie. You look like a hobo loitering there with all those bags."

Huh? Was someone talking to me? I stuck my head out of the shadows and surveyed the area. Someone was waving in my direction—a rather flamboyant red-haired man dressed in a purple silk shirt.

"No, this simply won't do. Don't you think, Francoise?" he said, turning to the man next to him.

The man I assumed was Francoise nodded.

I pointed at myself. "Are you talking to me?"

"No, Nora, I'm talking to the girl standing next to you!"

Red jumped up and sashayed over to me.

"A virgin, right?"

"What?"

"First time in a strip club? You have that poor, frightened Dora-in-the-headlights thing going on. Nothing to be ashamed of. We all need a little man candy from time to time." He winked at me.

"No, no, no…" I laughed nervously. "It's not like that at all. I'm not even supposed to be here. It's a total accident. Huge, *huge* misunderstanding." More nervous laughter again. "I mean, I had no idea I was even coming to a place like this. I don't come to places like this."

"Mmm." He eyed me suspiciously. "That's what they all say, sweetie. Come sit with us. I swear we won't bite." And then he quickly added, "Unless you want us to!" He threw his head back and shrieked with laughter. Without giving me much of a choice, Red grabbed my bags and dragged me to their table. "Come, it looks like you're in desperate need of rescuing."

And he was right. I definitely did need rescuing. I had been ripped so far out of my comfort zone that I wanted to scream. I'm not one of those open-minded watch-a-porno-with-your-partner types. I'm just not in touch with my sexual side in that way. Or in any way really.

"I'm Mark, and this is my ball and chain, Francoise." I looked at Francoise. He was a man in possession of the type of jaw that could easily secure him a starring role in a soap opera. It was *that* square. He was also a man of few words—perhaps his jaw impeded his speech in some way—he just nodded.

"Champagne?" Again, Mark gave me no choice and simply poured me a glass. Though I wasn't complaining—I think I needed the social lubricant.

"Is that fake Chanel I see?" Mark said, leaning over and practically climbing into one of my shopping bags. "Don't you just love how cheap everything is here? Hey, Fransi?"

This time Fransi gave a muffled grunt. Mind you, I'd probably also grunt if I was a grown man with that nickname.

I sipped my champagne and looked at my new friends and was very glad they'd saved me from the embarrassment of looking like a pervert leering from the shadowy sidelines. I was just about to thank them when…

The lights dimmed.

"Here we go, here we go," Mark said, downing his champagne and squealing with delight.

I felt a series of frantic tap-taps on my shoulder. "Hold on to your panties, sister. It's about to get steamy."

Multicolored lights illuminated the stage and a loud puff of smoke came billowing out from behind a red velvet curtain. Some slow and sleazy Rihanna song filled the air and everyone started screaming like high school girls. All I could think about was what a cheesy choice of song it was, but looking around, it was clear that no one else shared this sentiment. But my train of thought was cut short when I saw Damian burst onto the stage, dressed in a suit and tie. The shock was instant and I buried my face in my hands, no doubt going bright red in the process.

"Oh no you don't," Mark said, pulling my hands away from my eyes. By this time, I wasn't sure if I was more embarrassed for Damian or myself. But I was cringing so badly I didn't think I'd be able to watch.

Now in my mind, a strip show is a seedy affair, punctuated with much grinding and thrusting and rubbing and gyrating. But this wasn't the case at all, because as soon as Damian started moving around the stage, it became obvious he was hamming it up. He started his routine with a cartwheel, which made the audience laugh, whoop, and whistle. And then in a very dramatic move, he whipped off his jacket and waved it around his head like a lasso, which caused even more laughter and whistling. I felt an elbow in my ribs. "Oh my God, he's delicious."

Next came the tie, which he made one of the very obliging men in the audience remove. Damian then used the tie as a whip and gave the air a few playful lashings; of course this just caused more mirth.

The whole event was ridiculous; he danced around the stage like a clown and at one point did something that crudely resembled the Macarena. By now my initial anxiety had left me, and I was starting to relax and get into the spirit of things, when, without warning, Damian changed it up and pulled out the big guns...

He suddenly slowed *everything* down.

His face became serious.

His black eyes dark and broody.

Then one by one, and very, very slowly, he undid his shirt buttons. He looked directly at the audience this time; a wicked, naughty-boy look glinted in his eyes. I buried my face in my hands again—all I could think about was how I was about to see his penis. But Mark was on it.

"Eyes to the front, this is the good part."

Damian's movements were slower, more fluid, and highly seductive now. He pulled one of his shirtsleeves down and a surprisingly muscular shoulder slid out. And then another one and then the shirt dropped to the floor and...

A collective gasp of appreciation rose up from the crowd.

They were all silent for a moment; I think it was awe and wonder.

He was lean and ripped and chiseled and muscled and lined in all the right places. Who knew that hiding under those dirty, ironic T-shirts was such a perfect male torso? His most striking feature, by far, were those two lines that went straight from his sides down into his pants. The hot lights were making him sweat just enough that his body was moist and slightly glistening.

My heart started to pound, and my breath kept getting stuck in the back of my throat. I'd never felt like such a blatant perv before. I reached for the champagne and took a sip in a desperate attempt to rehydrate my dry mouth and distract myself. I felt a little dizzy looking at him. And the dizziness only escalated when I remembered holding hands with him and the way he had looked at me. Damian ran his hand through his hair and his six-pack responded by tightening and rippling; this only accentuated those two defined lines that ran all the way down to his…I was officially a pervert.

At this point, the crowd was going ballistic; the mania had built to a fever pitch. But then Damian's mood changed to playful again as he reached for the button on his pants and started teasing the audience, until a collective "Take it off, Take it off" rose up from the crowd. I felt another elbow and another whisper.

"You can tell he's dirty in bed. That guy would give you a good spanking if he could!"

The mere suggestion of Damian in bed was enough to make me wiggle in my seat. I swallowed hard as the button was undone and the zipper slid down. He taunted the audience a little longer before dropping his pants to reveal a rather silly pair of boxer shorts.

Another roar of laughter rose up and, as if it had been rehearsed, men began pulling out their wallets and hurling wads of cash at him. If ever a strip show could be described as funny, sweet, sexy, and silly, this would be it. The song was coming to an end and I assumed the show would, too, but for me it was only just beginning.

The house lights flicked on, illuminating the room, and I saw that Damian was looking directly at me. I must have flushed the color of a fire truck and looked as coy as a toddler trying to get out of trouble. I averted my eyes and my eyelashes fluttered. Yes they did, they bloody fluttered, and they had a mind of their own. There was no controlling them.

He smiled at me, standing there in nothing but his boxer shorts.

And then he moved toward me…

Oh please, oh please do not let this be happening.

Too late. Damian had jumped off the stage, and he suddenly appeared at my table. The crowd went mad and Mark jumped up and down like a possessed teenage girl at a One Direction concert. There was no way I was going to be dragged onto that stage; I would rather die!

Famous last thoughts. I dug my heels in to resist. I held on to the chair and I begged and pleaded, but Damian was too strong. He pulled me all the way through the now-standing, clapping men and onto the stage.

"Please don't do this. Please," I begged Damian, but alas, I was completely ignored.

Instead he swung me around as if we were doing the tango and then dramatically dipped me until the world was the wrong way up. The song had ended by now, and I saw the upside-down figure of Mark stand up and shout.

"Kiss her! Kiss her!"

Oh, holy crap.

"Kiss her. Kiss her, kiss her!" He chanted and clapped until the rest of the club joined in. Damian pulled me up. We were face-to-face now. My body was pressed against his, and I was acutely aware that he was practically naked. He looked me straight in the eye and said, "Well, you heard the men."

I was simultaneously excited and panic-stricken. Earlier we'd shared that brief lip brush, but it was nothing like this. He was going to kiss me, right there, right then, in front of all those people. He took my face between his hands and looked at me for what seemed like forever. I wished I knew what he was thinking.

"Kiss her, bloody hell!" Mark's shrill voice pierced through the chanting.

He leaned forward, and I closed my eyes.

I waited to feel his lips.

The chanting in the club seemed to fade away into the distance.

All I could hear was Damian's breathing, just inches from my face.

His lips finally touched mine, and I felt a flame of red-hot fire lick my spine.

They were soft.

Gentle.

Tender.

He let his still lips linger for a few seconds, before lightly planting another soft kiss on mine.

My lips parted slightly and I let out an involuntary breathy whimper, which I wished I hadn't.

The tips of our noses touched.

I felt him run his hand through my hair and around the back of my neck.

He pulled me a little closer; you couldn't have gotten a sheet of paper between us if you tried.

His other hand dropped down and I felt it slink around my waist.

I let out another breathy whimper. (God, I wished I hadn't.)

He pressed his lips against mine again and my legs went weak. I'd never wanted to kiss someone so badly in my entire life.

His lips parted ever so slightly and he gently kissed my bottom lip. The tip of his tongue came out and met mine. I gasped and opened my mouth for him. My control was slipping and I didn't care. The kiss deepened and sped up, becoming almost frantic as his hands tightened around me and he pulled me even closer and then...

And then he let go of me.

Completely.

Took a step back.

The spell was broken.

The bubble had popped.

I was giddy and confused and looked at Damian. He had the strangest look on his face now.

Regret?

"I'm sorry, Lilly. I should never have done that." His voice was deeply apologetic.

Why was he sorry for kissing me?

I felt my heart crack a little.

I wasn't sorry. That was the best kiss of my entire life.

CHAPTER TWELVE

*W*hen I was six, I was the only girl in my class who didn't get a Valentine's gift. I'd started at yet another new school, because my mother had moved us halfway across the country to be with her yoga instructor, an old white guy named Abhijat (try to pronounce it, I dare you). He was a freak, and my mother forced me to do his morning yoga classes, where he said things like:

"Breathe in through your toenails and out through your ears, Lilly."

"Imagine your buttocks are flowers, Lilly, blossoming in the spring."

"Your spine is a rainbow and it wants to be outside in the rain, Lilly. Release it. Set it free. Let it fly."

A week before Valentine's Day, the boys' craft teacher had them make gifts for the girls. It was very sweet—one of the boys made a heart from bent paper clips and someone else made a necklace with bottle tops. Come Valentine's Day, they whipped out their respective creations, brimming with pride and accomplishment, and handed them over.

But they'd forgotten about me—yes, I was new, but it still hurt.

I remember standing there among the sea of shiny crafty things feeling like no one cared about me. It was so embarrassing, and I didn't want anyone to notice, so I snuck outside and hid in the playground.

And that's how I felt right now as I stood outside the club.

It hurt that Damian regretted kissing me. It was the sharp pain of rejection, mingling with the sting of embarrassment, mixing with the dull ache of disappointment that took me right back to being that little girl who'd climbed into the colorful tunnel and cried softly to herself.

I felt pathetic. But I was also angry with myself for letting it get this far. I was clearly vulnerable and this was no time to open myself up to anyone, certainly not to Damian. And I didn't even like him...*did I?* Whatever feelings I *thought* I had for him were obviously of the rebound ilk. I couldn't afford to go there, not with Damian, not with anyone. No, what I really needed right now was to close all the doors and windows, bolt the shutters, throw away the key, and retreat into a padded cell for my own safety.

I felt so alone and was overcome—once again—with a need to spy on Michael. I took out my phone and realized that it was flooded with messages: Mom, Dad, Val, Jane, Annie, and even Stormy (which is odd because she is suspicious of cell phones). I flicked through them quickly, not really absorbing much, although I did see that Stormy had cast a spell on Michael and with any luck, she said, he should have genital warts within a day or so.

I logged on to Facebook and was about to go to Michael's page when I saw I had a friend request. I clicked. Damien Bishop.

Damien with an *E*. I'd spelled his name incorrectly. My heart conveniently forgot that it was meant to be on lockdown and I accepted his request, went straight to his page, and opened his photos (as one does).

And there he was. Beautiful Damien with an *E*. I got this strange feeling as I scrolled through his pictures. It was a feeling of familiarity—as if I was looking at photos of my oldest and dearest friend. But then I stopped. All the blood that usually pumped around my body drained out of me in one fast whoosh.

A photo caught my eye. It was of Damien, happy, smiling Damien, with his arm around a hot chick. Did I mention she was super hot? She looked like his type, too: She was petite and her dark hair was cut into a severe bob with dead-straight bangs.

She had huge blue eyes and was dressed in black skinny jeans and a casual T-shirt with a Barbie doll print. Is there a shop somewhere that sells ironic T-shirts to cool people? I kept scrolling and she kept making more and more appearances. Yep, there they were in London together; yep, that's them in front of the Eiffel Tower; and yep, that looks like them having lots of fun at some party somewhere. It hadn't even occurred to me that Damien might have a girlfriend…or *two*?

My mouth fell open as I flipped through more pictures and another girl appeared. She was equally gorgeous, and her undeniable coolness intimidated me all the way through the phone screen. She had long, blond hair with blue tips. She wore bright colors and cute Gangnam-style clothing. The three of them were hanging on to one another as if they had all been surgically attached. Then I saw a picture that actually made me feel physically ill. A selfie. All of them. In bed. Together.

Suddenly, I felt cheated on. Damien was cheating on me with

some hot, skinny hipster chicks. They were probably cool, but in that *I so don't care what's cool* kind of way. They were probably fun and rebellious and had tattoos and nipple rings. They probably tattooed each other as foreplay. They probably didn't even need to read *Fifty Shades of Grey*; they'd moved on from whips and ties years ago and were doing something that hadn't even been invented yet.

Clearly they were having wild, hot, loud threesomes while hanging upside down like vampire bats and listening to obscure bands that made pretentious ukulele music on vinyl. I continued to scroll through the pictures, and they were everywhere. Wearing more ironic T-shirts, big black-framed glasses, and strange vintage shoes that might have been worn by a vagrant, but with the addition of knitted laces made from reclaimed wool, the look went from homeless to hipster.

But the photo that grated me the most was the one of dark-haired hipster chick lying on the beach wearing a yellow polka-dot bikini, *ironically*. She had one of those thin, wispy ballet bodies and you just knew she'd probably Instagrammed a photo of herself eating some kind of fattening vegan treat just minutes previously.

I was so jealous of her!

The door swung open and Damien stepped out. I jumped as if I'd just been caught doing something naughty, which I had been—I was cyberstalking his hot girlfriends. I had this sudden mad urge to confront him about his infidelity, but then sanity slapped me in the face. I turned the phone off quickly and slipped it back into my bag. After the painful sting of my public humiliation, the only reason I was still there, standing outside the club waiting for him, was that I didn't want to attempt escaping the red-light district alone—who knew what could happen? If it hadn't been for that, I would have been long gone by now.

But instead of walking straight up to me, he stopped and started typing on his phone. Sending someone a message? My first thought was that he was texting his cool girlfriends. I felt so unbelievably jealous I could scream.

"Do you think you can help me get back to my hotel?" My statement was curt and I deliberately avoided eye contact.

"Sure," he said, striding out into the road, barely looking at me while he continued to type away. There was definitely a weird vibe between us now. Gone was the comfortable familiarity of the lunch we'd shared earlier.

Damien finally finished his sexting and slipped his phone back into his pocket. He kept walking and I followed him closely, watching him walk. I wish I hadn't seen him half-naked, because now I knew what lay beneath those clothes and this had only ignited a full-blown war in my head. My primitive reptilian brain was waging a fierce war against my logical self, fighting for control. Images of a shirtless Damien flooded my mind, and then some kind of superhero avatar of myself jumped in and beat him away. This went on and on until I felt positively exhausted. I tried to focus on something else, so I looked around.

There was a mangy, flea-bitten cat with half a tail scrounging in a dustbin to my left, a group of sexy women to my right. We walked past a giant red flashing light that said GIRLS and past a group of drunk, stumbling guys.

"Hey, baby." I heard a whistle followed by a shout and turned around. One of the drunken guys had changed direction and was veering toward me, so I quickly put my head down and sped up.

"Hey, hey, baby. Don't run from me." I could almost smell the alcohol, even though he was still a few feet away.

Damien stopped walking and swung around. He wasted no time in grabbing me by the arm and pulling me behind him with such force that it actually hurt.

"Is there a problem here?" His tone was menacing, and I'd never heard it before. It clearly took the guy by surprise, too, because he held his hands up in resignation.

"No problem, bro. Just trying to say hello to a beautiful lady. No crime in that."

"Well, don't." Damien glared at him and took an intimidating stride forward. The man stepped back.

"Hey, buddy, no worries. No harm meant." The drunken guy turned and stumbled away, but Damien carried on standing there, staring after him. I walked around and looked at him. He had a terrifyingly dangerous look on his face. His eyes were squeezed together into thin black slits, and his face had contorted into a look that *could* kill. I shivered. Damien definitely had a dangerous streak, that's for sure.

"Come." Damien sounded forceful. He grabbed my shopping bags, took me by the hand, and yanked me hard. I resisted and pulled away. This hand-holding thing had to stop. Now!

"What are you doing?"

"I'm more than capable of carrying my own bags and walking alone without you holding my hand," I said as indignantly as I possibly could.

"I'm sure you are, but I'd rather you didn't. If you hadn't noticed, we're not exactly in the most kosher part of town. Come." Again, his hand came for me.

I pushed it away. "No!"

"Do I need to pick you up and throw you over my shoulder?"

"You wouldn't dare."

"Try me." He glared at me without blinking, his poker face revealing absolutely nothing that led me to conclude he was joking.

"Why do you even care?" I started walking again, striding ahead as fast as my short legs would take me.

Damien caught up to me quickly and grabbed me by the elbow. "What are you talking about, Lilly? Of course I care. I'm not going to let some drunken guy take advantage of you."

This was killing me. I couldn't bear to look at him and focused all my attention on a little puddle by my foot instead. "Please just get me back to my hotel."

There was another one of those awkward moments, and I heard Damien fill it with a loud sigh.

"Do we need to talk about the kiss?" His tone was calmer and even though I wasn't looking directly at him, I could tell his demeanor had changed, too.

"No," I said, trying to put on a brave face. "You made it perfectly clear that you regretted it and wished it hadn't happened."

"You think I wished it didn't happen?"

"Yes."

"You've got it *so* wrong, Lilly. I don't regret kissing you. I could *never* regret kissing you. It was…" He paused. "It was…" I looked up at him now and could see he was struggling to find the word. I could offer him a few: nice, great, amazing, hot?

He continued without finishing his sentence, but the implication was there. "And you're beautiful, but…" Our eyes met. "I just didn't want you to think I was taking advantage of you. I know you're hurting…" He took a deep breath and paused for a moment. "That's why I'm sorry it happened. Not because I didn't enjoy it or want it. Because I really did. Enjoy it and want it."

I couldn't believe what I was hearing. This moment couldn't be more perfect if I'd written the script myself. I was about to let him know that I, too, had enjoyed it, and I, too, had wanted to do it and that I would very much like to do it again, when…

"But I know it can never happen again. *Ever.* This is supposed to be your honeymoon, for God's sake. You've just been through hell and I don't want to hurt you more. So I promise that I will never kiss you again, you have my word. So…"

He stepped forward and extended his hand.

"So…friends?" He looked up and smiled at me innocently. Friend-like.

Hang on a moment. Let's stop here. What just happened? We'd gone from "I wanted to kiss you, I like kissing you" to "I will never kiss you again, let's be buddies."

I sighed internally but extended my hand. "Fine. Friends." Deep down I knew he was right. Then why did it feel so wrong?

A tuk-tuk drove up the street and Damien waved it down. I wondered what was going to happen now. Would we continue hanging out together? Should I reinvite him on my so-called honeymoon? Offer to put him up for the nights ahead?

"Damien, would you like to come back to the hotel again, as friends? I know you have nowhere to stay still."

"As much as I'd love to crash your honeymoon, Lilly, I'm going to be leaving Phuket soon."

"Leaving? When?" I wasn't sure I liked this news.

"I'm leaving in the morning."

My heart sank. I looked at my watch, it was already one thirty a.m. How the hell had that happened? "Where are you going?"

"I'm not sure yet."

"How can you not know where you're going?"

A mischievous smile lit up his face. "I'm going to this party, they just haven't sent out the map yet."

I shook my head at him. The information was not computing.

"Once a year a big party is held, it's always in Thailand, though. But the precise location is kept a secret until just before the event. Last year it was on top of a mountain—took me two days just to hike there."

"That sounds terrible," I said, thinking about all that outdoorsy exertion and the potential close proximity to snakes and spiders.

Damien shook his head. "No, it's pretty amazing, actually. It's two days of music and partying, and you meet really cool people."

Oh wait, something about this was starting to sound very familiar. I remembered Stormy-Rain telling me about these amazing parties held in Thailand. She's always wanted to go. "Oh, like those Black Moon parties," I offered.

Damien *tsk*ed loudly. "Nothing like those Black Moon parties. This is much, *much* better. They only invite a limited number of people and you have to qualify for an invitation."

"Oooh," I said in a mocking tone. "So exclusive and cool, no wonder you're going."

And then Damien jumped up excitedly. "Hey. Why don't you come with me?"

"What?"

"Yes, come with me." He pointed at my shopping bags. "You're already packed."

"Um…" I was thinking fast. There were about a million reasons why I shouldn't go.

"Um… what about my hotel?"

"It's not going anywhere. You'll be back in a few days."

"But I can't just go with you!"

"Who says?"

"But I don't have any sun cream."

"I'll buy you some. I have pockets full of money now, remember?" He patted his bulging pocket.

Mmm, how could I forget.

"But, but…" I was searching still. "I don't have a toothbrush."

"I'll buy you one, too."

I was running out of reasons. "I don't know, Damien…I just don't think I can."

Damien deflated like a balloon. "It's cool, Lilly. I understand. It's a pity, though."

Damien took my bags and started packing them into the tuk-tuk. The action had such an air of finality to it. This was it. He was going away for a few days and by the time he got back, I'd be on my way home to South Africa. I would never see him again.

Should I? Shouldn't I? Should I? Shouldn't I? Should I? Shouldn't I? An inner mantra began. *Why not go? What harm could it do?*

"Okay, fine! Fine!" I quickly pulled my bags out of the taxi and told the driver he could go, before I could I change my mind.

Damien's face lit up. "Seriously?"

"Why the hell not? Caution to the wind and all that stuff, right?"

"When in Thailand," he offered and we both smiled.

"But if it's by invitation only, how will I get in?"

"Don't worry, I know the guy who runs it."

"Of course you do."

Damien turned to me. "You're going to have the time of your life, Lilly. I promise."

Mmm, that's what I was afraid of.

CHAPTER THIRTEEN

amien and I wandered through the still action-packed streets of Patong. This nocturnal town seemed to be in constant motion. The frenzied energy that spilled onto the streets from the clubs and bars was like nothing I'd ever seen before. Everywhere you looked, something was going on.

Damien spun around and faced me. "Do you want to grab a drink somewhere?"

"Drinks?" That sounded so very date-ish. "Sure."

"I was hoping you'd say that. I can't wait to show you this place." With that, Damien picked up pace, weaving skillfully through the crowds and street vendors who seemed to be selling all types of foods on sticks. I followed him down the infamous Bangla Road until we arrived at the bottom of an almost vertical escalator. I hesitated. I disliked heights. Immensely.

"It won't be that bad. Just hold on to the rails," Damien said in an encouraging voice.

"Hold on to the rails! Ha! Do you have any idea how germy an

escalator is? They've done tests on it and they've even found—"
I stopped midsentence. I was about to tell him that an escalator
belt is basically a mobile sperm bank. "I hate heights. Okay? Hate
them."

"Then look at the floor and hold my hands." Without asking,
Damien took me by the hands and led me onto the escalator. I did
exactly what he said, not daring to look up for a second.

I held my breath the entire way up and as soon as we reached the
top, I sprinted away and put my back up against the nearest wall. I
let out a massive sigh of relief and closed my eyes. But when I opened
them again, Damien was staring at me curiously.

"What?"

"Nothing. You're just one of the funniest people I've ever met."
His smile broadened until it had taken over all of his features.

"I don't think anyone has ever called me funny before. Pedantic
maybe. A perfectionist. Organized, definitely. Not funny."

"Well, they don't know you like I do then."

"Oh please… You hardly know me."

"I know all the important stuff. You like baths. Prefer savory
foods, your favorite color is cream and—"

Damien proceeded to rattle off the list from earlier with an
almost perfect recollection. He really did pay attention to everything I said, or maybe he had one of those savant-style photo-
graphic memories?

"Do you remember everything people tell you?" I asked.

"No. Just the interesting ones that I like."

"I am so *not* interesting. I assure you."

He walked over and leaned against the wall next to me.

"If anyone is interesting and confusing, it's you, Damien Bishop."

"How am I confusing?" He looked me in the eye and all those strange, fluttery feelings inconveniently returned.

"Well, you come across as this dark, mysterious creature with all your strange faded clothes, terrible shoes, and tattoos. To be honest, when I first saw you, you scared the hell out of me."

Damien laughed. "So did you."

"Hey, that's unfair. There were extenuating circumstances."

"Fair enough." He smiled at me gently. "Please, do continue. I'm fascinated."

"I thought you'd be cold and strange and disturbingly dark—no offense."

"None taken."

"But now I suspect you'd probably risk your life to save a fluffy kitten from a cliff."

Damien remained silent for a while before he spoke. "I think when my sister died, I built up these walls around me. Tried to keep certain people away. Besides, I quite like making bad first impressions."

"Why?" This statement confused me. Why would anyone want to make a bad first impression? It didn't make sense.

"It keeps people at bay and lets me be selective about who I get to know. I only put energy into people I really like and feel a connection with."

I nodded. I understood this. My sister Stormy behaved in the exact same manner, keeping certain types of people at bay with her appearance.

"Well, I think you're depriving a lot of people from getting to know you. I think you're really…lovely."

Damien turned and looked at me with something that

resembled…*what the hell was it*…coyness? He looked so shy and cute that I was overcome with a desire to hug him. "Thanks, that's one of the nicest things anyone has ever said to me."

Damien slid closer to me until our shoulders were touching and our faces were just inches apart. Our eyes met and it felt like a meteor crashed into my stomach leaving me totally winded.

"So…" Damien suddenly cleared his throat and pushed himself off the wall. "So, shall we not lean against a wall all night then?"

"Sure." I gave him a faint smile. The moment was over. Damien had deliberately ended it because we were *friends*.

He held his hand out again for me to take. I was getting so used to holding hands with him, and it was happening with increasing frequency.

Michael and I hadn't been great hand-holders. In fact, we hadn't been that affectionate with each other lately at all. It suddenly dawned on me that I'd been more physically affectionate with Damien in the last few days than I had been with Michael in months. It started to make me wonder, *wonder if*…

I dislodged that thought from my head. I wasn't ready to think about it yet.

We walked into one of the fanciest bars I'd ever seen, and immediately I knew why Damien loved it here. It was situated on a high rooftop and was entirely open to the night sky above. The view in every direction was spectacular. For a moment I totally forgot where I was. It was hard to imagine a place like this existed above such a busy, bustling road. I looked up, and the night was clear. Stars bright. Moon fat and silver. It looked bigger tonight and seemed to be hanging even lower. I glanced over at Damien—he was looking up with that same boyish expression of awe I'd seen the night before.

"So, do you have any cool moon facts?" I asked, feeling a genuine interest in all things astrological.

"Sure. Did you know that the moon is moving away from the Earth by 3.8 centimeters every year?"

"I do now."

"And what about this one: Only twelve people have set foot on it. Can you imagine that? We see it every single day and yet it's so unexplored. Imagine setting foot on a place like that."

"Is that why you travel? To set foot on the un-set-footed?" I asked.

Damien smiled at my made-up word. Michael would never have appreciated that; in fact, he'd probably have corrected me immediately.

"There's nothing better than experiencing a place for the first time," Damien said, looking up at me with a very loaded, meaningful look. Another inappropriate feeling began rising up from my belly.

He turned away, which I was downright grateful for. I doubted I could hide the now-crimson shade of my face—even in the subdued atmospheric lighting.

I eyed Damien as he sauntered through the place. He stopped at the bar and then proceeded to lean against it so nonchalantly you would have thought he owned the bloody place. He seemed to have blasé down to a fine art. Nothing seemed to faze him, whereas everything fazed me.

I'd always wished I could be a cooler and more composed person, but the truth was, on the freak-out scale, I could go from one to *disaster/the world is about to end and we're all going to die* in a matter of minutes. His devil-may-care disinterestedness gave him such an air of self-confidence. It was both intimidating and undeniably sexy at the same time.

"So what will it be, Lilly?"

"Huh?" It took a moment to realize he was talking to me. "I'm not sure."

"This then—" He pointed to a colorful drink with an unreadable Thai name. "I have no idea what's in it. But when in Thailand, right?"

Exotic-looking drinks in hand, we made our way to the comfortable red chairs by the window.

"So what's the plan? For the party?" I asked, feeling somewhat lubricated from the strong, unusual-tasting drink.

"We should be sent a map soon and then it's up to us to make our way there." Damien whipped out his phone and scanned it. "No map yet but"—a smile played at the corners of his mouth— "one Lilly Swanson seems to have accepted my friend request on Facebook."

Damien fiddled on his phone for a while, mm-hmming and nodding and then eventually grinning from ear to ear.

"Hey! What're you doing?" I jumped up and looked down at his phone. One of my old, less-than-flattering photos stared back at me.

"It was for a dress-up party. *Okay!*" I jumped to my own defense. "I don't usually wear blue eye shadow and...that!" Damien turned and smiled at me with another roguish grin that screamed naughtiness.

"I bet you've already looked at all my photos."

"What? That's such crap. Why would I look at your photos? Please. That's ridiculous." And that was way too much protesting! But I suddenly realized that this might be my one legitimate opportunity to ask about hipster chicks casually without coming across as a psycho stalker.

"Well... okay, maybe just one or two." I took a sip of my drink, hoping for a tiny drop of Dutch courage. "But since you bring up the topic, now that we're on the subject of photos..." I stopped myself again. What the hell was I doing asking about his possible girlfriend? Girlfriends? I'm not sure I wanted to know. I downed the last bit of my drink and almost choked on the fruity thing at the bottom.

Damien continued to fiddle on his phone and then stopped. He looked at it curiously for a moment or two. "Is this Michael?"

He turned the screen to me, and my stomach tightened.

"Yes." I nodded. "It's him."

"You look... you look..." Damien paused and pulled the screen closer to him. "You don't look like yourself."

I was momentarily stunned. This was the last thing I'd expected him to say.

"What do you mean?"

"Your hair is so perfect... and straight?"

"Michael liked it that way." My hands instinctively went up to touch it. It was wavy from the sea air and I'd scraped it back into a loose, messy bun. I usually wouldn't be seen dead like this.

"And that necklace, Lilly?"

"Oh. That. It's a family heirloom from Michael's side." Truthfully, I'd hated the thing. It was a big, Baroque pearly affair that I'd always felt obliged to wear on special occasions and family functions.

"Stormy-Rain is always threatening to pull it apart and turn it into a wind chime."

Damien let out a small chuckle. "I think I'm going to like her."

He put his phone back into his pocket and leaned all the way across the table. "This looks like you."

"A much messier version," I added quickly, tucking a lose tendril of hair behind my ear.

"Mess suits you." He gave me a playful smile and I started melting. I couldn't afford to melt right now, so I sat up straight and crossed my legs.

"So now what? Are we just going to sit here all night waiting for the map to arrive?"

"No, I was hoping to get a bit of sleep at some stage."

"Where?"

Damien smiled. "I'll show you."

***

"Where the hell are we?" My eyes widened in shock as I surveyed my new surroundings.

"Backpackers lodge." Damien sounded cheerful.

"We do have a perfectly good hotel, you know."

"But where's the fun in that, Lilly?"

"Fun?" I snorted. This place looked more like a postapocalyptic nightclub than somewhere one might actually sleep. A few people were dancing, some lazed on the bright DayGlo beanbags that were scattered across the floor, and others were playing loud drinking games while girls in bikinis cheered them on. Glass sliding doors opened onto a pool area that was filled to capacity with laughing, splashing, jumping people and, *look*, there went a naked man. Delightful.

I stepped over someone on the floor who was clearly on the wrong side of consciousness, and I tried not to trip on the beer can by my foot. *Classy!* I'd never been to a place like this before. Nor did I want to. I didn't care how much "fun" everyone looked like they were having. I could *never* have fun in a place like this.

And that was only further confirmed when I saw the "rooms." A large gray dormitory reminiscent of a prison cell, packed floor to ceiling with wire-framed bunk beds stretched out before me.

Some of the beds were inhabited; a few girls looked up from their magazines and smiled at us (or maybe they were smiling at Damien). A shirtless man nodded in our direction, a dreadlocked fellow rolling "something" between his fingers gave us a "Yo man" greeting, and the body that dangled from one of the top bunks gave a loud grunt.

I felt dirty just looking at it all. Coed communal living wasn't exactly my thing. What was next…eating dried rations and sharing a solitary bar of recycled soap?

But before I could open my mouth to protest, Damien said, "Come on, where's your sense of fun, Lill?"

"Fun? Here? I don't think so."

Little did I know how wrong I was.

CHAPTER FOURTEEN

❧

What's going on?

My head was pounding and I was vaguely aware of a persistent dripping sound near my ear. I tried to roll over. Owww…my stomach hurt as if someone had kicked me in it.

I tried to open my mouth, but it felt like I was at the dentist getting a cast of my teeth taken. *Was I at the dentist?* I struggled to open my thick, swollen eyelids. What was wrong with them?

They finally opened. But nothing looked familiar.

Oh God. Why was I so confused? I started to become aware of my extremities. One arm, another, a leg, another leg, and feet…*Hang on*, why were my feet wet?

Something strange dangled above my head. It looked like…*but how?* Why the hell did it look like my shoe was hanging from a palm tree above my head?

I looked around. *Where was I?*

Okay, I was lying on a bright-pink lounger by a pool. A few lively folk seemed to be splashing in the water; some were sleeping on other loungers, but most looked like they were nursing a hangover from hell. I felt like I had a hangover, too. But I can't remember drinking. *Did I drink?*

I stood up and winced in pain. Every muscle from my calves to my thighs, up to my bum and some other muscles I didn't even recognize or knew existed were on fire. *Why was I in so much pain?* A serious gym workout? A marathon?

I must have drunk last night. And then exercised. There was no other possible explanation for this feeling. *Unless...* No! Get a grip, Lilly. You aren't the victim of one of those black-market organ-stealing backstreet operations. *Fuck, remind me to stop watching so much reality TV.*

My head was *so* heavy. Someone had poured cement into my skull. I looked around again and vague recollections started coming to me.

Damien brought me to a backpackers lodge. I remembered walking into the dorm, thinking it was dirty... *But what happened next?* And where the hell was Damien?

German men? I remember now... I'd played a drinking game with a bunch of rowdy German tourists. Beer. I remember beer. My stomach lurched. *I hated beer.*

"Lillllyyyy..." A distinctly macho voice made me whip around. The voice belonged to a rather hairy shirtless man who was a making very quick beeline for me.

"Lillyyyy," he said again in a tone that concerned me and with a smile that quite frankly disturbed me. His smile seemed to hold a secret that I wasn't privy to, and the way he was looking at me was just, just... he reminded me of some sleazy, hip-thrusting lounge singer. He was walking toward me as if he was about to use my body as a stripper pole.

"Lil, babe. You were great last night, babe." I stood dead still as his clammy little hand came up and squeezed my waist.

"Mmmmmm. So good…" He pursed his lips and gave me a slow wink before he turned on his heel and walked away.

What did he mean anyway? *"You were great last night…"*

"Hey, Lilly." Another male voice startled me and I spun around. Dreadlocks the size of my arms flapped in front of me. I could barely make out what was behind them. And then a hand came up. And another. And then without any kind of warning this man had taken me in his arms for a hug. He pulled away and gave me two enthusiastic thumbs-up and a knowing wink.

"You were awesome last night," he said, before planting double kisses on both my cheeks and walking away.

Oh God—their words punched me through the face like a knuckle sandwich. NO! Surely NOT! I would never…*would I?*

I scanned my brain again, trying to remember what I'd done next, but nothing came to me. Not a single image to allay my fears that I may have…but I couldn't have, could I? I wasn't that type of girl and where the bloody hell was Damien?

I turned when I heard a whistle. Across the pool, a group of more shirtless guys were waving at me. Two of them raised their glasses in a kind of toast and another blew me a kiss.

What the hell had I done last night?

I took a few steps and suddenly became aware of a terrible sensation. I wasn't wearing a bra. I looked down…I wasn't wearing my clothes—I was wearing a man's shirt. This was a very bad sign.

I glanced around frantically. My dress was hanging from the back of a chair and the floor was scattered with other people's clothes. My fears had been confirmed in one ugly fell swoop. I had officially lost it, and in the process, had clearly slept with half of Thailand. I was mortified.

I crossed my arms and rushed inside as fast as my humiliated self would take me. I bumped straight into another smiling person…this time it was Damien.

Not him…*please*!

"Morning," he said cheerfully. I glanced behind him and a few more smiles were being thrown in my direction. Some from women. *Could I? Would I?*

"Damien…I think we need to talk."

"Sure." He put his arm around me and led me to the nearest table.

"What's up?" He pushed a cup of coffee toward me, and I immediately grabbed it.

"I thought you would need it this morning, especially after all that energy expending you did last night."

"Energy?" I half choked on the black liquid.

"Yeah. You were really going for it." A massive smile broke out across his face and I immediately face-palmed.

"Oh God. I'm so fucking embarrassed! I never, ever, I mean *never*, do that kind of thing. I've never…I can't even believe it…!"

"Don't worry." Damien laid a consoling hand on my shoulder. "You were really good. Everyone said so."

"EVERYONE?" A mouthful of coffee shot out onto the table in front on me.

"How…how…how many were there? Did everyone see?"

"See? Everyone joined it!"

The walls of the room felt like they were going to crash down around me. My ears started ringing, my tongue started swelling, and my face started burning with the kind of humiliation that made being left at the altar feel like child's play.

"I…I don't remember."

"How can you not remember that? I've never seen anything like it!"

"Did you…um…also, I mean…?"

"Totally! I was your leading man. You really don't remember?"

I hung my head in absolute shame waiting for the sordid details to be regaled to me.

But then Damien did something very odd. He burst into sudden loud song…

"Mamma mia, here I go again—"

Then the whole room joined in…*"My my, how can I resist you?"* They all sang loudly and jumped up, gesticulating wildly with their arms.

I looked around in absolute shock; the whole room had burst into an ABBA song. My mother had starred in an ABBA musical years ago. I'd hated that play, more than anything. I'd lived in it. Every single rehearsal. Sleeping on the theater chairs late at night while my mother flung herself around the stage like a prima donna.

I turned back to Damien. "I reenacted a song from a musical?"

"Not just that. You taught it to everyone and the whole place joined in. It was hysterical. You even jumped into the pool fully clothed. Everyone did." Damien laughed and relief began to creep in.

"Is that all I did?"

"You entertained the whole place for hours."

"Oh thank God!" I exclaimed, as the full force of my relief rushed in. "Phew! I'm so glad I didn't sleep with you." I glugged the coffee down enthusiastically.

The smile on Damien's face melted off and was replaced by a look that I'd never seen before. "You thought we...?"

"Had sex? Yes, for a moment there! What a relief we didn't!" I laughed out loudly at the ridiculousness of it all. Of course I'd never do anything like that. No matter what state I was in. "For a moment I thought I might have had sex with everyone here."

"Really?" He sounded shocked.

I nodded. "Yes, even with that guy with the massive dreadlocks."

Suddenly Damien looked wildly offended. He got up and walked off to the other side of the room. What the hell was going on? I jumped up and followed him.

"Have I said something wrong?"

"I can't believe you thought I'd let that happen to you." He sat on one of the beanbags, and I flopped down next to him.

"Let what happen?" I asked.

"Do you really think I would've let you sleep with anyone last night?"

"You wouldn't?"

"Of course not. I'd never let you do something like that to yourself. And I would never, *ever* sleep with you..." He paused for a moment and looked over at me meaningfully. My heart thumped in my chest. "...not in that state."

Had Damien just said he would have sex with me? He looked away and sudden images from last night came popping in. Small fragments at first, then a little more, and a tiny bit more, until I could remember everything. I remembered Damien.

The way he'd stayed by my side the entire night and made sure I was okay. The way he'd warded off that hip thruster when he'd come up and grabbed my ass. The way he'd taken me into the bathroom, removed my wet clothes, towel dried my hair, and put me in one of his shirts. Wait, had he taken my bra off too?

I remember him sitting on the lounger with me, and most of all, I remember his hands. He'd rubbed my back and stroked my hair until I'd fallen asleep with my head in his lap.

"I remember now. You were so sweet last night." I turned and smiled at him. "Thanks for looking after me."

"I would never let anything bad happen to you, Lilly. Ever." A solemn look washed over his face and he moved closer to me. He gazed at me in a way that caused a shiver to navigate the entire length of my spine.

I swallowed hard, my throat going even drier than it already was. I looked at this man sitting next to me, and I felt so incredibly cared for. He made me feel safe in ways that Michael never had. A sudden loud *beep beep* rang out and broke the moment, sending Damien reaching for his phone.

"They sent the map out, by the way. So we should probably get going soon." He quickly rose and pulled me up.

"Thanks again for looking after me." I leaned in and kissed him on the cheek, letting my lips linger. God, he smelled good.

"So are you ready for an adventure, Lilly?"

"Ready as I'll ever be." I finished my coffee in two last big sips and quickly flew up the stairs, despite the stiff muscles. Everyone I passed greeted me with a big hello. Some even broke into song and hugged me.

Who the hell was this messy Lilly that did such wild, crazy things? I quite liked her, even if I didn't recognize her, and I definitely didn't recognize the—

"*What the hell!*" I couldn't stifle the shocked scream as I looked down at my stomach in the shower. I had a belly ring! An actual honest-to-God ring through my belly button. I jumped out and ran for the mirror.

Who had done that? Why would I have let them? And I hope it had been done under sterile conditions.

Oh shit, maybe one of my organs was missing!

"Damien?" I screamed out the bathroom door.

Loud laughter came echoing down the corridor in reply. "Don't worry, she's a professional body piercer and you said you really, really wanted it."

"I did?" I stared at myself in the mirror. This new Lilly was surprising me more and more with each passing moment. What the hell was she going to do next?

CHAPTER FIFTEEN

$\mathcal{I}$'m usually the girl who's on time.

The girl who doesn't go out on weeknights.

The girl who files her books according to the Dewey decimal system.

The girl who takes her rented movies back on time. Sometimes even early.

I'm the girl with a plan.

I'm the girl with a routine.

I'm the girl with the well-ordered, well-arranged, well-organized, well-placed, well-structured, well-controlled, well-everything'd life.

So what the hell was I doing on a boat with Damien, speeding across the waters to some island, somewhere, out there, on the way to some strange, wild, mysterious party where, for all I knew, the requirement would be going totally nude, fire dancing, fire breathing, drinking alcohol filled with worms, belly dancing with snakes, having orgies, swinging with your partner, swinging from the trees, drinking blood, and participating in human sacrifice—okay, so maybe that last part was extreme, but then again, I've seen stranger things on the reality channel.

We'd left the hostel to a round of very enthusiastic hugs and a loud chorus of good-byes. Dreadlocks Guy had made one last desperate attempt at a sleazy waist clench, but after Damien had flashed him a very loaded look, he retreated.

We'd then taken a tuk-tuk across the island all the way to Rassada Pier. Once there, we boarded a ferry and sped off to the famous island of Phi Phi. From there we were to board another boat and go off to a more isolated island where the party was going to be held. It sounded pretty simple.

The scenery on the ride was incredible. The waters were a deep blue and dissolved into an incandescent light blue the closer they got to land. Small islands rose straight up out of the water; most of them simply looked like enormous rocks. Some were covered in tropical plants, while others had sheer white cliff faces that plummeted into the swirling waters below. Although spectacular, the islands looked completely uninhabitable; there was no way you would be able to access them with all those vertical cliffs.

The boat sped through the water, sending a soft, warm spray into my face. A large island came into view and soon we'd docked in a busy bay. This was clearly a very popular tourist destination, but there was no time to explore and we immediately started looking for another boat that could take us on to our final destination.

Damien found a small boat that took private tours, and after some more calculator negotiation, they agreed on a price. The tour guide scrutinized the map on Damien's phone and assured us with many happy nods and a lot of broken English, he knew *exactly* where the island was. In fact, he said, a lot of tours went past that island every morning en route to more popular destinations.

And with that, we were off again, speeding across the waters and headed back out into the open seas. It was all so very pirate-y; following a map to some secret somewhere. The island of Phi Phi started to disappear behind us, and the tourist boats became fewer and fewer. I had no idea what time it was when we finally reached the island. I barely knew what day of the week it was. My phone had been off for ages, causing my usually precise sense of time to feel completely muddled. And I didn't care. It felt liberating. I didn't even know where in the bloody world I was exactly.

We thanked the man for taking us and stepped off the boat and onto an island littered with boulders. There was barely any sand on the beach, it was so covered in rocks of different shapes and sizes. Behind the boulders, a thick jungle sprawled out.

There wasn't a sign of life anywhere. Not even a solitary set of footprints to indicate that a human had ever been here. Damien started looking around and I took the opportunity to inspect my surroundings.

It was magical here. Picture perfect, in fact. Like one of those computer screen savers that seem to show places too perfect to be real. But this was real. The beach was covered in massive gray boulders. They looked like they had haphazardly landed there from a game of ancient intergalactic marbles.

The sea here was particularly blue. A powdery baby blue that looked almost silky to the touch, and in places it was perfectly translucent. The sand didn't seem like sand, either; it was far too white, too fine and luxuriously soft. I watched, in an almost trancelike state, as tiny swells of water lapped against the rocks, producing a soft, rhythmic swishing sound.

But I wasn't able to relax fully. I was aware that Damien seemed to be buzzing up and down behind me on the beach. I heard a gentle rustle and glanced over my shoulder at the thick, mysterious-looking jungle. Damien had just stuck his head into it as if he was looking for something. He'd started to look, *dare I say it*, concerned.

"Um…what's wrong?"

"Nothing just yet," he said in a voice that was hardly reassuring. "Give me another five minutes and then I'll let you know if we have a problem or not."

"A problem?" I didn't like the sound of that one little bit. I watched him intently as a growing feeling of impending doom gnawed at the back of my neck.

"What are you looking for?" I asked nervously.

"A sign. They always have a sign to let you know you're in the right place. I can't find a sign."

The doom morphed into a supercharged bolt of panic that shot from my head to my toes and back again. "Are we on the wrong island?"

Damien stopped pacing. He looked around thoughtfully, as if he was really considering that option. It frightened me. "We could be."

"What!" I almost fell off the rock I was sitting on. "The wrong island?"

"It's possible."

"How possible?" My voice was quivering.

"I would say *very*, since I can't see a sign anywhere."

"I'll help." I jumped off the rock, and like Damien, began frantically scrutinizing the perimeter. Looking on, under, through, and

around anything I could find. But there was nothing. The full implications and true gravity of our situation began revealing itself to me,
slowly at first…

Okay, we're on the wrong island.

The wrong island.

But then, like a tumbling pebble picking up mass until it grows
into a full-blown avalanche of catastrophic proportions…

We're on the wrong island.

Lost!

In the middle of the sea.

Somewhere in the middle of Thailand.

And no one is looking for us!

No one is ever going to find us!

We're going to die here!

"Oh my God." The start of a panicky seizure was building. "*On
the wrong fucking island!*" I yelled with the kind of sound that might
shatter glass on the other side of the world.

Damien smiled and I wanted to smack it right off his face. How
could he be grinning at a time like this?

"Okay…" I breathed in, forcing my brain to return to a more
grounded logical place. "Phone someone and get them to fetch us."

"No phone signal. Island in the middle of nowhere, remember?"
He waved his phone at me with another grin.

"Damien! This is serious. What the hell are we going to do?"
I tried to think back to all those survivor-style TV shows I'd
watched, where someone gets dumped in the wild and has to survive for a week. But all I could think about was the guy who had
to drink his own urine and eat raw buffalo meat. "Do you have
matches?"

"No."

"Crap! We could have sent off smoke signals." I paced up and down the sand a few times. *"Right* . . . this is what we need to do. We need to gather rocks and make a giant SOS sign on the beach and—"

"Lilly, chill. That won't be necessary."

"Chill?" Damien's relaxed attitude was seriously starting to piss me off. "Do you realize that if no one finds us, we might be stuck here for the rest of our lives? We'll have to fend for ourselves and live off the land like those feral people who are raised by wolves. You'll have to catch fish with sharpened sticks and nets made from jungle vines like they do in *Survivor*. Rub stones together to make fire. I bet you can't do that."

"I've never tried," Damien said, still looking decidedly amused.

"Well, don't you dare expect me to weave us clothes from spiderwebs and moss. *And what about shelter?* Think you can whip us up a little bamboo house strong enough to stand up to a tropical storm, huh? And you'll definitely grow a big, filthy beard and then we'll probably turn on each other, too, like in *Lord of the Flies*. *Oh God, I don't want to drink my own wee!"*

Damien burst out laughing. "I think you watch too much reality TV. Besides, you heard the guy; boats come past here all the time. We'll just flag one down and be on our way again in no time."

"Just flag one down?"

"Sure."

"And what about food? We might starve in the interim."

Damien patted his backpack. "I have some snacks."

"Water? Or shall we dehydrate in the sun while we wait to be rescued?"

"I have a bottle, too."

He was still smiling at me. "Stop smiling, Damien. This isn't funny. At all!"

"Fine." Damien forced his face into a serious grimace.

I slumped down on the sand and took my head in my hands. I couldn't believe this was happening. Of all the bad, crappy, crazy things that could possibly happen to someone, this had to be right up there on a list somewhere just under "being digested alive...slowly." I felt Damien sit down next to me and put an arm around my shoulders.

"Don't panic, I bet a boat will come past in an hour or so." Even though the tone of his voice was gentle, it did absolutely nothing to allay the terror that had taken up residence inside me.

"Lilly, it's going to be okay." He pulled me toward him. The close proximity did seem to take the edge off my terror, especially when his hand began rubbing my back in a very reassuring way.

"Besides, for all you know, there's a village on the other side of the jungle. We could go and look?" Damien added, trying to sound upbeat.

"I'm not moving," I said. I was going to sit there and watch those waters for any sign of a passing ship or boat or canoe or bloody rubber dinghy. Any kind of flotation device would suffice. I would even take a buoyant log at this stage and fashion oars out of coconut shells if necessary. Anything to get us safely off this rock.

"I'll go and look." With a swoosh he was up again, as if this didn't faze him in the slightest. In fact, it looked like he was actually enjoying himself. He probably was with his happy-go-lucky-adventure vibe.

"Wait. You can't leave me here."

"You'll be fine." And with that he disappeared into the jungle like a man on a mission. If I wasn't so damn panicked, I might have found it vaguely attractive.

"There might be large poisonous snakes in there," I screamed after him, only to hear a laugh. It wasn't the reaction I was hoping for. "And I forgot to bring the antivenom."

I sat on the beach not daring to take my eyes off the water. I didn't even move them as I reached into my shopping bags and riffled for a sarong I could drape over my head. The sun was relentless and the heat almost unbearable. But as the time passed, I started to worry. Damien still hadn't come back and I was starting to feel that familiar panic again.

I stared up at the jungle; it looked like the kind of place that if you ventured into, you might emerge with an extremity missing and a deadly insect bite between your eyes. It spread out in all directions, and I wondered how deep it went. On top of my own feelings of worry, I also started to worry about Damien's safety. I hoped nothing bad had happened to him. And then I was overwhelmed by an irrational compulsion to go and find him.

I abandoned my bags on the beach and cursed the fact that, like a magpie, I'd been so tempted to buy all the pretty, shiny things. And now I was just lugging them around with me. I walked in Damien's footprints all the way to the edge of the leafy darkness. I took a deep breath and stepped inside. I was no tracker, but it was easy to follow Damien's path. The squashed plants and bent branches were a dead giveaway.

I followed the trail for only a few minutes before seeing a clearing ahead and heard someone splashing in the water. I pulled a giant palm leaf away and looked into the clearing. Damien was swimming in a small pool of water. He looked like he was having fun. How could he be frolicking merrily at a time like this?

Then in one swift, splashy movement he climbed out of the water and...*Oh God!* He was naked. My hands immediately flew over my eyes just as he turned around. Luckily, it was just in the nick of time. Thank God I hadn't seen his...

Giant penis!

I jumped back in absolute shock-horror, as I caught sight of the rock that was poking out of the thick bush and staring straight at me. The rock in question looked like it should be starring in an ad for Viagra. Not just that, but plastered across a giant billboard, or one of those ad banners that covers the entire side of a massive building.

"Lilly...is that you?" Damien called out.

My hands flew over my mouth this time, and I wished he hadn't heard me. It would've been nice to silently run back to the beach, pretending that I hadn't been anywhere in the general vicinity of his naked body. I didn't want to get into an awkward conversation about whether or not I had just seen his manly bits. Which I hadn't! Let's be clear, I had not seen *his*...

But instead, I was staring at a giant penis-shaped rock and thinking about it anyway.

"Yes. It's me."

"Hang on, give me a second," he called out. I could hear him fiddling with clothing.

"It's okay...I'm still...well, I hit a rock, I'm still a little way—um..." I stood dead still for a few moments, hoping to convey the sense that I was still en route. I stamped a few times for authenticity as I "approached" him.

"Here I am." I walked into the clearing, making sure I didn't let my eyes wander below his waist. "I see you found water."

"I hope you don't mind that I had a bit of a swim in it?"

Oh God, he'd been swimming free willy in our drinking water...I wasn't sure how I felt about that. I watched him put on his shirt and I hoped I wasn't gawking, because all I could think about was his skinny-dipping self. I had also become acutely aware of the unsubtle rock sculpture right behind me. I looked away from Damien and immediately wished I hadn't.

It was as if the universe was conspiring to play the sickest joke imaginable. The joke was so sick, I wondered if I wasn't hallucinating.

But after blinking a few times and squinting, I realized that it was neither a joke nor a figment of my imagination. There, surrounding the clearing, rising up from the underbrush, poking out of every nook and cranny, jutting out of the ground, peeping out from behind the palm leaves...*rocks*.

All with one thing in common.

They looked like penises.

To make matters worse, Damien had taken to leaning casually against a massive one that jutted straight up. My mouth fell open and all I could think about, as I gazed from Damien to the rock and back to Damien and then to the rocks, was...*well*, it was pretty damn obvious what I was thinking about! This was making me feel so awkward I wanted to crawl out of my skin...

...*penis, penis, penis, penis, penis, penis!*

"I know, right! They look like giant dicks," Damien suddenly said as casually as ever.

"I've heard about these but haven't seen them before. They're pretty famous in Thailand actually." He flashed me a smile, but I certainly wasn't ready to reciprocate, nor was I ready to acknowledge the fact that we were surrounded by a pack of penises. Penii?

"Really..." I shrugged. "I hadn't noticed." I tried to look casual, but inside I was freaking out.

Damien laughed. "You're not a very good liar, Lilly. It's plastered across your face. You're gaping at the giant penises."

"I am not! Not. Okay? Not."

"Mmmm...I'm sure that's what all the girls say," he added with a mischievous smile that did nothing to distract me from the fact that *I was surrounded by massive dicks*! I must have blushed, or something equally embarrassing, because Damien laughed again.

"Lilly, you're so squeamish." His tone was distinctly mocking and playful.

"I'm not." But truthfully I was. I was very squeamish when it came to things like strip clubs and phallic-shaped rocks. Truthfully, a traumatic childhood experience had completely altered my perception of sex and sexuality. My friends were always trying to get me to loosen up, especially Stormy. She'd even suggested I go to someone who could help unblock my root chakra—whatever that was.

"They're just rocks, Lilly. They look like that from all the friction caused by wind and grinding against other rocks for thousands of years," he said very calmly, as if sensing my terror.

I swallowed hard. *Great!* I wasn't just thinking about the phallic forest now, but I was also thinking about bumping and grinding and all manner of different frictions.

"There's also a famous vagina-shaped rock on Koh Samui. They're very common here."

"Stop!" I threw my hands in the air. "Can we not talk about...you know. It's enough that we have to be surrounded by the bloody things without you giving me a geology class, too…so did you find a village?" I quickly tried to change the subject.

"A village?"

"You went looking for a village," I reiterated. "Did you find one?"

"Oh. No, I didn't."

"So now what?" I sighed and threw my hands in the air, bumping one of the rocks. I pulled away quickly.

"Why does this freak you out so much?" he asked, looking up at me curiously. I held his gaze for a while, wondering if I should tell him. His face suddenly softened and he smiled at me gently.

"You don't have to tell me."

"I know," I said. But suddenly I wanted to tell him. There was something about Damien that made me feel safe to open up and be myself.

"When I was about ten, I went on a camping trip with my mom and her new boyfriend. We were all staying in a caravan together and…" I cringed just thinking about it and Damien jumped off the rock as if something had shocked him. He started coming toward me.

"No. It's nothing like that," I said quickly. "My mother and her boyfriend…*well*, let's just say it wasn't pleasant when they kept me and the entire camp up all night with their disgusting noises. And worst of all, the guy had a running commentary going throughout the whole thing. He was very clear and specific about what he was doing, what he was about to do, and what he wanted to do, and trust me, it was very *Fifty Shades*. And it went on for hours, and then for the rest of our vacation. It was disgusting. So yes, you can say that my attitude about sex is a little bit damaged."

"That's really terrible, Lilly. I'm sorry," Damien said. He looked genuinely upset by my story. This was such a change from what had happened when I'd told Michael. He'd laughed and told his friends and soon it was turned into a joke. Michael also didn't think it was a very legitimate excuse for lack of sex, either, I might add.

Damien slipped his shirt back on and grabbed his things. "Come, let's get out of here then." But as he said it, we both heard the roar of an engine. I practically threw myself through the thick foliage and straight back onto the beach. Damien was in hot pursuit and we both barreled onto the soft sand and ran for the shore screaming and waving our arms widely. But it was too late. The second we'd managed to get close enough to be seen, the tour boat was gone.

"Crrraaaaappp!" I struggled to deflect the waves of frustration and anger that had just smashed through me. "Craaappp!" I screeched again before collapsing onto the ground in the manner of a soap opera actress. Or my mother. I quickly preempted Damien's response, which I was getting all too familiar with by now. "This is not funny, by the way!"

But he wasn't smiling this time. Maybe he was finally taking this "stranded" thing seriously. My heart jumped. I think I preferred it when he thought it was all a big fat joke. He flopped down onto the sand next to me. "So we missed this one. At least we know they come past. We'll wave down the next one. Promise."

"Promise?"

"I promise we're going to get off this island."

I nodded tentatively. I wished I had his confidence right now.

"Remember what I said. I would never let anything bad happen to you."

We smiled at each other for a moment, and I felt mildly better. The sand was warm and didn't feel unpleasant, even if the situation was. I ran my fingers through it. It was so fine and soft that it reminded me of cotton candy that melts at the touch.

"It is beautiful here, though," I offered, looking back up at the sea. A familiar-looking shape bobbed up and down in the current.

"Well, there go my new shoes," I said, pointing. "And there goes a handbag." I didn't even flinch; in fact, I was somewhat relieved I wouldn't have to lug them around anymore—who needs high heels when you're stranded on a pile of sand anyway?

But then the waves started lapping dangerously close to my bag of clothes. Those I did need! Before I could make a move to save them, Damien was already jumping into action. He waded into the water and started pulling them out, stuffing them back into the bag.

"That's about as close to fishing as I'll ever come." He strode out of the water and headed for a palm tree that was growing horizontally across the sand. I watched as he carefully hung my clothes over it to dry.

"This is so domestic." He turned around and flashed me a massive smile before returning to his task.

He was right. I was totally domestic, and suddenly I imagined Damien like that. Coming home from work after a long day in the physics lab, or whatever you call it. I would cook, we would have a glass of wine and laugh and chat about our days and…

What was going on? What the hell was I thinking?

I tried to stop the thought dead in its tracks, but to no avail. The thought plowed into me with such force that I jumped up.

I was…*no, this was not happening.*

Too late…*it had already happened.*

I liked this guy.

A lot. Maybe more than a lot.

CHAPTER SIXTEEN

The sun was starting to set over our little lonesome rock. We hadn't seen another boat go by in the last couple of hours, but after constant reassurances from Damien that a whole bunch would come past in the morning, I was vaguely starting to relax. Vaguely. I had no option, really.

The air was still warm, despite the sun taking its final bow. Damien and I had made our way through two bags of big chips and a slab of chocolate already and he was on his way to top off our water supply. We were both physically fine. No one had had their limbs gnawed off by passing indigenous cannibals, or sustained any deadly insect bites. All in all, our exile was going rather well.

I'd been stealing glances at Damien all afternoon, trying to figure out whether I really liked him or whether the whole marooned-on-an-island-and-possibly-facing-death situation was messing with my emotions. How could I like someone so quickly, and so damn much, after being left at the altar only a few days ago?

Right now, I was supposed to be Mrs. Lilly Edwards. A wife. The

wedding seemed so far away now and so did Michael. It was so surreal, like a bad dream you can't shake.

God, how had it all happened?

"What are you thinking about?" Damien was standing next to me
with a full bottle of water; I hadn't even noticed him return. I had
disappeared down a trail of thoughts that left me feeling very uneasy.

"The wedding. Or lack thereof," I half grumbled.

"If you don't mind me asking, what do you think happened?" he
asked gently, sitting next to me on the sand.

"I think…I think that maybe the relationship wasn't as good as I
thought it was. Maybe he wasn't ready to get married…" Then the
painful part to admit to myself. The bit that had been biting at the
back of my mind for a few days now. "I don't think he ever wanted
to get married. Maybe he'd felt pressured."

The engagement, marriage, and wedding had been my idea. Settle down, start a family, get a dog, a manicured lawn, and perfectly
pruned roses. *Wasn't that how it was supposed to work?* Maybe I'd
wanted that life so badly that I'd had blinders on.

Looking back now, there had been some signs. I just hadn't noticed them at the time. The closer we'd gotten to the wedding, the
more distant he'd become and the more time he'd spent working
late and on weekends. He constantly forgot wedding appointments,
and whenever I excitedly showed him a picture from a magazine or
asked his opinion about something, he'd just said, "*Do whatever you
want, honey.*"

"Even if he felt pressured, he still shouldn't have proposed,"
Damien said.

"No."

"And he shouldn't have waited until your wedding day to tell you, either. That's just cowardly." Damien sounded genuinely angry. "Bastard."

I smiled. There was something so sweet about Damien getting upset like this.

"Do you want me to hurt him?" he asked.

"What would you do to him?" I turned and looked at Damien with an excited smile.

"It depends. Do you want him permanently or temporarily maimed?"

I burst out laughing. Damien had a way of making me feel better about everything. "You know what…right now, I actually don't care about him. I don't care where he is or what he's doing…I just don't give a flying fuck!"

I threw my head back and looked up at the sky. I took a long, deep breath. Warm, salty sea air rushed into my lungs, and a feeling of absolute freedom washed over me. It was almost euphoric.

"Do you still want to get married, though?" Damien asked.

This was a good question. *Did I still want to marry Michael?* These last few days had made me realize that I hadn't been as in love with him as I'd thought. I'd been in love with the idea of love. I'd been in love with the big, romantic white wedding. I'd been in love with some strange notion of a perfect husband and family.

Did I still want it all, *a family life with all the trimmings?* Yes, and hopefully I would find it one day.

"I do. Just not with Michael," I said faintly. "And you?"

"I'm not sure. I've never thought about it before," he said after a long pause. "Maybe. I guess. One day." He didn't sound that convinced, though.

Suddenly, the desire to ask him about those girls overwhelmed me.

"And do you…I mean, have you…with relationships…woman, and—?" I mentally slapped myself on the side of the head after I'd vomited out that hot mess of a sentence.

Damien turned and smiled at me. "You're asking me about my relationships?"

"Only if you want to tell me. No pressure!" I defended quickly.

"I've had a few relationships over the years, but they never really get serious."

I had sudden visions of Damien being a man-whore, chewing up and spitting out women like gum that had lost its flavor. I think this subject was better left dropped.

"What I mean is," he continued, "I don't think I've ever really let anyone get close, or let myself get close."

"Why?"

"I guess I have this fear. The people I love tend to…go away." His voice was steeped in sadness and I knew he was referring to his sister.

"I get that. How your past affects your relationships. I think mine has, too, just in opposite ways. I think my life was so messed up as a kid that all I wanted was this perfect life and a family of my own…but there's no such thing as perfect, is there?"

"Like I said, Lilly, we're both damaged little souls." His voice sounded sympathetic and affectionate and sexy all at once and it made the tiny hairs on the back of my neck stand to attention. *Bloody hell.*

With each passing moment I seemed to be feeling closer and more attracted to this guy.

Despite all outward appearances, and the different ways in which we both lived our lives, I'd never felt that I'd had more in common with anyone. And I'd never felt so understood before.

The sun completely disappeared and darkness settled in. It was time to start thinking about our sleeping arrangements. We decided not to attempt building anything from palms and stalks (we both agreed we would fail dismally). The night was warm and the breeze was even warmer. The sky was so magnificent that it made the Sistine Chapel look like a spray-painted mural on a wall. And when you combined those things, lying on your back on the beach was perfect. My unnecessary clothes purchases finally came in handy, and we made a makeshift bed on the sand with sarongs. We both lay down—not too far, not too close.

"This is pretty cool, though," I said.

"*Pretty* cool?" Damien raised himself up on an elbow and shot me a sarcastic look. "*Pretty?* Lilly, this is something that you and I are going to remember for the rest of our lives. How many people get to say they slept under the stars on an uninhabited island?"

Damien lifted himself even farther off the sand and inched a little closer to me. "I'll certainly remember this forever." He flashed me the kind of smile that could stop traffic, and possibly even stop the world from spinning on its axis. "I've never had so much fun with anyone before."

"Me either," I said breathlessly.

"I'm really glad fate threw us together, Lilly."

"You believe in that stuff?"

"Not until now." Damien collapsed back down in the sand, but this time he was definitely closer to me. I could feel the heat coming off his body, and when I adjusted slightly, my hand grazed his. Instead of pulling away, though, I kept it there. Gently touching his.

"This has got to be the best bed in the world," Damien whispered.

"Best bed in the world." I seconded that.

He pointed up at the night sky. "See that. That's one of the arms of our Milky Way galaxy. I've never seen it this clearly before."

"It's incredible."

"Do you know what's even more incredible? In the center of every galaxy is a supermassive black hole. They're the most destructive things in the universe, but they're also what holds it all together and makes it so perfect."

"I like that," I said. It was a beautiful sentiment, and I stared up at the sky thinking about it as my eyes started getting heavier and heavier. "Damien, I still wouldn't mind getting rescued tomorrow, even though it's so pretty here."

"We'll be rescued. I promise. Night, Lilly."

"Night, Damien."

***

I woke up the next morning to the roar of an engine and the sounds of voices. I jumped up immediately, and to my absolute joy Damien had delivered on his promise. He was standing waist-deep in the sea and had successfully waved down a fishing boat. After some more explications and more waving the map around, the fisherman looked at us curiously before pointing.

We both followed the direction of his finger. There, within an easy swimming distance, lay an island.

"That's where it is?" I couldn't quite believe it.

The fisherman nodded profusely and seemed absolutely convinced. I turned to Damien and burst out laughing. "We could have swum there!"

It had been staring us in the face the entire time and we hadn't even realized it. Damien joined in until our laughing escalated to mad hysteria. I clutched my sides, I was laughing so hard. The fisherman recoiled, as if we might be dangerous crazy people.

Even though we could have probably swum to the island, we decided against it and jumped into the boat, and after a literal minute, we were there.

Two enormous pillar-like rocks came into view; they rose straight up into the air and were only a few feet apart, creating a thin passage between them. We entered the passageway, and it was so narrow that if I stuck my hand outside the boat, I could touch the cliff face.

We finally popped out the other end and entered a huge crystal lake enclosed by a large island that wrapped around it completely. Long white beaches ran the entire length of the shoreline and, from them, imposing rocky faces rose vertically. The boat stopped at one of the beaches and Damien and I climbed out. I indicated to the driver that he should wait while Damien took in the lay of the land and found the elusive sign. But within seconds, we both saw it; a bright-pink arrow painted onto one of the rocks. The fisherman turned and left us.

"Beautiful," Damien said, looking around.

"Where's the party?"

"Ahhh, patience, we're in no rush to get there. Besides, I am sure it's going to be quite an adventure getting there."

"What do you mean?"

"Oh, that's part of the fun. They always choose a really remote location that's hard to access—keeps the rabble away."

I looked around nervously; the only way from here was up. And that didn't thrill me at all.

"Do you think we'll be going up…there?" I looked up and pointed nervously.

"Well, there's nowhere else to go, is there?" He was nonchalant again, despite the fact that climbing one of those things would be madness and potentially detrimental to your health—i.e., you might fall and die.

"Don't worry." He draped his arm around my shoulder. "I'll be there. It'll be fine. But"—Damien put his backpack down on the warm sand—"I'm not going anywhere until I've had a swim." And with that, he started peeling off his clothes. First the shirt and then the pants. Although this was the third time I'd seen him half-naked, it still had the power to elicit the same silly, dizzy schoolgirl response from me. I tried not to stare, but there was no way I could ever become immune to the effects of a shirtless Damien, no way I could ever grow used to or blasé about seeing Damien like this. Immediate blush.

He was wearing only his boxer shorts now and confidently strode into the water. I involuntarily bit my lip and was glad he hadn't seen it. As soon as the water reached Damien's thighs, he dove in. I watched him disappear and found myself waiting breathlessly for him to pop back out of the water. He finally emerged, his back was to me, and for the first time I noticed—well, it was impossible not to notice—a huge tattoo on his back. It completely covered the top half of his back and both shoulder blades. It was so complex and intricate, containing lines that curved, intersected, and wove their way around and through one another, coming together to form an abstract pattern. It's hard to describe, but let's put it this way, his naked back was now officially my favorite part of his body. He turned to me and I quickly wiped the stupid look off my face.

"Well…aren't you coming in?"

"I'm not wearing a bathing suit."

"So put it on. I know you have one, I rescued it from the water, remember?"

I looked around; there were no obvious trees or rocks to change behind, only wide-open beach.

"There's nowhere to change," I shouted back at him.

"Change there. I won't look."

"No! Are you crazy? I'm not just going to change on the beach! What if someone sees me? What if another boat comes?"

"I'll keep an eye out. Besides, we'll hear the boat long before we see it."

"I don't know…"

"Lilly, you're missing out big-time, trust me. And we've probably got a long, hot walk ahead of us, so…come on." He paused for a moment and looked at me very seriously. "I'm not going to look…you have my word."

I looked around once more, but I couldn't see anyone, and Damien had his back to me. I slipped my recently purchased bikini on and it immediately became apparent that it was at least one size too small for me. There was no way I was going to let Damien see me in this, so I put a T-shirt over it. But he was right, the water was amazing. Once it had reached waist height, I told him to turn around.

"Interesting choice of swimwear. Why are you wearing a shirt?"

"Just…you know…"

We smiled at each other for a moment. "You have to see the reef down here, the fish are amazing. Come." Damien disappeared and I followed him. The water below was crystal clear. The sand was snow white and powdery. One big rock poked out of the sand and was covered in multicolored coral and hundreds of beautifully patterned fish fed on it. I wanted to have a closer look and then…

I was blinded.

T-shirts should come with warnings that say, *If you swim underwater with this, it will billow and puff and cover your face.* I resurfaced to peel the wet, sticking fabric off my face with Damien close behind me. The T-shirt was clinging uncomfortably, and I was forced to tug and pull it back into position.

Damien looked at me curiously. "You know, you really can take it off. I'm not one of these guys who gawks and whistles—no matter how good the view is."

My stomach moved up into my chest and my heart fell into my stomach. Damien disappeared under the water again, and I continued to fiddle with the wet, uncomfortable shirt, which was really starting to piss me off.

Why the hell not, right? And so I whipped the thing off and followed him under.

We swam and laughed and splashed each other like little kids, and I couldn't remember the last time I'd had so much fun. It also dawned on me that I hadn't thought about Michael the whole day. Not once, well, until right now.

And then Damien abruptly ended our fun. "Come, time to go."

I'd completely lost track of time, so I quickly stood up out of the water and headed back toward the beach, and then I realized…

I was walking in front of Damien in my bikini, and stuff was probably (no, definitely) wobbling.

Crap. I suddenly became very self-conscious and took a deep breath, hoping that would suck it all in somehow. I started to walk in a rather robotic way in an attempt to minimize any unwanted movement of my subcutaneous fat cells. I put my feet down gently in case the impact would jiggle something loose, and I tensed my muscles in the hopes it would give me the appearance of sleeker legs and a perkier bum (wishful thinking). At this stage, I was concentrating so hard on defying nature, gravity, and all known laws of physics that it was already too late by the time I saw the rock. And so I walked straight into it, stubbed my toe, and stumbled backward.

And then—you couldn't have orchestrated a more clichéd-yet-perfect moment if this had been a Hollywood rom-com—I felt two strong hands catch me. I found myself pressed, hard, against Damien's naked chest, and I'd never felt more turned on in my entire life. Which was a very odd sensation for me.

Right now, squished against his naked chest, the feel of his arms wrapped around me, the intense sensation of his hot hands resting on the small of my cold, wet back, and our wet bodies pushed together tightly, every inch touching, made me feel like all the blood rushing through my body had changed direction and was suddenly swirling around my nether regions. I wanted him so badly it literally hurt. I wasn't looking at him yet, but I willed my face to tilt upward and my eyes met his. The air between us was electric. His eyes moved down to my mouth and although he wasn't touching my lips, they were stinging…

We'd both been fighting this feeling for days now, and it was officially no longer possible to fight it. It was too big. Too overwhelming and I was certainly giving up. And judging by the look in Damien's eye right now, it was clear that he had given up the good fight, too, and was ready to surrender. Kissing Damien was all I wanted. And I'd never wanted anything more in my life…

"Lilly." His voice was a whisper.

"Yes, Damien…"

He was still staring at my lips, and moved his hand up to touch my face. His finger traced its way down my cheek, and I shivered in response; my skin rose up in goose bumps that covered my entire body. He moved his fingers down to my mouth and I felt his thumb trace my bottom lip.

Then he moved his mouth closer to mine. Our lips were now only inches apart. I could feel and smell his breath. And it was sweet and hot and I wanted to drink it in.

"Do you mind if I kiss you, Lilly?"

"Yes…" I whispered back to him. "Kiss me."

CHAPTER SEVENTEEN

Wooooooo-hooooooo!

Yeah!

Aaaaaahhhhhhhhhh!

Woooooooooo!

Screams reverberated around us. The sounds bounced from one cliff to the next like a psychotic Ping-Pong ball until it felt like the screams were coming from above, behind, between, and in front of us.

What the hell?

Damien stared toward the tunnel; the screams grew louder and the roaring engines were coming closer. The boat finally burst into sight, sending white rippling waves out in every direction as it sped toward us. I could see four people on board, and judging by all the whooping and woo-hooing, they were all in party spirits. And then...*hang on*...suddenly Damien sprinted across the beach.

Why? Why was he waving and shouting? And then I looked closer and my heart not only dropped, but it climbed out of my body, jumped into the lake, and sank to the bottom to sleep with the fish. Leaping—no, springing gracefully like a baby gazelle in a tiny bikini—was the brown-haired hipster chick. I pressed pause in my head and she stayed suspended in midair. I looked closely at her. She was smiling. She was springing with open arms. She was excited and she was about three sizes smaller than me. I mentally pressed play again and she went pirouetting onto the beach and into Damien's arms, the arms that I'd just been in! My arms! Not hers.

They hugged. It was gut-wrenching.

He spun her around in the air. It was heartbreaking.

They tripped and collapsed onto the sand. It was nauseating.

Suddenly I really hoped there would be a human sacrifice tonight.

I was glaring at them so intently that I hadn't even noticed that Blondie-Blue-Tip was also there. She also went leaping and flying and diving onto the sand with them. I cringed.

I looked back at the boat and a guy stepped off it and started walking toward me.

When my mother gets sent a play, before even reading it, she goes through the character descriptions. These are short, concise tidbits that give you an exact image and understanding of the character. And if the guy walking toward me was a character in one of my mother's plays, this is what it would say…

Name: Chad "The Man" Matthews

Age: 29

Height: 6'2"

Weight: 200 lbs. of pure hard rippling muscle

Hair: Blond and shiny

Eyes: Crystal blue and dreamy

Characteristics: Chad is a jock. He is wealthy, healthy, and enjoys working out. In his spare time he loves cooking, spending time with orphans, rescuing stray kittens, and feeding the homeless. He's also incredibly well endowed and is a very giving lover.

Flash back three days ago: If I'd seen this guy walk through the door, I would have melted. Dissolved into a puddle and looked up at him with puppy-dog eyes, but now, I couldn't care less about him even if he took all his clothes off and did jumping jacks in front of me so that his willy flapped in my face—no matter how big it was.

There was only one person in the world I wanted, and he was frolicking on the beach with Hipster Barbie.

"Hey, I'm Jerry." Suddenly he was in front of me.

"Huh? Oh…yeah, yeah…Lilly, whatever." I sounded totally disinterested, but I didn't care.

When Damien and the slutty slut-sluts finally emerged from their dry-humping session, Damien dragged them across to me and I had a sneaking suspicion I was not going to cope with the encounter very well.

"Hey!" The brunette was running toward me smiling. "You must be Lilly."

I was thrown, especially when she hugged me. Why was this strange woman hugging me?

"Uh…how do you know?"

"Damien hasn't stopped telling me about you. I basically get a message every five minutes."

"Really?" I perked up a bit and looked to Damien; he was blushing and moving his toes around in the sand.

"Yep. He's been going on like a stuck record. Besides, you're also pretty famous."

"Famous?"

Suddenly Damien elbowed her in the ribs and shushed her.

"What's going on?" I asked suspiciously.

"You haven't seen the pictures?" Strange Slutty Girl asked with genuine surprise.

"Jess," Damien hissed under his breath at her.

"What pictures?" I demanded.

"Sorry, I didn't know you hadn't seen them…" the Jess character said to me.

Now I was worried. Something was definitely up and I didn't like the sound of it.

"Damien, what's going on?"

"Show her," he said to Jess, who immediately proceeded to take out her phone. She pressed a few buttons then held it up to me.

I gasped. "You took a photo of me on the plane in my pajamas, with my hair like that, and you sent it to her?"

Damien jumped in quickly to correct me. "No! I would never. But someone did, and it's kind of gone viral."

My eyes widened in shock. "What do you mean, viral?"

Damien and Jess exchanged another look—it was one of those loaded looks that not only contained subtext but a whole thousand-page novel and then some.

"Guys…" I just knew something bad was going on.

"Remember that photo of Angelina Jolie's leg and how everyone started Photoshopping it onto things like the Venus de Milo statue? Or the photo of that woman who fell asleep at the mall and got Photoshopped onto a stripper pole?"

"Yes…" I said tentatively.

"Well it's kind of like that," Damien said as gently as possible.

"I don't understand. My leg is on a stripper pole?"

"No, not your leg." A quick look passed between Jess and Damien.

"You're making no sense!" I grabbed her phone angrily and started flipping through the pictures.

And there I was. In my SPOONING LEADS TO FORKING pj's with my massive hairdo, my black-stained mascara cheeks and lipstick-smudged face standing next to Shrek…and there I was riding a giant spoon through the air, Photoshopped onto the *Mona Lisa*, climbing up the side of a building swatting planes out of the air, and yes, someone really had put a flock of seagulls in my hair.

My jaw fell open.

I was an Internet meme. I was everywhere. I was viral, like the angry hamster and Psy. I know I should have been totally morti-fied, but I was still too focused on Damien's plus one. Correction, plus two.

"You kind of have a hashtag, too," Jess added tentatively.

"Really?"

"Hashtag spoonforker."

"I see." I felt surprisingly calm about the whole thing, especially for someone who was viral. "How long have you known?" I turned to Damien.

"Since yesterday morning, a few people at the hostel showed me. Sorry, I should have told you but—"

I shrugged. "It's fine. What can you do, hey? So I'm trending, so millions of people are looking at the worst picture ever taken of me…So what!"

"That's the fucking spirit!" Little Miss So-and-So smiled and hugged me again.

Who was this chick, and why was she hugging me?

"Lilly, this is my best friend, Jess," Damien finally said.

"So nice to finally meet you." She was smiling at me again. "Oh, and this is my girlfriend, Sharon," she said, pulling the other chick toward her.

Now, it took my brain a while to compute the information: Sharon was Jess's girlfriend, they were a couple, so that meant that *she was a lesbian.* I'd never been so happy to meet someone in my entire life. I threw my arms around her and hugged her way too hard before moving to Sharon with the same enthusiasm and then declared that I was "delighted, simply delighted, ecstatic, in fact" to meet them.

This seemed to make Damien happy and he beamed at us.

"Oh…" Jess piped up again. "And this is Sharon's brother Jerry and his friend Chris."

The introductions were finally over, but I still hadn't gotten my kiss. There was a lot of chatter, some laughter, some general catching up, and some more hugging while Damien helped the *lesbians—yay!*—get their bags out of the boat.

I watched Damien intently, like a lioness might watch her prey before pouncing and biting off its head, but out of the corner of my eye I could see Jerry inching closer. And then he started trying to make conversation with me. So in between my adoring Damien stares, I grunted a few words here and there. There was nothing wrong with him. In fact, he seemed polite and nice and interesting. Well, at least that's what I would have thought a few days ago, but not now.

"Ha-ha-ha-ha, that's so true, Lilly!" Jerry suddenly burst out laughing and playfully hit me on the arm. *Huh?* I must have said something funny to him, but what?

The laughter obviously caught Damien's attention, because he turned around and glared at us with a rather strange look. In one swift movement he was off the boat and making a speedy approach. And then seconds later he was at my side, arm around my shoulders, pulling me closer and eyeing Jerry. And then it became awkward. Jerry took a step back.

"Oh, sorry, dude. I didn't know you guys were together."

Automatically, without even thinking about it, I quickly replied, "Oh, no, we're not—"

But Damien cut me off. "Not together…yet!" He pulled me even closer, and those were the best words I'd ever heard spoken.

Jerry smiled at Damien. "Sorry."

Damien held out his hand in truce. "No worries at all."

And then he pulled me closer and put his mouth to my ear.

"I want to kiss you so badly."

I melted.

"So kiss me." I'd never been so brazen before.

"I don't think we want an audience, do we?"

I liquefied. My body turned to unstable, watery jelly and my legs shook. I could feel his lips touching my ear.

"Lilly, if I kiss you, I don't think I'm going to be able to stop there."

Damien looked at me meaningfully. I hadn't thought beyond kissing Damien, but now I was. Suddenly I started having these thoughts, unfamiliar…*naughty thoughts*…about sex. Hot, naked, sweaty, acrobatic, porn-star sex.

I wanted to have sex with him, fuck him, make love to him, in whatever way, shape, and form I could. (OMG, I couldn't believe I was even thinking these things. What had happened to me?)

I wanted to.

I needed to.

And it felt right.

It also didn't feel like it was coming from an impulsive, mad place that was reeling in shock and in rebound mode, desperately seeking out a male to fill the hole. And I mean that in the purely figurative sense.

I wanted to do this with him. I put my lips to his ear and whispered, "I don't think I'll be able to stop there, either."

Damien's hands tightened around my waist and his body stiffened against mine. I'd never felt sexier and more desired in my life.

I was floating on cloud nine; nothing could touch me. I was in a Damien daze and it was so intense I barely noticed that I'd climbed a rickety string ladder up a cliff face, or that I had waded through waist-high water and hiked through a dense—spidery—jungle. All I was aware of was Damien and the intense looks that were flying between us. Every now and then he would come up behind me and wrap an arm around my waist. He would hold my hand, he would stroke my back, and at one stage he came up behind me and whispered, "Jesus, you are so fucking sexy it's killing me."

And then finally Jess announced that we'd arrived at the last hurdle. We were standing in the middle of a clearing in the jungle, and in front of us was a small brilliant blue lake. Like the others we'd seen, it was completely surrounded by high cliffs, but looking around, I saw no string ladders or steps anywhere. Jess bent down and began feeling the ground around her, until she found a rope and pulled it. A trapdoor of sorts opened up, and I burst out laughing.

Everyone turned and looked at me.

"Seriously, are we on *Lost*? Is the island going to start spinning and going back in time, and am I going to see black smoke coming out of the jungle?" This whole thing was ridiculous: "Mysterious party" was an understatement. Everyone laughed with me and agreed that it was all indeed a little like *Lost*, but hopefully without the unwatchable final season.

"Okay, so the map says we can leave all our bags and electronics here and just take our essentials."

"Leave our phones here. Why?" I asked.

"Well"—Jess looked at her phone again—"it says, 'Swim across the lake to the white cliff directly in front of you. Look for an arrow carved into the rock, take a deep breath, and you'll find a tunnel under the rock. Make sure it's a deep breath, because it's quite a long tunnel. There's an air pocket halfway where you can take another breath, and then swim the rest of the way. See you guys soon.'"

"Um…" I hated the idea of swimming under a giant rock. What if I ran out of air and started to panic?

"Don't worry. It's gonna be fine, hon." Jess put her arm around me and gave it a squeeze. "Besides…" She was smiling now. "You have big, strong Damien to rescue you if anything goes wrong." She followed this sentence with a playful eyebrow raise, which made me blush like an idiot. "Think about it, if you started to drown he could give you mouth-to-mouth, maybe even slip you some tongue." Jess then looked at us, flicking her eyes between Damien and me. "Ah, that would make such a cute story to tell your kids one day. 'I almost drowned your mommy.'"

Damien lunged toward Jess. "Jess, you're such a troublemaker."

"I know. That's why you love me!" And then she winked at us and jumped into the water with a loud splash. I avoided all eye contact with Damien now; I was worried that if I looked at him, he'd notice that I'd been reduced to a dithering puddle of hormones. So I jumped in and followed.

We found the arrow easily and then we all counted to three, took a deep breath, and submerged. The tunnel was dead ahead and not as long as I'd imagined. I soon saw the sun rippling on the surface of the water and knew that the air pocket was close. We emerged into a small space that was just big enough for the six of us. Everyone started taking their next big breaths and disappeared. I was about to do the same when I felt Damien pull me back.

"Finally, I have you alone," he said in a gravelly voice that did nothing to hide his feelings and thoughts. He pulled me closer. We were both treading water and as we got closer, our legs bumped into each other. Damien pulled me closer still and tried to kiss me, but we soon succumbed as the effort of trying to kiss and keep our heads above water with vigorous treading became too difficult. We sank under the water together, our knees knocking and feet tangling, and attempted another kiss. It was clumsy and pointless and our mouths filled with water. We both burst out laughing, which caused our faces to disappear behind a shroud of bubbles. This was the worst failed kiss in history, and we both emerged laughing and spluttering.

"Okay, so maybe that wasn't the best idea I've ever had," he said between fits of laughter. "I don't want to be the guy who ends up drowning you in the throes of passion. Then there'll be no story to tell the kids."

Kids, dot, dot, dot. And even though I knew it was just a clever reincorporation of the joke that was being thrown around, my mind couldn't help going there for a second.

Damien was still laughing, clearly oblivious to the fact that we now had three daughters with blue eyes and black hair and their names all started with a *D*.

"So how about we just forget that even happened and we'll try again later?" he said, his laughter finally tapering off.

"Sure," I said, and then I almost fainted when I heard the words come out of my mouth. "But you have to promise to make our first *real* kiss the best one of our lives…"

Damien came closer to me and I felt his hand on my stomach. I flinched—but in a good way. His hand moved down and he hooked his finger into the top of my bikini bottoms and pulled me closer.

His gaze intensified and he gently parted his lips. "I promise."

When we finally resurfaced on the other side, we entered into a world that was amazing and bizarre and beautiful. We were in yet another small crystal lake, which was also enclosed with rocky cliff faces and had the same huge wraparound beaches. Beyond the beaches were giant palms filled with hammocks and strings of colored lights. Multicolored tents were erected all over the beach, which also had big, comfy-looking cushions and giant beach balls scattered on it. An enormous bar dominated the center of the beach and people were milling about; some were floating in the water on bright inflatable loungers, others were sleeping in hammocks, some were playing volleyball, and a few were already dancing on the beach to music being played by a DJ.

I looked around, amazed.

"Welcome to Burning Moon, Lilly." Damien turned to me. "I'm going to make this the best night of your life."

CHAPTER EIGHTEEN

*R*emember all those millions of years ago when Tom Hanks won the Oscar for *Forrest Gump* and for the next while every Tom, Dick, Harry, and uncle's tree squirrel's monkey walked around saying, "Life is like a box of chocolates, you never know what you're gonna get."

Well, that's ridiculous! Of course you know what you're gonna get—just read the bloody box. Turn it over and look at the little pictures of the chocolates and their descriptions. I'm not sure where Forrest was buying his boxes, but really, it's not that hard.

But I finally got it. Because the chocolate I was currently unwrapping, and was about to take a bite out of, wasn't on the box. It wasn't on any box, anywhere. In fact, it was a totally new flavor that hasn't even been invented yet and will exist only in the future when we taste with our fingertips.

Because I would never—in a million years—have guessed that my life was "gonna get" this.

The party preparations were in full swing. More and more people were arriving and the music was getting louder and louder. The water thrashed with partygoers—swimming, floating, splashing, and jumping. Dusk was creeping up and the sparkling lights in the trees had been turned on. They scattered rainbow beads of color across the white sands and cliff faces. The tiny dots of color bounced across the surface of the reflective water, and it looked like everything had been coated in millions of brightly colored M&Ms.

But I still hadn't had my alone time with Damien, because he seemed to know everyone here. We spent the whole afternoon moving from person to person. "Hello…How are you?…Great…Awesome…Long time…Glad to see you…This is Lilly…" etc. A couple of people recognized me thanks to my newfound Internet fame, and they'd all thought it was just about the coolest thing they'd ever seen. Suddenly, I was the "cool chick," the celebrity. Some guy even asked me to autograph his chest. These people were so accepting; I thought about what Michael would say if he saw the picture. It would not be complimentary, and I'm sure he would have been mortified to be associated with me.

We went around like this for hours, and I was thrilled to see my strip-club buddies Mark and Francoise there. We got so wrapped up in girl talk that when I looked up again, Damien was gone. He was nowhere to be found. Nowhere. So I wandered around aimlessly, drank two tall purple drinks, and then went to the toilet. The bathroom was a rather junglelike affair. It was a temporary structure made up of reed walls built around a large palm tree. I wondered how all this stuff had arrived here. There were only two possibilities: Either the guy who ran this was very rich and everything had been airlifted in, or this party was *that* mysterious and strange that everything had been beamed here through a transdimensional portal.

Either way, it was pretty spectacular and I was in absolute awe of it all. You couldn't help but get caught up in the energy and exhilaration of the night.

You really felt like you were a part of something. Something unique. A secret underworld that was completely separate from everything else. Here people were happy. They were free. They made their own rules and marched to the beat of their own drums. (Literally—a drumming circle had been formed out on the beach. What is it with hippies and drums?) I looked around at the people and was struck by how diverse they were: from your arty, poetry-reading, shell-earring-wearing types to your hipster Kens and Barbies, a few Rastafarians, some really cute Asian schoolgirls with pink hair, a few emos for good measure, and then the most bizarre of all, a few people who looked like ordinary moms and dads.

I caught sight of myself in the bathroom mirror and stared back at someone who looked nothing like the Lilly I knew. I didn't have a scrap of makeup on, for starters, which was very unusual. The sun had sprayed freckles across my nose and cheeks and my hair was messy and wavy from the humidity. I walked out of the bathroom running my hands through it, trying my best to tame the unruly beast, but I was interrupted.

"Leave it. It looks nice like that."

It was Damien. He was casually leaning against a palm tree waiting for me. Somewhere along the way he'd managed to change, and it was the first time I'd seen him in anything other than his uniform black. His knee-length shorts were still black, but he was wearing a ludicrous Hawaiian-style shirt with a pink hibiscus and tropical parrot print. He looked ridiculous yet outrageously sexy and simultaneously adorable.

"Do you like my shirt?" he asked, doing a little turn.

"I love it."

"I borrowed it from this real surfer dude, right after he showed me the scar on his leg where a shark bit him."

"Oohhh. Hardcore," I said, stepping closer.

"I figured that if we were going to make out, I should at least be wearing a clean shirt."

"Make out?" I burst out laughing. "I haven't heard anyone say that since I was twelve." I'd never laughed with anyone as much as I did with Damien.

"So…how did you know where to find me?" I asked.

Damien winked at me. "I've been watching you from a distance, Lilly."

A chill ran up my spine. "Really?"

"No, not really. But it's easy to find a celebrity. You're the talk of the party." He laughed again, and I was pretty sure I wasn't ever going to live down that now-infamous photo.

The laughter subsided and, once again, we found ourselves in yet another awkward moment. (God this was getting old.)

Silent.

Staring.

Looks loaded with expectancy.

We both knew what was coming next. It was just a question of time. Now it was about who was going to make the first move, and when.

You know how that moment before you kiss someone for the first time can be so terribly awkward that you actually feel sick to your stomach? Well, that's how I felt. In the silent, expectant looks I mentally screamed at him to kiss me, willing him so I wouldn't have to make the first move. Even though I knew he wanted to kiss me, it's human nature to be filled with just the tiniest bit of doubt that tells you if you lean in to kiss him, he's going to pull away. (And consequently, you will die of embarrassment.)

Then Damien walked toward me and took my hand. "Come, I want to show you something."

"What?"

"I want to show you why it's called Burning Moon."

Damien pulled me across the beach, through the crowds who were dancing to the hypnotic music. I hadn't noticed it before, but there were some steps curved up the side of one of the smaller cliffs. Damien still had me by the hand and was carefully leading me up them. We reached the top and I gasped. Out loud. I felt like we were standing on the top of the world.

The sea stretched out around us in every direction as far as the eye could see. The sun had just taken its final bow and the fat, silver moon was creeping over the horizon. I stood there in silent wonder and watched as the plump moon came into full view, but as I stared at it, I noted a subtle change in its color. The silver flushed with a warm pink.

"What's happening?" I turned and looked at Damien. He had the same look on his face the night he'd told me about the galaxies.

"You're about to see a full lunar eclipse," he said, still staring at the moon. "And if we're lucky, we'll have a big blood moon tonight." Damien turned and looked at me. "But this isn't the best place to watch it from." He took my hand again. "We need to get to higher ground."

Minutes later we were standing in a small alcove carved into the rock. It was perched on top of the cliff, only a short distance from the sheer drop into the waters below. Damien had spread a blanket out across the ground and scattered a few cushions around. He'd lit some lanterns, which drenched the walls in a warm glow.

"Welcome to the party," he said, ushering me into the alcove and pulling out a cushion for me to sit on.

"So is this where you disappeared to?"

"It's always the first thing I do when I get to these parties."

"What is?" I suddenly had images of him making love nests for women.

He smiled at me; he seemed to have this uncanny ability to know what I was thinking.

"The main reason I come to these parties is to watch the lunar eclipse."

I was surprised by this revelation, especially after everything we'd been through to get here. "So every year you come to a party just to sit alone and watch the moon disappear?"

"Basically. Some years it's only a partial eclipse, but this year is going to be special. I told you, Lilly, I'm a bit of a nerd."

"You know, I think you're the weirdest person I've ever met."

"Really? I was thinking the same thing about you."

"What?" I shrieked in genuine shock. "I'm about the most normal person you'll ever meet."

Damien shook his head smiling, "Not a chance, Lilly. You are by far, *by far*, the strangest girl I've ever met!"

"Oh please. How?"

"Okay, first, I've never seen anyone dress like you did on that plane—"

I cut him off quickly. "You know I had a perfectly good reason for it."

He continued. "Not only that, but then you somehow managed to become an Internet sensation, wearing arguably the worst pajamas ever created. And then to top it off, you are the clumsiest person I've ever met. You set yourself on fire, for heaven's sake. Who does that?"

I laughed. I couldn't argue with that one.

"You're a little bundle of contradictions, because you're also the strongest woman I know."

"How's that?"

"You made the decision to come on your honeymoon alone— that's pretty brave. I don't think there're many women who could have done that."

Damien had said this before, but now I was starting to believe it. "And I'm very glad you did, come on your honeymoon alone…" Damien crept closer to me and I could feel the excitement churning in my stomach. He leaned in a little closer and my breathing quickened. He smiled at me. It was the sexiest, scariest, naughtiest smile I'd ever seen, and it made me shiver in the warmth of the evening air. The soft-pink light around us was changing with the moon and being whipped into a deep red. The color in the air only intensified Damien's features and the sharp red shadows that trickled across his face made him look dangerous. Powerful.

And then he leaned in and kissed me. The kiss was gentle at first. It was slow and soft and tender and warm. His hot breath licked my lips and made my body tremble. He wrapped his arm around me and pulled me even closer, intertwining his fingers in my hair. He tasted sweet and salty, and I let out a moan as I felt his hand tighten around my waist.

And then everything changed. As if that little breathy sound had ignited something.

The kiss became frenzied.

We grabbed at each other.

Tore.

It was chaos.

It was hungry, angry, and frantic.

Our lips and tongues engaged in a kind of desperate, erotic dance that went faster and faster and faster. Speeding toward something. Toward everything.

It was so animalistic and insatiable that I no longer felt in control.

It was the dizziest, most erotic moment of my life.

"Is this okay?" he whispered, in between the kissing.

I answered by arching my body toward him, and the pace of the kiss escalated until I felt Damien bite my lip, and then everything stopped.

He pulled away panting. I was gasping for air and my body was heaving from the exertion. I finally managed to open my eyes, and when I did, everything was red. Our bodies were painted crimson and the world looked like it was on fire. The rocks were embers. The sea was churning blood; the sky looked like it had been ripped open, exposing what lay beneath its skin. And the moon…the big red moon hung low and ripe in the sky. He smiled at me. It wasn't a scary, sexy smile anymore. It was something else.

Something quieter.

Something that enveloped us in our own little world.

And then he kissed me again. It was slow, soft, and deep. There was nothing frantic or angry or rushed about this kiss; instead it felt like we had all the time in the world. That time was standing still just for us. He ran his hands through my hair and touched the side of my face, as the kiss became even slower…

But the slower it became, the more exquisitely intense it became.

The intensity overwhelmed me.

I reached up and put my hands on the sides of his face; it was the first time I'd touched his face, and his hair felt rough against my hands. The kiss ended, and just the tips of our noses were touching. We looked at each other, our hands cupping each other's faces.

He looked through me.

In that silence, not a single word was uttered, but everything was said, and I'd never felt closer to another human being before.

The light around us had become even redder. I looked at Damien. His shirt was off, and he was bathed in the glow of the moon. He looked otherworldly, ethereal almost. The light accentuated the strong black lines of his tattoos, and I reached up and touched one. I ran my fingertips up his arm, following the lines and shapes all the way up to his wrist. When my fingers reached his wrist, he opened his hand and I ran my fingers over his palm.

He looked at me with eyes that seemed to ask a silent question. And I understood.

"Yes," I whispered.

The faintest smile made the corners of his mouth twitch, and his hands went to work on my sarong. He was quick and it soon fell to the ground. He moved closer to me still, wrapping his arm around my back and tracing his fingers down the length of my spine before stopping at my bikini strap.

I felt it loosen.

Both of his hands went to work on the straps, which he pulled down slowly, savoring the moment and letting his fingertips run over my shoulders and down my arms as he freed me.

A bolt of panic shot through me as my bikini top started to fall;

instinctively I crossed my arms over my breasts. I felt so exposed, so naked, and suddenly crippled by shyness.

But Damien wrapped his hands around my wrists and pulled my arms away. "I want to look at you."

I shut my eyes tightly, not able to look as I felt my breasts tumble free into his gentle hands.

There was a slight breeze and the warm air caressed my nakedness.

"Open your eyes, Lilly." Damien's voice was gentle yet commanding, and it gave me the courage to look at him.

That dangerous, hungry lust was gone now. Instead, he was looking at me the same way he'd looked at the stars.

Damien smiled at me. "You are so fucking beautiful, Lilly, and…" He looked so vulnerable right now. "…and I think, I think I'm falling in love with you."

And with those words, I gave myself to him. Fully. I would let him take control and do whatever he wanted to do with me.

I felt safe and cared for and…and, *I couldn't believe he'd said it*, I felt loved.

The red light drenched us both and we melted to the ground kissing. He never stopped kissing me, not for a second, as his fingertips encircled my breasts and lightly touched my nipples. So lightly sometimes that it felt like a gentle breeze. I threw my head back as his lips left mine and worked their way down my neck to my breasts.

I could see the moon now. And I could feel the heavy bass of the party below, as the sound pulsed around us.

The air around us prickled my skin and I was lost in the moment.

His hands seemed to be everywhere all at once, and I was putty in them. The speed of the kissing increased again as he ran his hand down my stomach and then pushed my legs apart. I gasped as I felt the cool air rush between my thighs. His kissing grew deeper and faster still as he pushed my legs apart even farther and in one fluid motion, was inside me.

I could feel all of him. It was slow and deep and every movement was deliberate and purposeful.

"Are you all right?" Our eyes met, and the fact that he was being so gentle and considerate just made me want him even more.

So I wrapped my legs around him, bringing him closer and deeper still. I wanted him to claim me.

Our legs and arms and lips tangled, and I no longer knew where I ended and he began.

We moved as one.

The thick red light started to dim and blacken as our bodies moved faster and faster to the invisible beat that controlled us.

The shadow's black fingers were reaching out and leading us into their darkness as the moon began to slip into the blackness.

I could feel it rising up inside me and I knew it was totally out of my control.

It was not something I could stop, or temper or tame.

Damien's breath grew faster and louder as we dipped into the blackness together.

"Look," Damien whispered in my ear.

I opened my eyes just as the moon completely disappeared into the void, and everything went black.

The darkness awakened us.

There were no longer rules or inhibitions.

I felt free.

I clawed at him, grabbed and pulled.

Our bodies writhed and thrashed and I opened my legs as wide as I could, hoping he would disappear into me.

We were now a singular entity, and we'd both lost control.

I threw my head back and arched my back as the sensation slammed through me, almost breaking my body in half.

I cried out his name over and over again until it was too intense to even speak.

The music from below grew louder and the crowd roared.

Damien lifted my hips off the ground and pulled me onto his lap.

He let out one long guttural moan in the darkness.

We held on to each other, shaking.

All I could hear was our panting and thumping hearts.

Our bodies went limp and he lowered me gently onto the ground and collapsed on top of me.

He put his head on my chest and I ran my hand through his sweat-drenched hair.

"Damien, I love you." I hadn't even been aware that I'd said it until I heard the words. It felt so good saying them out loud. Better than it had ever felt with anyone before. It was different with Damien. This was real. *Damien was real love.*

CHAPTER NINETEEN

⌐

A lunar eclipse can happen only if a number of variables all come together in perfect symmetry, at the perfect moment in time. The full moon passes directly behind Earth and is swallowed up by its shadow. But for this to happen, the sun, Earth, and moon have to align precisely. This is known as *syzygy*.

And that's how my relationship with Damien was. So many things had to align perfectly, at just the right place, at just the right time, and in just the right order for this moment to have happened. For this moment to even exist. Look a little closer at the seemingly disordered chaos of the past few days and a pattern emerges. A pattern that is ordered, structured, and has a singular purpose.

Michael needed to leave me at the altar. I needed to be so distraught that I wore my pajamas onto the plane, thus attracting Damien's attention. I needed to enter the toilet at the exact moment that he was exiting so we could bump into each other and be introduced. I needed to get sick on the plane so that I would have a reason to talk to him later at the airport when I tried to apologize.

We needed to be talking together and standing at just the right place and time for security to have seen and arrested us. We needed to be arrested so that Damien would lose all his money trying to save his dignity, and so that I would offer him a place to stay for the night. The following day we needed to be at the same restaurant, at the exact same time, and he needed to have brought me to Burning Moon.

It was all so clear now. Everything had happened exactly the way it was supposed to. Coincidence. Synchronicity. Call it what you like. But this whole time when I'd been cursing Karma for causing my life to fall apart, it was actually all coming together. I just didn't know it…until now.

In fact, you could say that my entire life had been orchestrated so that this moment, *right here*, *right now*, could happen.

***

The light from the sun crept toward us, bringing with it the early morning humidity. I opened my eyes and saw that Damien was up and sitting on a cushion staring at me.

"How long have you been awake?" I mumbled, still half-asleep.

"A while." He smiled at me, and his face looked completely different this morning. Or maybe I was looking at him through cheesy rose-tinted lenses of love. "I've been watching you sleep."

This was one of those true Hallmark moments. The soft-focus final scene in the Hollywood romance where the music swells and the characters declare their undying love for each other. It was butterflies in your stomach and a whole new world of beautiful possibilities, and the anticipation of tomorrows spent together.

It was all that and much, much more. The night before, I'd

opened myself up to him and he'd filled me with love. *God*, I actually blushed at that thought. It was official, people: I'd been reduced to a puddle of corny sentimentality. A whispering-of-sweet-nothings, swooning, sighing, heartbeat-quivering kind of gal. And looking at him looking at me, I could see he felt the same way.

Big sigh.

"What are you thinking about?" I asked as the staring intensified.

And, *oh my God*, Damien blushed.

"Now I *have* to know what you're thinking," I said, perking up.

The blush again. "Honestly, I feel a bit overwhelmed actually. Probably like someone who suddenly finds out they won the lotto or something. It almost feels too good to be true and it's all happened so quickly. This has never happened to me before."

"Me neither." Now it was my turn to blush. "I…I…also feel the same way," I managed to stutter.

"I'm glad," he said with a smile that lit up his whole face. "So, Lilly, what to do today?"

"What is there to do?" I said, holding my hand over my mouth for fear of morning breath.

"There's usually a big breakfast, followed by some more swimming, more partying, some more partying, and then a little more."

"Sounds good to me."

But then his eyes suddenly darkened. "You're so sexy in the morning, I think I'm going to have to do something with you first, though."

I was suddenly a coy schoolgirl. "What are you going to do with me?"

"Everything. Absolutely everything I can think of."

He leaned over me and pushed me into the hard ground. He

wasted no time and I felt his hands move down my body, pushing my legs apart. I gasped as he moved aside my bikini bottom and touched me. I surrendered to the feelings. Michael and I had done all this before, but never with the same kind of physical intensity I was experiencing now. Damien knew what he was doing, and with only the soft touch of his fingers, he broke me in half again. But this time I felt more comfortable with him, and all the shyness and modesty I once possessed were gone. My sexuality had lain dormant up until this moment, and it felt like Damien had turned on a tap that was not going to be closing anytime soon. I wanted him to show me and teach me everything I didn't know. I wanted it all.

And he gave it to me. He explored every inch of my body with his hungry hands, mouth, and hot tongue.

When he finally gave me what I was now loudly and repeatedly begging for, I cried out instantly as he pulled me on top of him. He was strong. Stronger than I'd thought, and I felt like a rag doll in his arms. His hands gripped my waist so tightly that I was sure he'd leave bruises. I hoped he would, because I wanted to walk away from this with his mark on my body. I wanted to be branded by him. His possession.

Sometimes he was slow and deep, and other times fast and forceful. All inhibitions were gone now and I told him what I wanted, how I wanted it, and when it felt good. I never thought that I'd be the kind of girl to do all that. But Damien made me feel like the sexiest woman on the planet and with him, I was alive. More alive than I'd ever been.

There was nothing tender or gentle about what we were doing now. It was about fulfilling a desperate need. And we couldn't get enough of each other. I'd never imagined that sex could be this good. Mind-blowing.

The pace built, and during the heavy breathing and moaning I heard Damien say, "You're amazing, Lilly." I wanted to say something back, but I couldn't speak. We were racing toward the finish line now. Damien had somehow managed to get me up against the wall; I can't even tell you how or when he'd lifted me up, but I was pinned. The cold wall felt hard against my back, and Damien had wrapped my legs around him.

As he was coming, he grabbed my face between his hands and stared into my eyes. I watched as they glazed over and it was beautiful. He was beautiful. He kissed me when it was all over. "I'm so fucking in love with you, Lilly. And I don't think I'm ever going to get tired of saying that to you."

My heart screamed in my chest, every neuron in my brain fired and was flooded with intoxicating dopamine, and every nerve ending stung.

No words had ever meant so much.

***

Breakfast was a rowdy affair. Partygoers were still drunk and happy after the night's festivities. Damien and I were in high spirits, too, walking around like a young couple in love—which we were—holding hands and whispering sweet nothings. I felt so proud to have him on my arm. He was my guy. Mark and Francoise also seemed pleased, judging by the wolf whistles we got.

Jess and Sharon were a bit worse for wear when we finally found them in a tent on the beach with hoodies and sunglasses on. Jess was cursing those red-and-yellow cocktails, and Sharon was cursing the fact she'd mixed them with a brownie obtained from the Rastafarian contingent. They both declared that this had been the best Burning Moon ever and, much to my delight, Damien had jumped in quickly and said that it had been not only his best Burning Moon, but also probably the best night of his life.

Of course this made me flush a deep crimson that didn't go unnoticed by Jess.

"Best night, huh?" Jess teased.

Damien reached forward and pulled her dark glasses off, exposing her vampire eyes to the blinding sun. She winced and threw her hands up in defeat.

"That will teach you," Damien said, waggling a finger at her.

"I know the perfect cure for that." A loud voice startled us and we all turned. The voice was coming from a young, cool-looking guy who seemed very pleased with himself. He was flanked by a small group of eager-looking followers. They looked as if they were there to recruit people, like a cult might.

"The best hangover cure in the world," he said again, and then looked down at us with a sly smile, the kind a charismatic cult leader might have just before he talks you into skinning your granny's cat. I was trying to imagine what kind of "hangover cure" this guy was peddling when Damien chirped up.

"Oh yes. I think I've heard about this, too," Damien added with an equally sly smile, followed by a knowing, mischievous look. Why did they look like they were sharing the world's biggest secret?

"What?" I asked abruptly.

"Come. We're all going there now." The guy beckoned for us to follow him and his little group. Damien immediately shot up, pulling me with him. Jess and Sharon seemed more reluctant, though; that is to say that Damien had to practically pry them off the sand with a spatula.

Our strange little group strode across the sand. I had no idea where we were going or what the hell we would be doing. And every time I asked Damien, I was met with a blanket "you'll see."

With each step, I was starting to feel more and more suspicious. Not to mention I had the distinct impression that I wasn't going to like what lay ahead. We marched past Francoise and Mark and, not being the kind of folk to be left out of an adventure, they joined in.

"It's like following the pied piper!" Mark added with sheer delight as he skipped next to me. A few more stragglers got up and followed us, too, when the words *hangover cure* were mentioned. This guy clearly had some kind of animal magnetism that drew people toward him. Perhaps he gave off a pheromone? We walked all the way across the beach to the edge of the thick tropical jungle. Our pack leader paused for a moment. He turned and looked at us with a satisfied smile.

"Let's go!"

But it soon became obvious that this was turning out to be *far* from a hangover cure. It was more hangover-inducing. The terrain had gotten very rocky and the walk had become distinctly vertical. A few followers threw their hands up in despair and mumbled expletives before turning back. Jess and Sharon had almost done the same thing, but Damien had mysteriously insisted that it would be worth it.

"Damien, where are we going? It's sort of getting very high and steep and the path is getting very—"

He placed a finger over his lips and silenced me, then slid an arm around my waist and whispered in my ear, "You look so sexy when you're worried."

Well, that about did it; I almost forgot where I was for a dizzying second and my fear of heights seemed to magically disappear.

The climb continued until we finally broke out of the vertical thicket and walked onto a flat plateau. I got the sense we were high up, and my suspicions were confirmed quickly. The plateau ended very abruptly. A steep white cliff face plummeted a million miles down into still, dark waters below. I looked from the waters to Damien and back again, and that's when I got it.

"Nooooo." I backed away from the edge of the cliff. "I don't even have a hangover."

"Jesus!" Jess suddenly exclaimed when she caught on a second or two after me. And then gasps and curses and exclamations rose up from the small party as they also began to realize what was afoot. Surprisingly, some people seemed excited by the prospect of throwing their bodies off a deadly cliff.

"It's totally safe. Just keep your arms and legs tucked in," our fearless leader said. He gave us all the thumbs-up and then threw himself off the ledge. Everyone rushed up to the edge and looked over. I crept there, slowly. The cliff was so high that it looked like he was falling in slow motion.

If it were so safe, I wondered why the hell he was screaming at the top of his lungs as he plummeted to what could be his death. A few more gasps and shrieks rose up from the audience as he hit the water with an almighty bang. He went under and everyone held their breath until his head finally popped back up. He gave a loud victory cry that reverberated around us.

"No fucking way!" Mark was backing off, pulling Francoise with him. But Francoise had a little twinkle in his eye that I'd never seen before. All of a sudden he broke away from Mark's protective grasp and jumped off the cliff.

"You're going to die!" Mark screamed after him as he disappeared over the edge. "Fine! We'll die together." And with that, he dramatically flung himself off the cliff. Their bodies disappeared into the water. I held my breath for a few tense moments until they bobbed back up and proof of life was confirmed. The shouts of adulation and excitement that rose up from the pool below were earth-shattering. They whooped and screeched and this just caused more bodies to go flying. They reminded me of lemmings.

"Hangover cure, hey?" Jess asked, tentatively gazing from Sharon to Damien and back again. What was going on? Was everyone out of their minds? Jess looked at Sharon meaningfully and they both nodded at each other.

"And in one, two, three…" I watched in horror as they, too, flung themselves off the cliff. There was no way I was going to do this. But the crowd around me started to dissipate, as one after the other went flying over the edge. And soon it was just Damien and me.

"No, no, no, no!" I backed off as if I were retreating from a blazing inferno. "There is no way, *no way*, none, no!" I had expected Damien to have an amused smile plastered across his face, but he didn't. Instead he looked at me very solemnly and held out his hand.

We stayed like that for what seemed like minutes, my eyes fixed on his hand as I tried to decide whether or not to take it. The thought was totally terrifying in that way that paralyzed my entire body from top to bottom. My stomach rose and fell a few times, giving way to a slightly nauseous feeling.

"Do you trust me?" Damien finally broke the long silence.

My eyes came up and met his and he smiled at me…God, I was so in love with this man. A man that was asking me to jump off a cliff with him.

"Sure." I half swallowed the word down, hoping that he hadn't heard it. I took a tiny step forward and put my hand into his. The second our hands touched he intertwined his fingers with mine and locked them together. We walked up to the edge of the cliff and a cheer rose up from the waters below.

I couldn't believe I was about to do this. This was the single most mad, insane, frightening thing I'd ever done in my life.

"When in Thailand…" Damien whispered. My heart jumped into my already constricted throat and adrenaline started to surge.

"AND one, two, three, go!" I closed my eyes and suddenly the ground was no longer under my feet. The air rushed past me so fast that it stung my body like a million needles. I could hear myself screaming, even though I wasn't aware of doing it. I closed my eyes tightly, gripped on to Damien's hand for dear life, and waited for the plummeting feeling to stop…

WHOOSH.

My body was consumed by water and I slipped farther and farther down until I finally lost momentum and came to a halt. I cautiously opened my eyes. I was submerged in the clearest, warmest water. I looked up and could see the blurry outline of the cliff through the ripples on the surface. I'd just leapt off a cliff and I felt so fucking alive in that moment. More alive than I'd ever felt. I felt like a superhero. I stayed under for a while, enjoying the feeling of being suspended in the warm quiet. The calm after the storm, the quiet after the chaos. But then a hand came toward me and I gripped it. Damien and I swam up to the surface together.

My eardrums almost burst when the cheers and screams assaulted them. I looked at Damien and my face felt like it was going to rip open from my smile.

"That was the fucking coolest thing I've ever done in my life." The words just flew out and they were followed by another massive cheer.

We all swam to the edge and climbed out. Once on dry land we hugged and compared notes and I felt so close to these total strangers. I felt connected to something that was so much greater than me. It was both a happy and sad thought; this all had to end at some point. This utopian life we'd all been living.

We made our way back to the party in high spirits and everyone swore that their hangovers were all but a distant memory. The smell of food filled the air, and I walked straight over to the nearest barbeque—what's with Thailand and this desire to serve every food imaginable on a stick? But I grabbed a few things. Not the prawns, though; I have a no-eating-animals-with-their-heads-still-on policy.

Damien disappeared for a moment and it gave me the opportunity to grab some quiet time. I sat on the sand eating my meaty stick and looked around. A few days ago I would never have imagined myself in a place like this, not to mention enjoying it and not wanting it to end. And I certainly never imagined that I would be in love with someone else, the strange guy I'd met on my honeymoon.

"Come, Lilly, let's swim." Damien came up behind me and planted a kiss on the back of my neck. But he didn't wait for me to respond; instead he put his hands under my arms and pulled me to my feet. I shrieked as he picked me up in his arms and ran toward the water.

The water was warm.

The sun was bright.

And I drank in my surroundings.

"This is the most beautiful place in the world," I said.

"Wait until you see some of the temples in the jungles of Malaysia."

"I'd like to see them one day."

"Not one day, next week."

I looked at Damien, confused. "What do you mean, next week?"

"Well, we're all off to Malaysia next week." He was still happily splashing in the water.

"We?"

"Yeah, sure. Me, you, Jess, and Sharon."

My stomach plummeted.

"I'm going home tomorrow…" I said tentatively. "My flight is booked."

Damien suddenly stopped and the color drained from his face in one swift motion. "But I thought…" His eyes betrayed his feelings. "I assumed that you would be coming with me. Aren't you?"

My heart started racing and a desert formed in my mouth.

"I, I hadn't thought about it."

"Well think about it now." He sounded anxious.

"But I have a life. I…I…" I was stammering. My tongue felt twice its usual size and it made the words stick.

"But I thought, because you didn't get married, and you came on your honeymoon alone, I thought you wouldn't be in a rush to get back."

I couldn't believe what I was hearing. "I have work, though. Family. Friends. I can't just up and leave."

"It's not forever. It's only a year."

"A year! That's a long time."

Damien suddenly swam away from me.

"Where are you going?"

He disappeared under the water. This was no time to be running away from the conversation, and suddenly I was pissed off. I folded my arms and waited for him to resurface.

"Sorry, I just needed a moment of silence to think," he said, standing up and running his hands through his wet hair. God, he was beautiful.

"You're only twenty-four, Lilly. You have your whole life ahead of you to work. One year isn't going to kill you. It will be an adventure. I mean, you just jumped off a cliff with me."

"Just because I jumped off a cliff doesn't mean I'm prepared to jump and leave my whole life behind."

It suddenly dawned on me that Damien might have seen the whole *Trust me, jump with me* thing as some kind of metaphor for our relationship.

"Come on, Lilly. Didn't it feel good to let go like that?" He sounded like he was pleading.

I couldn't believe what he was saying. But then I suppose I hadn't thought about what would happen after today. I hadn't once thought about the actual logistics of having a relationship with Damien. We hadn't discussed it. But we hadn't exactly planned this, either.

Tears welled up in my eyes. "I…I…" That bloody stammering again.

Damien stared at me as if he was trying to read my thoughts.

"Shit!" he said, and made a sudden and very hasty exit for the beach. I followed him. "I knew this would happen. It always happens."

"Where're you going?" I was struggling to keep up, he was moving so fast.

"Somewhere where we don't have an audience."

He walked across the beach to one of the tents and sat down inside. I followed.

"So let me get this straight." I didn't like his tone now; it was cold and angry. "After last night, you're just going to go back home?"

"I could say the same for you." I lashed out. "Why don't you come back with me?"

"That's totally impossible. I have a year's worth of flights booked. Friends I'm meeting in China, more friends in Japan. A friend's wedding in Russia. I have plans."

"And I don't have plans?" I hissed back at him sarcastically. "My life is somehow inferior to yours just because it's not all jumpy and cool and spontaneous? That's very judgmental of you."

Damien paused and the mood changed again.

"Just come with me, Lilly. I know you're not the dishwashing-for-money, backpacking type of girl, but I actually have lots of money, shitloads, in fact—we can do it in style. Not the dirty student way. We'll stay in nice hotels, I won't make you strip in nightclubs to earn travel money. We'll fly business class. It will be fun." He grabbed a fistful of sand and let it run through his fingers. I could see he was hurting. "I can't offer you marriage and kids and stuff like that. I'm not saying that stuff won't ever come, but not in the near future, that's for sure. But what I can offer you is my love and the biggest adventure of our lives."

My heart broke as I listened to him. I wanted nothing more than to go with him, but I had a whole life back home. How could I just pick up and leave? Rent, bills, job, friends, family. I couldn't just press pause for a year.

"I can't." The words felt physically painful to say.

Damien looked away from me.

"So what was last night about? I thought it was…" He cut himself off and tossed a handful of sand against the tent wall. "Never mind. Clearly I was wrong."

He started getting up and I felt the panic rise again. I grabbed him by the wrist and pulled him back.

"Wait. Stay. Let's talk about this."

He sat down again. "What's there to talk about? I knew it was too good to be true. I meet a girl, a fucking amazing girl, and I've never felt this way about anyone before, and we wake up the next morning and realize that our lives are totally incompatible. We're on different paths and they are so far apart that…"

My tears came.

They ran down my cheeks as his words sunk in.

Damien leaned forward and wiped them away. He was so tender and loving that it only made the situation a million times worse.

"It's okay, Lilly. It's life. The timing is off for us. What can I say?"

"But I don't want it to be." I wept.

"But you can't come with me and I can't come with you, so what can we do?"

The gravity of this situation was starting to sink in.

"But I love you, Damien."

"I guess love's not enough." He paused for the longest time, and I could sense something bad was coming. "As good as last night was, I kind of wish it hadn't happened. Because it's just taken this whole thing from disappointment to…" He paused again. "Heartbreak. The people I love always seem to go away."

His words struck a chord and guilt flooded me. He'd opened himself up to me and his worst fears had been confirmed.

My crying intensified and Damien wrapped his arms around me. We held each other tightly. And I wondered if this would be the last time.

"I'm not sorry about last night." I loosened myself from his grip and looked up at him. He stood up again and the sense of finality hit me like a bowling ball in the stomach.

Why couldn't I go? Why couldn't I just say fuck it and go with him? But no matter how many times I mulled the thought over in my head the answer stayed the same. I just wasn't capable of leaving my whole life behind. Maybe I was a coward, maybe I was stupid, but that was my reality right now. I just couldn't.

"Do you want me to come with you to the boat? I know there are a lot of people leaving today…"

I looked out at the water. Large groups of people were starting to leave. "No. It's okay. I'll go with one of the groups."

He smiled at me. "I'm sure they'll all be very honored to have a celebrity in their midst."

I felt a stabbing in my chest.

A tightening in my throat.

Nausea.

And then lots of pain.

He knelt down next to me and kissed me. One last time. It was so soft and tender and so full of love. But it was also just a painful reminder of what I would be missing.

"Take care of yourself. Keep in touch over Facebook. I'll be back in a year and, well…who knows?"

"You'll probably have found some hot chick by then and forgotten all about me," I offered jokingly, even though the thought had just ripped a hole through my brain.

He looked very serious suddenly. "That is very doubtful. *Very*. You're going to take a very long time to get over, Lilly."

And then he was walking away from me across the beach.

I sat there for a while, shell-shocked at what had just happened.

Devastated.

My heart had been ripped out of my chest and was lying next to me in the sand, and I had no idea how I would ever, *ever*, get it back.

CHAPTER TWENTY

I felt like a shoe.

An old, decrepit shoe.

A rejected, redundant, superfluous shoe that had been tossed out into a cold, muddy puddle on the side of a busy road in rush-hour traffic.

A sad shoe with scuff marks down the side and a peeling sole. A shoe that finds itself in the mouth of a pug with bad breath, on the foot of a homeless woman with bunions, and on the unfashionable hoof of a sweaty glam rocker with a fungal infection.

Now times all that by one hundred, throw in two extra zeros for good measure, and add it to infinity, and then maybe—*maybe*—you can begin to understand how I felt right then.

Oh, and did I mention that the shoe had also been regurgitated by an anaconda after it accidentally ate the glam rocker?

The boat ride back to the mainland had been a painful affair, literally. No longer in the Damien daze, I was very aware of the steep incline that we had to climb down to reach the boat. No longer in possession of the hero's hand, I'd slipped down some steps and grazed my elbow, bruised my bum, and had a lovely little bump smack-dab between my eyes. And to top it off, there was now a lovely crack down the screen of my phone, which was thankfully back in my possession.

The misery that I felt as I sat on that boat, in between someone's soon-to-be seafood supper and a raver on too much Ecstasy, was... was...

I mentally ran through the thesaurus looking for a word that made *excruciating* sound like something used to describe the sensation of a raindrop falling on your head. But nothing. The pain I was experiencing now was nothing like the pain of Michael leaving me at the altar. This was on an entirely different level.

By the time I'd disembarked, it was already early evening. Phuket had turned her lights on and the night creatures in short skirts were filling up her streets. I walked up the road in search of a tuk-tuk, and I couldn't believe that a few days ago I'd been afraid of taking one on my own. Bad karaoke rang out and the smells of street food filled the air.

Since I'd been away, my Internet fame had clearly escalated, because despite my current state, I wasn't oblivious to the staring and pointing aimed in my direction. At first it didn't bother me, but when a woman walked up to me with a concerned look in her eyes and asked me if I needed help, I lost it.

I claimed center stage in the middle of the street, held my arms open wide, and screamed. (My mother would have been so proud.)

"Yes, people! It's me. Get over it, okay?"

They all stared. Some people took a step back, and an alarming number of them took out their phones and started dialing. *Oh, shit!*

Surely they weren't going to call the cops over a tiny public display of emotion. A tuk-tuk came toward me and I jumped in quickly. I had no desire to be arrested twice in one week.

"The White Sands Hotel and Spa, please," I managed to mumble to the driver as I got in.

The driver glanced back at me. "You look like you need drink," he said in a thick Thai accent.

"Damn right. I just wish I had one." A strong one.

"Here." The little man reached over the chair and passed me a cigarette and a lighter.

"I don't smoke."

"Looks like good time to start."

And for some reason, that sounded like a very bloody brilliant idea. He was right, it was a good time to start. Yes, smoking cigarettes would surely make me feel better.

So I lit one. It was disgusting. It made me cough, and it gave me a queasy, nauseous, head rushy feeling.

I loved it!

Having a dreadful physical sensation to focus on made the emotional pain seem *so* much smaller. So I demanded that the man stop at the nearest shop so I, too, could come into possession of my very own box of cigarettes.

And he did. And I smoked all the way back to the hotel, which gave me a blinding headache, a sore throat, and a throbbing lung.

It was exactly what I needed.

We pulled up to the reception area where I paid the driver and thanked him for the cigarettes. I climbed out of the tuk-tuk and then caught sight of myself in the mirrored door…

Imagine an undiscovered wild woman who's been living in the

jungles of Papua New Guinea her whole life and was raised by apes.

But who the hell cared, right? Certainly not me. By this stage, I was so used to looking like shit that it no longer surprised me.

There was a very large NO SMOKING sign on the door, so I was forced to stand outside and finish my cigarette. Only ten minutes as a smoker and I was already starting to feel the discrimination! While I waited, I pulled out my phone and realized that it hadn't been on in days, so I fired it up and watched a million messages flood my cracked screen. I tossed my cigarette away and started walking and reading.

Hey, Lil. Where are you? We're starting to worry. Jane.

Lilly, your mother and I are getting very worried. Where are you?

I'm having a panic attack right now and I can barely breathe. Are you alive? Please come back to my motherly arms.

Stormy is lighting protective sage sticks everywhere. She almost set your curtain on fire. Where the hell are you?

WTF? There is a really weird photo of you on the internet. Are you okay? Annie

Lilly, Annie has shown me a photo of you and I am very worried. Call me.

We called the hotel and you're not there! Where the hell are you?

Babe, if you don't call us back TODAY we are all getting on a plane to Thailand.

Okay, that's it. We're all at the airport and we are coming over.

I was nearly at my room when I lit up another cigarette. The nicotine had obviously affected my brain somehow, because it took several more reads of that last message before it clicked. I opened the door to my room...

It was a circus.

Val and Jane were sitting cutting out pieces of paper with my photo and the word *Missing* in red above it. Annie looked like she was nervously folding and unfolding clothes. My father and brothers were standing with the hotel manager and talking, while three police officers rushed around dusting for prints. My sister-in-law rushed past, talking to a strange-looking woman who was taking photos of everything and typing away frantically on her iPad.

I cleared my throat and they all looked up at the same time.

I looked at them. They looked at me.

We looked at one another.

And they all looked very worried.

Out of the corner of my eye, I saw my brother Adam approaching with his little bottle of white pills. Val and Jane were inching closer, too, but my dad stood dead still.

"Sweetie." Worried little voices. "Are you okay, babe?"

"Hey, sis." Adam was desperately trying to hide his panic and worry under casual lilting inflections. "Did someone hurt you? What's that on your forehead? May I have a look at it?"

They all inched closer, even the cops and manager. The scene was totally bizarre, and I had been so caught off guard that I hardly knew what to do.

"Sweetie, can you understand what we're saying?" Val started talking very loudly and very slowly.

"Yes. Lilly, do you know who we are?" My brother was unscrewing the bottle and a small white thing was coming toward me.

"Of course I bloody know who you all are. I'm not a loony!" I finally said, while exhaling a big puff of smoke. "But who are you?" I asked the woman who was still typing away on her iPad.

"Lizzy Brown. PI. I was hired to find you."

I was stunned. The severity of the situation hit me all at once. "You guys hired a private investigator? You all flew here? You called the police?"

"Do you know how worried we've been about you?" Annie shouted, sounding like she was on the verge of angry hysteria.

"It's okay," my dad said, moving closer to me. "The most important thing is that you're all right and that we've found you." And then my father burst into tears, leapt across the floor, and scooped me up in his arms. That seemed to be the cue for everyone to flock.

JAMES: Jesus, sis, we've been here for two days, we've hung up missing posters on every street corner. (*Aha, that explained the stares in the streets.*) We've been so worried. I'm glad you're okay.

ADAM: Can you tell me how you sustained that injury on your head? Did you black out or lose consciousness? Can you feel your extremities? Oh my God, I've been so worried about you.

JANE: We thought someone had kidnapped you and then taken a photo of you and put it online. We were waiting for a ransom note. I've been so scared.

VAL: I've been so worried. You look terrible, and smell like fish, and when did you start smoking? *Oh my God*, we've all been so freaked out.

ANNIE: Sorry I got angry; I've just been so worried. Stormy said to give you a kiss; you know how she can't fly. And your mom is passed out next door if you want to see her?

They all hugged me and while I was supposedly distracted, I saw my brother Adam relieve me of my box of cigarettes and throw it in the trash. I was so touched by everyone's care and concern, and I felt terrible for causing such an international emergency that I burst into the tears that I'd been holding back for the last few hours.

"I'm so sorry I wasted your time," I wailed at the policemen who gave me polite smiles and disappeared.

"I'm so sorry, guys." I turned to my friends and family. "I didn't mean for you to all get so worried and fly out here." A chorus of "Don't worry, at least you're okay" rang out.

And then I wailed. "I love him!"

The tears became a waterfall drowning my face. Unflattering snot bubbles came next. "I love him. I love him so much."

"We know. We know." Val was trying her best to soothe me.

"When we saw that photo of you online, we realized how bad it was, how much pain you were really in." Annie took me by the hand and led me to the bed. "So the private investigator tracked him down."

"Yes, and we all had a very, *very* long talk with him," my dad said.

"It was a very serious talk," James piped up, smashing his fist into his other hand. "If you know what I mean."

Adam held his hand up to silence James. "No one beat him up, but we did make our feelings very, *very* clear."

"Crystal!" my sister-in-law said with venom.

Then it was my dad's turn to add to the conversation. "He apologized, and we hashed the whole thing out for hours. I was furious with him at first, obviously, but he is very sorry and he explained what happened."

Then Adam jumped in. "It can happen to anybody, Lilly. Hell, I was nervous before my wedding. Committing yourself to someone for the rest of your life is a massive deal and it can be very overwhelming. I had cold feet, too, and wondered if I was ready for it—"

My sister-in-law cleared her throat loudly and shot my brother a sideways look.

"Obviously I didn't run away, though, and that was terrible of him. Terrible. But he panicked and he didn't know what to do. I'm not suggesting you forgive him right away, but it's also important not to just give up on a good relationship."

"Of course you don't have to take him back right away," Annie qualified. "You may need to go to some counseling, but he is very sorry. I can see that."

"*Wait!*" I screamed. I had to stop them; they were going around in circles and I was starting to feel like a little goldfish in a bowl. "What are you talking about?"

"About loving Michael," Annie offered gently.

"But I don't love Michael. *At all.* I love Damien."

There was an eerie silence in the room, and then I heard it.

"Who's Damien?" The voice came from the doorway behind me.

The voice made my skin crawl and made me feel violently ill and homicidal all at the same time.

I clenched my fists, and if I were the kind of person who could crack her jaw, I probably would have.

You know how in those spaghetti Westerns, when the two cowboys have their big standoff in the main road of the town all the folk come out to watch before that distinctive Western music fills the air? That's what was happening now.

I stood up slowly, with my back to Michael. In my head they were playing that music and I was fingering the trigger of my imaginary gun, ready to cock it, aim, and fire.

I closed my eyes and saw Damien's face. And then I turned very, very slowly and faced my ex-fiancé.

He looked exactly the same.

Blond.

Buff.

Beefy.

Blue eyes.

Big, straight, white smile.

Good, clean, fun, commercial.

Picket-fence commercial.

Boring bastard commercial.

"Who's Damien?" His voice had a biting quality to it that I didn't like.

"He's a guy I met." I spat the words out with flaming indignation.

"You met a guy on our honeymoon?"

"Well, you were nowhere to be found!"

Michael pulled out his phone with such smugness that it made me sick. He pressed a few things and then held it up to me. "Is this Damien?"

I looked at the picture on Facebook. It was of Damien and me—Jess had obviously taken it and tagged me in it.

"Why are you stalking me on Facebook?" I asked Michael and grabbed his phone, but only because I wanted to look at the picture of Damien closely. His shirt was off, I was in my bikini, and we had our arms around each other, laughing.

I heard another voice from behind me—it was the private investigator. "On ascertaining that you were in fact missing, the first thing

I did was check your Facebook and other social media pages. I noted that you had friended this character, one Damien Bishop, recently and—"

I cut her off. "Okay. Fine. I get that part. But why are you really here, Michael?" I pointed at him. Did he really think he could get me back?

And did my friends and family really want me to get back with him?

Had the world gone mad since I'd left?

"Look…" Michael started approaching me with a patronizing tone. "I get it. What I did was really, really wrong and I don't blame you for losing it—"

"Losing it?!" I cut him off abruptly. "Do you think I've lost it? Do you all think I've lost it?" I turned and looked at everyone, and they didn't need to say a word, because I could see the answer on their faces.

But I hadn't lost it.

I'd actually found it.

I was more myself right now than I'd ever been in my entire life.

In the last few days I'd seen a different side of myself.

And Burning Moon had changed me irrevocably.

A calmness washed over me. Not that weird, psychotic calmness that I'd experienced at the wedding, but a confident, silent calm. In fact, I felt pretty damn cool, calm, and collected right now. If this had been a movie, it would be in French and I would be one of those chic, powerful French women who sat at cafés drinking strong coffee, reading *Vogue* magazine, and smoking cigarettes.

What the hell…

I wandered over to the trash can, pulled the box of cigarettes out, and lit one. I inhaled like a pro and exhaled with an air of *I'm too cool for school*.

"Right," I said, slowly walking over to the window and opening it. I casually leaned against the wall as I flicked my ash out.

Everyone stared at me. I was probably just confirming their suspicions that I'd lost it.

"Michael." I turned my attention to him. "You left me at our wedding. *Our wedding*. In front of five hundred people."

"All men are totally bastards," the PI said with a disapproving headshake.

"I like you." I waved my cigarette at her.

"I'm not a bastard." Michael took a step forward. "I know I fucked up and I'm sorry, I freaked out. I made a big mistake, and I'm sorry—"

I cut him off with a wave of my arm. "No, no, please don't get me wrong. I'm not angry with you. In fact, I want to thank you for doing it."

You could hear the sound of jaws dropping to the floor.

"You did me a favor, actually. In the last few days I've learned so much about what I *really* want. I'd thought I wanted you, because you ticked all my boxes and fit into all my plans, but…I don't want you anymore, Michael." I took another drag and let the smoke billow out of my mouth. It made beautiful shapes as it curled and twisted in the breeze.

You could have heard an ant drop. You could almost feel the shock waves rippling through the room.

"So you want some tattooed junkie?" Michael's eyes flared with aggression now, and James instinctively took a step forward. Bless his overprotective heart. Bless all of their overprotective hearts.

But I didn't need them right now. I was more than capable of handling this by myself—I was smoking a cigarette, after all.

"Michael." My voice was so calm. "What I want is for you to leave."

Michael stared at me in disbelief. He couldn't have looked more stupefied it I were naked and mud wrestling another woman on the floor.

"One day you'll make some woman very happy, but I'm not that woman."

Michael opened and closed his mouth like a fish.

He blinked his wide eyes.

He shuffled from foot to foot.

I could see him trying to process the info, and when he finally recognized what was going on, I saw his wounded ego fluffing its feathers and puffing up.

He struck an aggressive male pose. "You're making a huge mistake. Huge!" This was his big clever retort. "You'll regret this, Lilly. Trust me." He turned and started walking out but swung around as he reached the door. "But…but when it doesn't work out with that weirdo, and he knocks up some hooker and comes home with a disease, don't come crawling back to me. Okay? Don't you dare come crawling back to me because it didn't work out with the junkie." He glared at me with such hatred.

"Junkie? Knock up a hooker?" I smiled at Michael's ignorance, and then I laughed.

This, of course, pushed him over the edge, and he said very some ugly things about me before telling my brother James that they should lock me away and he was glad he didn't marry me, because I was clearly unstable, etc. You know, the usual wounded-male-ego-type responses. James looked like he was going to punch his lights out and Annie grabbed him by the arm. God, this was all so dramatic!

Michael ran out the room and slammed the door behind him so hard that I thought the glass would fall out of the windows. The feisty PI looked at me, shook her head, and followed Michael out the door. I wondered if she was going to punch him instead. She looked like the kind of woman who knew how to throw a punch.

My sister-in-law marched out after them. "Don't worry, I'm still going to sue his fucking pants off."

I smiled and flicked my cigarette outside. The others all looked at me, and as much as I wanted to explain it all to them—where I had been, the amazing Damien, what he was really like, how he'd changed me, the party, the new Lilly—I was too tired and I knew they weren't going to get it or understand it all right away.

"I'm really sorry for causing all this chaos. I didn't mean to worry you guys and have you come here, but…" I turned to Val and Jane first. "I love you guys. You're my best friends. But right now, I need to be alone. I need some space to figure a few things out in my head. I promise I'll explain everything when we get back home, but right now, I need to be alone. Please try and understand."

I wasn't sure if they understood, but they both agreed to leave only if I agreed to tell them on the plane home the next day. And so I promised them twelve long hours of uninterrupted girl talk, which seemed to make them happy.

I turned to my family now. "And I love the way you all love me so much and are always there to protect me, but…I think from now on, you won't need to come to my rescue as much." I wasn't sure if they all understood, either, but they respected my wishes, too, and left.

But not without allowing Adam to examine my head wound first. He concluded that it wasn't life-threatening and it wouldn't leave a scar. My dad and Annie hugged me and told me that they were just happy I was all right.

And then I was alone.

I was totally alone for the first time in my life.

* * *

It was my last night in Thailand, so I walked down to the beach, sat on the sand, and looked at the moon. It would always look different to me now and would always remind me of my night with Damien. I wasn't sure if that was a good or bad thing, to have a nightly reminder of him, but then again, I also didn't want to forget him, *ever*. I wondered if he was also looking at the moon right now. And in the future, no matter where he was in the world, the same moon would always link us.

I looked at the calm, pale sea; it, too, was reflecting the moon's light. And even though this was one of the most beautiful places on earth, it did nothing to alleviate the complete heartbreak that was twisting my gut into knots. I took a deep breath. It was almost painful to breathe.

A tiny white crab ran past me on the sand; it stopped and looked at me for a moment before scuttling off and disappearing into its hole. I wondered what was waiting for it in its hole: Was there a Mrs. Crab and perhaps some bouncing baby crabs?

Or maybe it was also a sad, lonely crab.

I smiled at myself. Even though my heart was broken, I'd also never felt so strong in my entire life.

Before coming on this so-called honeymoon, I was the girl who'd never eaten at a restaurant by herself, always had a boyfriend and a group of friends around her. She'd never really done anything on her own, was afraid of change, and paralyzed by the unpredictable things that didn't fit into her plan. And sex, I was afraid of that, too. But I would be returning home totally different. I'd left the old Lilly behind at Burning Moon, but I'd also left a little part of my heart there. Sigh. Maybe you can't have it all?

I wanted Damien.

I wanted him so badly, but I also knew that I didn't need him.

I would be able to live without him; I wouldn't die in his absence. It would be hard and painful and there would be a lot of tears, tissues, and ice cream, but I would eventually get over him.

But I would never forget what he'd given me.

I was awakened. Changed. New.

I felt the warm tears start running down my face again. The breeze was picking up and the temperature was starting to drop. I looked around once more and, I admit, a part of me was hoping for the big Hollywood ending, that I would turn around and see Damien somewhere, illuminated by the million-and-one candles he'd brought and lit for me.

But I knew he wasn't going to be there.

And I didn't want him to be.

I loved him, truly and unselfishly, and I didn't want him to give up his dreams for me. He was the ultimate free spirit that couldn't be tamed, and that's what made him special and unique and so, so lovable.

As much as I felt different, I was also still not the girl who could disappear for a year and leave everything behind.

No amount of Burning Moons could change that, and the same applied for Damien.

It was like he said: The timing was just off. Maybe in a year from now…who knew? But right now, there was no magical alignment.

"Hey, Lilly." I turned and Annie was standing behind me. "I know you wanted to be alone but…are you okay?"

I nodded slowly and started standing up. "Sort of. I will be. *Yes*."

She rushed over and hugged me. Hard. "We're all here for you, you know that."

I held on to her tightly and out of the corner of my eye saw the bushes shake. I glanced over at them; Jane was so tall that her entire head and shoulders were sticking out the top of them.

"I see you hiding there," I called out.

"Sorry. Sorry," she said, bursting out of the bushes with Val close behind her.

"We just couldn't sit in our rooms knowing you were here alone."

I smiled at my little group of friends.

"I'm going to be fine, guys." I turned and took one last look at the moon, before we all linked arms and walked back toward my room together.

"We love you very much, Lilly, but you really, *really* need a bath," Annie said, bumping my shoulder affectionately.

I managed a little laugh. *Yes*, I was going to be okay.

CHAPTER TWENTY-ONE

All right, so maybe I wasn't going to be okay right away. But that was to be expected. My heart was breaking.

I'd been absolutely fine on the flight back home. In fact, this new brave Lilly was totally surprising me. I'd even managed to joke and laugh with my friends and family. I'd been able to think about it all in this deep, philosophical manner in which this was nothing more than a little learning bump along this path called life.

Halfway through the flight I'd even convinced myself that this was a good thing. A wonderful opportunity for character growth—*what doesn't kill you makes you stronger*—that kind of thing. I was so sure of myself and my ability to be A-okay...That is, until the wheels of the plane touched down and I disembarked.

But as I stepped onto the tarmac, it all came crashing down around me.

Damien was on the other side of the world. We were officially on different continents, separated by thousands of cold, lonely miles. This realization first crippled me with throat-strangling panic. I couldn't breathe and wanted to run back onto the plane and demand that the pilot turn it around immediately. But even in my state I knew this was impossible, and I began to weep.

The tears started and they didn't stop, even when I finally arrived home and was deposited onto my couch. This felt so familiar. I'd been sitting here crying only a few days ago, except I had been crying over Michael. This time I sobbed and wailed and blubbered and then got stuck in a repetitive loop of self-pitying babble:

"But I love him, guys."

"I'll never love anyone like him again."

"He's the one."

"I'm never going to meet anyone like him again."

I was finally dragged to bed at some stage. Stormy-Rain sang me some kind of ancient Tibetan chant that was supposed to calm me. Strangely enough it did, and I drifted off to sleep.

The next day tragically mirrored the day before, and the night was basically another stuck record session, but this time, I'd added another phrase to my self-pitying mantra.

"We would have had such cute babies."

Somewhere between eight and nine that night, I threw myself off the couch and started frantically packing a bag for the next flight to Thailand. I had to be talked down, as if it were a hostage negotiation, and I was finally lured off the brink of insanity, back into the real world, and straight into bed.

I woke up the next morning feeling just as bad as the day before. I shuffled through to my kitchen and found my friends sitting there—this was so familiar. But this time, instead of appearing concerned, they all had another look plastered across their faces.

"What?" I asked. Their eyes were boring holes into me.

Jane jumped up and pulled a chair out. "Have a seat, Lilly." This was all so formal. I didn't like it.

"What's going on, guys?" They exchanged a series of looks, as if they were trying to decide who should speak first.

"Guys…?"

"Okay." Annie stood up and moved closer to me. "I'll do it."

"Do what?" I was so nervous now I felt sick.

"After you almost ran off to Thailand last night, we all had a long chat." She looked to the others who nodded as if they'd been told to. "And we were wondering if, *perhaps*, just maybe…" She paused and looked around. "It's not that we don't believe you, per se. We believe that *you* believe and think that…and we're not trying to say this to hurt you and undermine your feelings in any way…*Oh, shit*, I can't do this." She turned and looked at the others, and Stormy stood up.

This was bad. Stormy didn't mince words. She confused them sometimes, but they were never minced.

"What she's trying to say is that you like guys who wear ironed shirts and shiny business shoes. You like guys who carry big corporate briefcases and drive their expensive BNW's to the country club to play croquet, and eat hors d'oeuvres with their colleagues while their trophy wives stay home with John Junior the second esquire."

"Um…" I blinked at Stormy, trying to make sense of her speech.

"You do *not* like guys like that…" She pointed at Jane, who slowly turned her computer screen to me. And there he was. I almost threw myself at the screen, I was so happy to see him.

He was dressed in his signature black. His messy, slightly dirty-looking hair fell into his face, obscuring his features a little. He looked exactly the same as when I'd first seen him on the plane. My heart exploded in my chest. I reached out and ran my fingers over the photo, but Stormy smacked my hand away. Jane clicked on another photo.

In this one, he was clearly in a nightclub and had been dancing. He was standing in a crowd with his arm around Jess. His shirt was off, and he was covered in sweat and tattoos. He was smiling that dark, dangerous smile and his skin was bathed in red light—it reminded me of our last night together.

"Lilly, that man does not eat hors d'oeuvres." Stormy pointed at the screen.

The others all let out a mutual "mmmm" and did some communal nodding.

"Is it possible"—Jane leaned across the table—"that maybe the trauma of what happened to you might have skewed your judgment a little?"

"We're just trying to protect you, Lilly," Val offered.

"What?" I couldn't believe what they were saying. Were they trying to imply that what I had with Damien wasn't real? That I didn't really love him?

Stormy, less than subtle, jumped in again. "I'm sure you guys had lots of fun and adventures, and let's face it, he looks like he's an amazing shag and is totally hot in that filthy kind of way—"

"Stormy," Annie interjected. "I think what she's trying to say is that he's not your type. *At all.* Maybe this is just some kind of passing infatuation brought on by the stressful situation."

"Post-traumatic stress from being left at the altar," Jane said. "It's very common and a very real affliction."

"What are you guys saying, that I don't really love him? Because I couldn't possibly love someone that looks like that, could I?"

"Well, he doesn't exactly look like the settling-down type. And he's certainly not someone to throw your entire life away for." Annie sounded firm.

"I'm sure you think you're in love with him, but you've only known him for a few days." Val tried to reach out and touch my hand, but I pulled away. I folded my arms across my chest to stop my heart from being ripped out of it.

"You're right, guys. Everything you say is one hundred percent correct. I have only known him for a few days, we did meet after a traumatic event, and he does look dark and strange and that's why you can't imagine the two of us together. That's why you assume that what I feel might not be real. It's perfectly logical."

They nodded, looking totally relieved.

"Thank Goddess you see that." Stormy leapt across the room and hugged me.

"What a relief." Annie smiled at me. "Now you can start moving on and try and—"

I held my hand up to silence them. "But it is real. *It is real.*" My voice was steady. I felt that same strange sense of calm and strength I'd experienced on my last night in Thailand. "What Damien and I have is real. I've never loved anyone like this before, and I've never felt more changed—for the better—by anyone. Damien and Burning Moon might have been the best things that have ever happened to me, and now I have to learn to live without them."

I stood up slowly and excused myself politely. I didn't blame my friends for what they'd said. If I was in their position and Jane had run off to Malaysia and fell in love with some exotic man that looked like a Hell's Angel, trust me, I'd be the first one to try to talk her out of it (not that she ever would). So I wasn't angry with them. Instead, their concern touched me.

But they were also right. I had to move on. I had to find that inner strength and courage again, and then cling on to it for dear life. And so I did, and the days got slightly better. Some days were still totally horrific, though, and all I wanted to do was climb into bed and succumb to the searing, pulling, ripping pain of my heart breaking.

But I didn't succumb. Not once. I climbed out of bed every day, put on a brave face, and got on with it, no matter how crappy and painful it felt. But whatever I did, it always felt like there was something missing. And just when I thought I couldn't miss him, or think about him any more, he sent me a Facebook message.

I wanted to make sure you are ok? I'm thinking about you. XD

My heart instantly inflated with the greatest joy I'd ever felt, but then immediately deflated when the cold, hard reality set in. I didn't answer his message for three days. I didn't know if I should. Eventually I caved in.

We started messaging each other every few days. The messages never escalated into full-blown declarations of love or despair; we were both being cautious. But as much as I was dying to hear from him and know that he was okay, I wasn't sure if his messages were making me feel better or worse.

Despite the shaky start, my friends continued to rally around me. I tried not to drive them too mad with all the Damien this, Damien that, and Damien the next things I was spouting every few moments. But they listened and never complained. God, I have the best friends in the entire universe.

As usual my family was also supportive; my sister-in-law was still offering to sue Michael, or Damien if I wanted to. It's her solution to most things in life, and I know it comes from a good place, but it's rarely the answer. James offered to hook me up with some "awesome dudes" he knew from the gym. Stormy also offered to set me up. She was convinced that a sexy one-night fling would get Damien out of my system. She fully subscribed to the motto "The best way to get over someone is to get under someone new." But that was the last thing I wanted to do.

Even my mother seemed concerned—well, as concerned as a self-obsessed narcissist can be. And when she could see I was still struggling to cope, she insisted I go to Esmeralda or her new hypno-regression therapist, who she had recently started seeing and who had taken her through her spiritual birthing, or some such crap.

Instead, I decided to take myself to a psychologist. I knew that I needed some extra help getting over this. Friends and family were one thing, but I craved the kind of objectivity that one can only get from a stranger.

I'd never been to a psychologist before. So at four thirty on a Monday afternoon, almost one month after returning home from Thailand, I found myself sitting in the waiting room of one Kevin Stanley, MD. I didn't really know what to expect.

His waiting room was an interesting place, and if I didn't know his profession, I would have said anthropologist or archaeologist. The walls were awash with tribal masks. One item in particular caught my attention. It was a disturbing thing with slit eyes and long fang-like teeth carved out of a dark wood.

"It's a North African voodoo dancing mask," I heard a voice say.

I looked up to see a man that looked nothing like Indiana Jones, and who I assumed could only be Kevin himself.

"It's said to be a conduit that allows the spirits to journey into their ritual ceremonies."

"Mmm, interesting," I said, not meaning that in the absolute slightest.

"Would you like to come inside, Lilly?" He gestured for me to follow him.

The office was exactly what I imagined: A massive mahogany table dominated the center of the room with a chair in front of it, facing a large, comfortable-looking couch. Next to the couch stood a side table, very well prepared with a bottle of water and a giant box of tissues. But by this stage I had no more tears to cry, unless I wanted to dehydrate and shrivel down to the size of a raisin. Kevin gestured for me to sit.

An awkward silence followed. Was I supposed to talk? I didn't really know how these things worked.

Finally he saved me from the toe-curling discomfort. "Do you know why I collect masks, Lilly?" he asked in a voice that you would imagine a psychologist to have. Soft, monotone, and purposeful, as if each of his words was deliberately chosen to elicit a certain response in you, which they probably were.

"Um…" I looked at the walls and noticed that they were also covered in masks. "Because you like them?" God only knew why anyone would choose this form of decor—it certainly wasn't to set his patients at ease, because I was now face-to-face with a gold, grotesque devil bird!

He shook his head slowly and jotted something down in his notepad. I wondered what the hell he'd managed to extrapolate from that single sentence of mine.

"Because my work, Lilly, is all about masks. We all wear them, and it will be our job to find out what Lilly's mask is and to remove it, so that Lilly no longer needs to hide behind it." He smiled warmly and jotted something else down. I mentally rolled my eyes, scoffed, and snickered—what the hell had I been thinking? I hated this kind of thing, this wishy-washy stuff that could neither be quantified nor categorized. And I also hated it when people used my name too liberally. What was going to happen next? Was he going to make me lie on the couch and discuss my earliest childhood memory and my sex life—or lack thereof, which was undoubtedly where the problem lay, since I was no longer wrapped up in the arms of Damien.

"What does your mask look like, Lilly? Let's find out how we can take it off, so that we can reveal the real Lilly. So, please lie back, *Lilly*, and make *Lilly* comfortable and tell me, *Lilly*, about your first childhood memory…*Lilly, Lilly, Lilly*."

Needless to say, I never went back.

I walked out of his office that afternoon and didn't feel like going home, but I didn't feel like going anywhere else, either, so I just stood on the sidewalk for a while and watched the people go by.

I wondered how they were feeling. Happy? Miserable? Maybe some of them had just left therapists, too? Had some of them had their hearts broken, had some just gotten back from their honeymoons in love? Had some just gotten divorced?

As I watched each and every one of them walk past, some to their parked cars, some to coffee shops, and some to meetings and maybe even home—it struck me that I had to start walking, too. Really walking. I'd been showing up for life every day, but not really living it. It was time for my life to go on. I could do this. I would be okay. I would get over this and move on, even if it was one small step at a time.

So in that moment of clarity, standing there on the street corner, I picked my head up, pulled my shoulders back, and started with one foot in front of the other, albeit rather shakily. I knew what I needed to do to get on with my life. I needed to cut off all contact with Damien, because as long as the two of us were sending each other messages on Facebook and I was looking at his profile every two minutes, the longer it would take to move on. But doing this would prove even harder than leaving Thailand. It was the severing of the last cord that held us together. The messages kept me tied to him. Kept me desperately, hopelessly, and devotedly in love with the guy that was a million miles away and totally out of my reach. So that evening, after a glass of wine (or six) to calm my shaking nerves, I sent him one last message.

Dear Damien,

I hope you're having fun.

This is really hard for me to say, but I think we need to stop talking to each other. I also don't think we can be friends on Facebook anymore. So I'm going to block you. I hope you understand.

Look after yourself,

Lilly

I pressed enter and watched the message pop onto the screen with that familiar pinging noise and then I unfriended and blocked him. I sat and stared at my screen in absolute horror. There was no way of taking it back. I momentarily panicked and started pressing buttons frantically in an attempt to undo it all. But I couldn't. I had actually done it. This was not something that the old Lilly would have done, and underneath the stomach-churning pain, somewhere buried deeply under the emotional mush of my brain, I felt a little twinge of pride. I couldn't believe I had done this.

***

I never heard back from Damien again. Not once. That was it. He was officially out of my life, and now I had to systematically pick up the pieces of my shattered heart—yes, it was *that* dramatic—and try to glue or tape or sew them back together somehow, even if it was a temporary patch-up job, until I could find something that would fix it more permanently.

So I threw myself into work, I redecorated my apartment, twice, and I even joined a gym and got a personal trainer—a scary-looking bodybuilder named Leonard who was an evil torturer. I sold my engagement ring and went out with Annie and splurged on an entirely new wardrobe and then spent the rest of the day at the spa getting mud wraps.

I systematically went through all the usual breakup steps; I read self-help books about healing my heart in a matter of minutes, I watched reruns of old romantic movies and sobbed, I went on a bizarre diet of kale and cardboard soup that promised to detoxify all my trapped negativity, and finally, I cut my hair. I *really* cut it. Pixie cut it.

I cried for the first two days after doing it, wishing I could find a time machine and go back and slap sense into the *Lilly* that had walked into the hairdresser so brazenly and said, "Cut it all off. And dye it too."

But after two or three days, I started to like it. It made me feel more energetic, if that makes sense? And with this newfound energy I started doing more and more things on my own. I went to movies a few times and even sat in a restaurant and ate dinner by myself. I also started going on dates again after about six months. Well, at the time I didn't actually know it was a date, thanks to the underhanded machinations of Val. It was supposed to be a simple dinner.

Brad was his name. And he was perfect. He was a med student, and he was ridiculously good-looking—blond, green eyes, big broad shoulders, a great smile. He should have been exactly my type—but I wasn't attracted to him in the slightest. And to top it all off, he was polite and funny and really interesting and intelligent. He wasn't the problem. The problem was that clearly my taste in men had changed.

I was confused. I barely knew what I liked anymore, and I definitely had no idea what I wanted. Six months ago I'd wanted marriage and kids. But now...I wasn't sure. I went on a few dates with Brad, we ended up kissing a few times, but it was nothing like it had been with Damien. I knew I had to stop comparing, but I simply couldn't help myself. That's human nature, though—it's the way we understand everything around us, by comparing it to what we know and placing it in a little labeled compartment.

After Brad, I went on a few dates with a guy Stormy introduced me to. Maxwell. He was an intense creative type who had directed a short black-and-white film about a lonely computer who fell in love with the telephone on the desk next to him. The whole thing made no sense. He made no sense. We made no sense.

Annie forced me to go on one more date—the third time's lucky, she'd said. This time it was with her new boyfriend's best buddy. Annie had recently fallen head over heels for a man named Trevv (we all assumed it was short for Trevvor, but that was currently still unconfirmed). Trevv was rich, successful, had model good looks and the kind of face you wanted to slam into a brick wall. No one liked him, especially Stormy, who had been very vocal about it.

But it was hopeless; no matter what I did, no matter how many dates I went on, how many aerobics classes I attended, how many hours I put in at work, or how many times I cut and dyed my hair (it was now platinum blond thanks to Annie insisting it was the latest color trend), it was still the same—I missed Damien. I missed him so much that it felt like a little piece of myself was gone. We hadn't spoken for six months, and it had been excruciating.

But if I looked at it holistically, some good had come out of it. I was much more independent now, not as reliant on my friends and family for support. I often went to movies on my own and even went away for the weekend alone once. I was fending for myself in the world for the first time ever, and I wasn't doing too badly, either.

Christmas came and went and the calendar ticked over into the New Year. I'd heard that Michael had shacked up with someone else, a girl that I had gone to school with. Actually, she had been a mutual acquaintance of ours, which of course sent Stormy straight into conspiratorial mode. She was convinced they'd had a little "thing-thang" during our relationship—but then she was naturally suspicious and believed that the government was filming us and that ancient aliens walked among us. It didn't bother me in the slightest, though. In fact, I wished him well.

February approached and Valentine's Day loomed and suddenly I was staring at the one-year anniversary of my failed marriage and painful breakup with Damien. I thought that after a whole year I would be over him, or I'd have at least moved on a bit to the point that I didn't look up at the moon every night wondering where on earth he was and if he had forgotten all about me.

It was clear now—if ever I was in doubt about it—Damien was true love. He was my one.

And the closer I got to the anniversary, the worse it got, until I was seeing him everywhere: on the street, at work, in restaurants. The last straw was when the prime cut of sirloin steak I had made for myself one evening also looked like him, in the right light. He was everywhere, and I couldn't stop myself from wondering when he was coming back to South Africa. He'd said a year, and that would mean now.

And then, as if the universe had been reading my mind, I walked into a coffee shop that I'd never been in before and immediately caught sight of someone familiar. Someone I hadn't seen in a whole year.

CHAPTER TWENTY-TWO

*M*y heart jumped into my throat and then into my ears where it started beating so hard and fast that I could no longer hear the clang of spoons against coffee cups and the idle chatter of the people around me. I felt positively nauseous from the panic-ment (excitement and panic) that had just gripped me.

I scanned the room frantically, looking, hoping, praying, wanting to see Damien. But I didn't. Instead what I saw was Jess, sitting at a coffee table with her blunt bangs and faded pink T-shirt, sipping on a tall latte and eating a giant piece of red velvet cake. How was she so thin? If I ate that, Leonard would have to tie me to a treadmill, weigh me down with ten-pound weights, and beat me for the next week while I ran nonstop without sleep.

Lucky bitch.

I eyed the back of her; she had a cute star tattoo on the base of her neck, and I wanted nothing more than to go over and talk to her, but a part of me was frightened. *No, frightened* wasn't the right word. Terrified.

What if she told me that Damien was great? Happy? That he'd settled down with some hot girl and they were going at it like porn stars all night long and spending all their other moments clutching on to each other like lovesick teenagers. I felt sick just thinking about it. I was so wrapped up in this torturous whirlwind of thoughts that I suddenly realized I was standing next to her table with no idea, or vague recollection, of how I got there; my legs must have done the walking on their own accord without consulting with my brain. *Crap!*

Jess looked up from the red velvet calorie hell and a huge smile lit up her face. She put her spoon down and jumped up immediately.

"Oh my God! Lilly!" She shouted so loudly that I'm sure not only the whole restaurant heard, but the entire block, too. She hugged me hard and then pulled back and looked me up and down.

"You look amazing. Wow."

I felt slightly self-conscious and instinctively ran my hand through my new, shorter hair. "Thanks, I got my hair cut. And the color is a little weird."

Jess looked me up and down again and then shook her head. "No, it's not that at all. It's something else." She paused for a moment and I could see she was thinking. "It's your whole vibe, I can't explain it, but you just look great. Sit! Sit, babes!"

I sat down with her and realized I'd forgotten how much I liked her. She was probably one of the most straight-talking people I'd ever met. There was no bullshit with her, ever. "So how've you been? It's been a year, right?"

"Um…" I was wringing my hands under the table in a desperate attempt not to bleat out the following:

"So how's Damien? Is he seeing someone else? Is he in love? Where is

he? When is he coming home? Does he know how much I love him and want to have thousands of babies with him and change my surname to his and live happily ever after and have amazing sex all night long and spend the rest of the time cuddling? Huh? Huh? Huh?"

So I mustered all of the cool, calm nonchalance I could find and simply said, "I'm fine," but then straight afterward felt like screaming, *"NOT!"*

Miraculously, my talented attempts at feigning nonchalance didn't stop there, "Mmm, great. Yeah. Just…fine. Totally, *so* fine." I nodded and tried to smile, but failed dismally when it felt like my face was made of putty and had a mind of its own. God knows what weird expressions it was contorting into right now.

We sat in silence for a second or two, as Jess stared at me with a suspicious look plastered across her face. And then she leaned toward me, slowly and deliberately. "Okay, I'm just going to say it for you then."

"What?"

"How's Damien?" The second the words were out of her mouth my sigh of relief was audible and my whole body relaxed.

"So…" All my pseudo nonchalance had left me and I didn't care. "How is he? How's he been? What's he been doing?"

"Honestly…" She hesitated for a moment and I could see she looked very conflicted. Oh God. He'd gotten married. He was lost to me forever. "What the hell, I'm just going to tell you the truth. I'm not going to lie to you or mince my words."

My poor little heart did some funny acrobatic maneuvering in my chest before it settled into the rhythm of a galloping racehorse.

I didn't want to hear this.

"He's terrible," Jess finally said. "I haven't seen him for about four months, and truthfully I'm a little bit glad. He's so fucking miserable, he's become unbearable to be around!"

It took a second to switch gears in my brain. "Really?" The word came flying out, and I mentally kicked myself for seeming so happy and enthusiastic about his misery. "I mean, really?" I tried to sound casual this time, but the giant smile plastered across my face was not helping to convey that sentiment in the slightest.

"Yep. Since you left he's just been moping around. To be honest, I love him, to bits. He's my best friend in the world, but if I have to endure another night of 'Lilly this' and 'Lilly that' and 'Lilly the next thing,' I might beat him."

This was the best thing I'd heard in almost 356 bloody long, depressing, painful days.

"And I'm not saying this to try and make you feel bad or anything. I mean I know you've gotten on with your life and started dating again—"

I cut her off immediately. "I'm not dating anyone!"

Jess looked genuinely confused. "Really?"

"Absolutely not. What gave you that idea?" I felt angry with her for even making that assumption.

"Okay, I'll be honest again. I've been stalking you on Facebook… on Damien's behalf, though. If I don't voluntarily go to your profile and scan your wall, he steals my phone and does it himself, since you blocked him. And we saw those pictures of you with that guy, that good-looking blond one that had his arm around you. We just assumed you were a couple, you looked like one."

I mentally ran through my Facebook photo album in an attempt to figure out what she was talking about. And then I remembered it. That "surprise" blind date, when Val had taken those pictures and shouted out, in a very not-so-subtle fashion, "Put your arm around her, Brad."

I was mortified then, and I was mortified now.

"I...I wasn't dating him, well, sort of...just a little..." Great! My nervous stutter made an untimely return. "I mean, we were kind of, but...not really, we only went on a few dates, but I didn't really like him."

"Well, Damien thought you did. In fact, it couldn't have come at a worse time for him. About five months ago he was planning on coming back to South Africa and then he saw those pictures, and, well..."

I gasped. I couldn't believe it; Damien had been planning to come to South Africa. I mentally cursed Val for her new obsession with Instagram and this uncontrollable urge she now possessed to take photos of everyone and then post them on Facebook with over ten dozen hashtags.

I could only imagine what Damien must have thought when he saw those pictures, and if the roles had been reversed, I'm not sure how I would have responded.

"Why...why was he coming to South Africa?" I finally managed to ask.

I looked at Jess as she moved a piece of red velvet cake around her plate, which left a thick snaillike trail of icing behind it.

"He wanted to get you back."

"Shit!" I put my head in my hands. "But he's coming back soon, isn't he?"

Jess shook her head. "He's decided not to come back for a while."

Her words stung me. "What? Why?"

"He doesn't think he has anything to come back to at the moment.

I think that at the back of his mind he was hoping you guys would get back together."

Everyone and everything in the coffee shop disappeared. Suddenly I was in the Matrix. The world around me was now just a series of numbers and flashing green dots, blurry images, monotonous droning sounds, and slow-motion movements. I took in the full implications of those words.

Damien was not coming back to South Africa.

I would never see him again.

There was no chance for us.

It's amazing what an impact social media can have on our lives. One photo of me—taken at the wrong time, and with bad hair—goes viral for the world to see; a few innocent photos of me with some guy I didn't even like has the power to stop Damien dead in his tracks. "So where's he now?" I asked Jess while waving the waiter down. I needed cake.

"He's in Japan, but he's going to Thailand tomorrow, it's Burning Moon again."

FLICK!

The sound of a lightbulb turning on.

The sound of clarity.

Brilliant, shiny clarity.

The same kind of clarity I'd had when I decided to go on my honeymoon alone.

"Where…where is it going to be?" I was getting fired up now and got up from my chair.

"Not sure. The map hasn't gone out yet."

"How do I get a ticket?"

Jess looked at me for a moment before her face lit up. "That's a brilliant idea. Please, please save me from the torture of having a miserable best friend and, for God's sake, go and get him. *Please*. I beg you."

"I need a ticket. Can I come with you?"

"Sharon and I aren't going this year. But I can get you one." Jess jumped up and grabbed me by the shoulders. "And please, when you get there, have sex with him as soon as possible—"

"Jess!" I hissed at her, looking around to see if anyone had heard.

"Sorry," Jess said. "But I think if a man goes without sex for a whole year it makes him mad. So go and do something about it! For all of our sakes. Please."

"He hasn't been with anyone this whole time?" My heart melted at the thought.

"Not that I know of. And we tell each other everything. And I mean *everything*."

I smiled at Jess. "Fine! I'll do something about it then."

"Oohhh." She playfully slapped me on the arm. "The new and improved, nonprudish Lilly. I like it. You're a nasty girl."

And then her face changed and her expression became serious for the first time ever. I'd never seen her like this before.

"He's crazy about you, Lilly. Completely head over heels. I've known Damien since we were kids riding our bicycles up and down the street. We've been through a lot together and I know him better than anyone on this planet—and that's why I know you guys are perfect for each other. So go and get him, hot stuff!"

CHAPTER TWENTY-THREE

~

*M*y mother said something to me once. Well, she'd burbled something to me in a somewhat slurred voice with the half-closed eyes of a mad, drunken woman, while trying to pick herself up off the floor. (It was a delightful sight, which is probably why her words have stuck with me through all the years.)

"Sometimes in order to move forward, you have to go back to the beginning again." *Hiccup*

At the time I'd paid her no heed. I never did. I thought the words were nothing more than the intoxicated ramblings of my liquored-up mother, the actress who talked incessantly but never said a single thing. At the time she'd said it, I thought she was just trying to justify the fact that she was being dragged into rehab for the fifth time.

But now, holding a ticket to Thailand in my sweaty hand once again, almost a year to the day, *I got it*.

The trip had been a very easy sell to my family and friends this time—they practically pushed me onto the plane. Any reservations they had once had about my feelings for Damien were all gone. I strode into the airport feeling happier than I had in nearly twelve months, and then I stopped. There was Annie, leaning against a pillar with a massive smile on her face and a bag at her feet.

"What are you doing here?" I ran up to her.

"I'm coming with you." She smiled at me playfully. "Someone needs to make sure you don't go missing again."

I threw my arms around my cousin. I loved the idea of having company on the trip. We linked arms and walked through the airport together. It felt strange—sort of familiar and yet totally different this time. *I* was different. For starters, I wasn't wearing my pajamas, but most importantly I wasn't scared shitless that my life was falling apart and that I was alone.

I had learned that life is a game of improvisation—you have to adapt to the unforeseen circumstances and roll with the punches. But I also learned that as you go, you learn to defend yourself. Until you get stronger and faster and better.

I felt better.

I managed to get onto the plane this time without causing delays and incurring the dirty death stares of the other passengers. Bizarrely, I was sitting in almost exactly the same place as the last time. Annie was nowhere near me, as we hadn't booked tickets at the same time, but it was very comforting knowing that she was there. As I buckled up, I couldn't help myself and immediately looked up the aisle in the direction that Damien had been sitting before, on the off (far, far off) chance that fate would have brought him back to me that easily, but she hadn't.

I looked around at my fellow travelers. To my left were obvious honeymooners, desperate for a horizontal surface, or perhaps waiting for the toilet to become conveniently unoccupied. Across the aisle from me sat an angry-looking teenage girl and her tired-looking parents. In front of me sat an old couple that appeared to be in their seventies. I wondered if Damien and I would ever be like that one day.

Everyone around me was settling in nicely now as the plane reached its cruising altitude. Books were opened, iPads were turned on, and TV screens fired to life. But as they were watching their movies and reading their novels, I was playing a totally different kind of movie in my head, over and over again.

It went a little something like this.

I arrive at Burning Moon, looking gorgeous, of course, and I immediately go to find Damien, who is no doubt already settled into his favorite moon-watching spot. I walk up to him confidently and call out his name. As he turns, our eyes lock and he smiles at me—that slightly crooked, sexy, sideways naughty-boy grin that is his trademark.

He is wearing black—a faded, torn, and slightly creased T-shirt. His hair has grown a bit, and it is messy. I smile back at him, and then I run and jump into his arms. We hug and tell each other that we love each other and that we no longer want to be apart. We kiss and it is amazing. The moon slowly starts turning red in the distance and we make love, and that is it.

Simple. Damien and I would be together.

End of movie. Roll credits. Applause.

I played this through a few more times in my mind's eye, each time adding a little something extra here and there as I went. By the third rerun Damien wasn't wearing a shirt, by the fourth he was completely naked—followed by several other variations of that scenario, which I'm not sure I should share with you. Just use your imagination…it was a very long flight, okay? But somewhere around the sixth rerun I think I managed to fall asleep.

***

We arrived in Thailand safely, despite some turbulence during the landing. I looked out the window and the rain was pelting down in thick, heavy sheets and the whole world was wet and glistening. It reminded me of my first night with Damien. I had thought about that night so many times over the past year. I hadn't wanted to forget a thing about our time together, or about Damien. I'd often imagined him down to the minutest detail, the tiny scar he had on his eyebrow, the cluster of freckles that were sprinkled across his shoulders, the twirling lines of his back tattoo, and the dark depth of his inky eyes.

The plane came to a stop and I jumped up and grabbed my bags speedily this time, eager to disembark as quickly as humanly possible. My destiny was out there after all, and I needed to go find it and claim it. I glanced behind me to see Annie muscling her way down the aisle. I was so glad she was coming with me. Maybe with a little luck she might meet someone in Thailand and dump that sleazy Trevv (confirmed as an abbreviation of Trevvor, with a double *V*—even his name was irksome).

The airport was exactly as I remembered it, but this time, as I walked past the guards they smiled at me. No one pounced or took my photo or pointed or stared. I went through customs without incident, but just as I was about to exit, I heard a familiar voice call my name.

CHAPTER TWENTY-FOUR

~

Leelee." The Thai accent was unmistakable, and I knew exactly who it was the second I heard it.

"Hi!" I turned around and came face-to-face with the three smiling guards from the year before, Ang, Ginjan, and Piti. It was uncanny how all of this was playing out as if it was an exact repeat of the previous year—except this time I wasn't being dragged off in handcuffs, looking (and I suspect smelling) like a hobo.

"You come back!" Ginjan said with such enthusiasm that it seemed to be our cue to start hugging each other like long lost friends—which I guess in a way we were.

"I did," I said, half squeezed to death in Gin's surprisingly firm grip.

"And who this?" They turned and looked at Annie.

"This is my cousin, Annie."

"Annie." They all sang out simultaneously, as if she was also a long lost friend.

"*Sawadee krap*," Annie said rather clumsily, gazing down at something scribbled on her hand. But it didn't matter, because they all lit up. "I've been learning some basic phrases in the plane."

"You know, you become very famous last year after you left airport," Piti said, and they all nodded simultaneously.

"Very famous."

"Yes, your picture was everywhere, and we all say, 'We know that girl,'" Ang added.

Yes, the infamous photo had had a life of its bloody own, even after I'd returned to South Africa. For a whole month it had been plastered across every computer screen, smartphone, and tablet across the globe. From Papua New Guinea to Patagonia, I was everywhere.

"So you have boyfriend now?" Ang asked me.

I shook my head. "No."

"So you and that other guy just become friends?"

"Which other guy?"

Ang pointed in the direction of the door. "The one that was just here. The one you with last time. The thin one?"

My heart started racing—could it be true? I glanced at Annie and she looked back at me with the same startled expression that I must have had on my face.

"Damien?"

Piti nodded. "Yes. One with tattoos and dark eyes."

My adrenaline spiked and my whole body woke up instantly. "Damien was here?"

I looked in the direction that Ginjan had pointed, but I couldn't see him.

Ang nodded and looked at her watch. "Only five minutes ago. He went through customs and Ginjan and I say to each other, 'Yes, we know him.'"

"What?" My shriek startled them, and some other tourists who were standing too close, too. I grabbed onto Annie's arm and squeezed it in sheer excitement.

My new set of BFFs looked curiously at me. "This is good or bad thing?"

"It's good. Very good!" Annie said.

"I came here looking for him."

Ang, Ginjan, and Piti all looked at me with doe eyes and then said a few things to one another in Thai. Before I knew it, they'd grabbed us both and were dragging us across the airport. I slung my bag over my shoulder; this time I'd packed light.

"That line take too long. We take you straight to the front. Come, come this way."

"This is so exciting." Annie squealed as we all raced past the long line of people and went straight to the front.

We all hugged once more and just before Annie and I went through customs, Gin shouted something that made me smile then and still makes me smile to this day.

"When you get that boy, you must feed him. Too thin."

Ang nodded in agreement and added, "Too thin. Too thin. He need sandwich. Or two."

If only they knew the punch he packed underneath that shirt.

Annie and I bolted straight for the door and toward my happy ever after (hopefully).

"Hurry. Run," I screamed as Annie fell behind. Clearly adrenaline hadn't given her the gift of incredible speed, like it had given me. I imagined seeing Damien standing outside the airport in all his black, dark glory, looking as hot and mysterious and deliciously dangerous as I had remembered him every night in my dreams—God, that was a corny thing to admit. But it was true; he was an almost nightly feature in all my dreams.

I ran out of the airport and was hit by that familiar wall of sticky heat, but this time it was accompanied by rain. I didn't let it slow me down, though.

"Oh wow!" Annie puffed behind me, getting drenched. "It's boiling here, yet simultaneously wet."

I immediately scanned my surroundings: tuk-tuks, confused-looking tourists pointing at maps and trying to decipher the signs, and of course, a few more of those lovey-dovey honeymooners who didn't care if they could read the signs.

But then I saw him.

"There he is." I pointed and Annie jumped.

"Where?"

"There…black hair, black shirt, and…*Oh shit*, he's climbing into a tuk-tuk. Fuck! Run!"

And so we ran as if we were the last runners of a relay race, tasked with carrying the batons over the finish line. We almost tripped over ten people as we went, and Annie ran straight into someone's suitcase.

"He's getting away."

And that's when Annie started screaming. Loudly.

"Damien, Damien!" She shrieked like a banshee and waved her arms in the air, almost swatting a few people along the way.

I joined her. "Damien. Damien." We both yelled, but it was too late, his tuk-tuk pulled off and started making its way out into the congested road.

Now I'm sure you're all familiar with another popular theme in Hollywood movies, where someone jumps into the back of a taxi, points, and shouts, "Follow that car!" And then the driver springs into action and the car goes careering forward. Well, this was not like that.

We jumped into the nearest tuk-tuk, sopping wet, and pointed. "Follow that car."

But the driver turned around and looked at us with a decidedly confused kind of a thing happening on his face.

"Not understand."

"Follow. Go after. Chase." I could see my words were still not getting through.

Annie pulled out her phone and started pressing buttons frantically. "Google Translate, Google Translate…*aha*, got it!" She held her phone up for the driver. He read it and started nodding.

"Yes, yes," I screeched again. "Follow!"

Naively I was still expecting a speedy pull-off. But no! The tuk-tuk chugged to life and spluttered and shuddered its way into the road—and straight into bumper-to-bumper traffic.

"We're never going to catch up to him like this," I said to Annie.

"Jump." She practically pushed me out and we both started running from tuk-tuk to tuk-tuk, sticking our heads into every opening and peering inside—and causing a lot of fright as we went. But no Damien.

We finally reached the end of the line of traffic and stopped. That was it. There was nowhere else to look. Annie threw herself down on the embankment next to the road. We were both wet and out of breath, and my ribs were killing me.

"Fuck. I didn't sign up for this, Lilly." She rolled over onto her back and lay there, not caring that people were looking at her strangely. "I taste blood. I actually taste blood. Is that normal?"

I sat down next to her feeling completely disappointed. We'd been so, so close.

Now what?" Annie asked.

"I don't know."

"You know him, where would he go?"

"Backpackers lodge," I suggested.

"Which one?"

But I didn't have an answer for her, and the only thing we could do was to systematically go to all the backpackers lodges and ask for him—and so began our long, tedious, and ultimately unsuccessful hunt for Damien through the backpacking underworld of Thailand.

Let me tell you a little something about backpackers—they can easily be divided into two groups. Hippies with dreadlocks and dirty feet and young, drunk students. By the end of the day, after visiting ten lodges, Annie and I had somehow managed to drink two rounds of shots with the students, who promised to relay my message to Damien if he checked in—although I suspected that two minutes after we left they would forget. We had also reluctantly had one very small puff of weed from a hippie who had insisted that the clarity of mind the magic herb would provide would help us find Damien. (I was desperate, okay, and by that stage maybe a little tipsy, too.) But as the day went on, I started to suspect that Annie might have had more than one puff.

"This is so much fun…" She was literally skipping down the street. "I feel like a student again, except that now I can afford *not* to sleep there and I don't have to hang something on my door handle when I want to have sex in my room and I don't need to eat left-over microwave popcorn for breakfast…" She laughed loudly and abruptly stopped. "Oh my God, I am *soooo* hungry." She turned and looked at me with this goofy grin, and I couldn't help but laugh at her.

Annie had always been the truly cool one. If ever you wanted to know what you should be wearing and what bag to have on your arm, she was your go-to girl.

The sun was setting over Phuket and the streets started to buzz and hum with activity. We passed a street vendor selling various types of foods on sticks. Annie bought several of them and wolfed them down in a few bits.

"Mmmm-aaaaah," she moaned. "This is so good. You want one?" She waved a meaty stick at me, but I had far too many butterflies in my stomach to even consider eating. "Oh please don't tell Trevv I'm eating this, we're supposed to be doing some weird liquid detox together." She rolled her eyes. "Lemon juice, maple syrup, and cayenne pepper, I kid you not."

I quickly wondered if this might be a good opportunity to talk Trevv with her. As Jane says, when all of your friends don't like your boyfriend, that's got to mean something.

"So you and Trevv, hey?" I tried to sound casual.

Her face lit up. "I've been dying to tell you, but didn't know if I should…he's asked me to move in with him. And I know it's only been a few months, but it just feels right." She squealed with delight and looked so happy I suddenly felt bad. Who was I to judge after all?

"So where to now?" she asked as we wandered through the market aimlessly, looking at all the pretty, shiny things but resisting the temptation to purchase them…Well, except maybe just that one handbag and an adorable little necklace that would look great with a pair of earrings I owned. We walked farther and farther into the night and I started to wonder whether I should try to find that strip club, on the off chance that I would find him there. The chances were slim, though, probably zero. But I had no other leads and nowhere else to go until they sent the map.

But in the red-light district, everything looks the same. It's red and luminescent and the streets are lined with boys in short skirts. We must have walked around in circles for an hour before finding the club. It hadn't been an easy find, and on the way we'd been solicited by at least five men. Well, at least I knew if my current career didn't pan out, I could move to Thailand, buy a pair of Perspex heels and a short skirt, and probably make a good living.

We stood outside for a few minutes. I was too nervous to go inside. What if Damien was behind this door? And if he was, what was I going to say to him?

I'd thought about it on the plane for hours, but I still wasn't any closer to figuring it all out. How would the logistics of a relationship with him actually work? Was I going to explore the world with him? Was he going to come back to South Africa with me? A long-distance Skype relationship?

Nothing had physically changed between us since last year. I still had a life and a job back home, and Damien also had a life. And our lives were still very different.

Last year Damien had said that maybe love wasn't enough…I hoped that wasn't true anymore.

"Hey." Annie clicked her fingers in front of my face. "Stop over-thinking it, Lilly. Let's just go inside." Annie pushed the doors open, and I took a deep breath.

But Damien wasn't there. Instead some blond beefcake was thrusting his G-string bum into the air and slapping it with his hand—a sight that I wish I'd never seen. This guy was so muscular that he had nothing even vaguely resembling a neck; his head just kind of attached straight onto his shoulders. We watched on as he bumped and grinded a bit more, with the same kind of horrifying fascination you get when you drive past a car accident—until the song was over and the houselights came on.

"So *not* my type," Annie said, sounding amused. I couldn't agree more. But judging by the wads of cash being flung at him, the crowd clearly didn't seem to share our opinion.

"Oh my bejesus, well if it's not Miss Infamy herself." I looked up and saw my two old strip-club buddies, Mark and Francoise. "You look beautiful, that hair of yours! Speaking of which"—he turned his attention to Annie now—"who is this stunning redhead beside you?"

"This is my cousin, Annie." Annie extended a hand and Mark pulled her into a friendly hug.

"It's always nice to meet a fellow red…and they say blondes have more fun." He winked at her and ran his hands through his hair dramatically. "Now come. Your cousin must have a drink with us. And I won't take no for an answer."

"I can't believe I found you here," I said, sipping the champagne that had already been shoved into my paw as soon as we sat down to join them.

"Oh, this is our little tradition, we always come here before the party."

"Do you have any idea where the party is going to be this year?" Annie asked.

"Nope, we haven't received the map yet. But that's half the fun, isn't it?" He winked at her.

"So…" A conspiratorial smile swept across Mark's face and although he raised his eyebrows at me, his forehead didn't move. It remained as smooth and silky as Botoxed marble. "So…where is Damien? We were secretly hoping to see him here tonight, I mean, who can forget that little show he put on for us, and of course, who can forget your little smooch. I think every man in this club harbors a secret crush on him."

"Smooch? You didn't tell me about that." Annie nudged me.

"It was so hot." Mark jumped in. "And I said to Francoise right there and then…they are meant for each other. You can just tell."

"Mmmm." I sipped my champagne melancholically. "It didn't really work out like that."

"No, my babes, that's shit. Don't you think, Fransi?" Fransi just grunted as usual.

"That's why I'm here actually. I'm kind of here to—"

Mark cut me off as he laid a tender hand on Francoise's shoulder. "Hear that, Francoise? She's here to win him back. Isn't that the sweetest thing you've ever heard?" Another grunt from him.

"I'm hoping that I will—"

Mark cut me off again. "Find him at the party. Ahhh. So divine." Suddenly he jumped up clapping. "Well, you guys must come with us, we must all go together! We'll help you find your guy and get you there safely. It would be mad fun! Don't you think, Francoise?" He looked at his partner and, this time, I noticed a small smile quivering at the corners of Francoise's mouth. I was completely taken aback. It was somewhat disturbing actually.

"We'd love to come," I said.

"Let's drink to it then!" Again another round of expensive champagne, which I must say wasn't mixing too well with the two shots from earlier and the puff of weed that *had not* given me clarity of mind—remind me to never do that again.

"I'll drink to that," I said slightly reluctantly before we all clinked glasses. Then suddenly, and almost scarily, Francoise opened his mouth, and it looked like words were finally about to come out.

And they did.

"*Pouvons-nous dîner avant tout?*" he said in a high-pitched voice that took me by total surprise, since it completely contradicted his über-manly exterior.

"Of course, dear," Mark said to Francoise before leaning over to us and whispering, "He's French. We've been together for five years and I swear I don't understand a word he says!"

CHAPTER TWENTY-FIVE

~

*D*o you remember when cell phones first came out? How they were the size of small children and how when you needed to talk on them, you had to pull out the long antenna that could easily poke someone in the eye? Remember when texting was cool and futuristic and predictive text was new and revolutionary? Phones didn't have cameras and GPS and Facebook, and you couldn't tweet that you had just posted a picture on Instagram while tossing birds into pigs and simultaneously tracking how many steps you were taking on your pedometer app.

Soon our phones will be capable of reading our minds and sending friend requests to people we haven't even met yet. I was terribly grateful for all this technology when Mark suddenly screeched…

"The map! They've sent the map." Within seconds we were all huddled around his phone looking at the precious GPS coordinates lighting up his screen.

Mark quickly typed the coordinates in and soon a polite-sounding American lady with a soothing yet strangely commanding voice was telling us to travel north. By now I was practically bubbling over with excitement, while next to me Mark seemed to be exploding with it.

"I've always wanted to do this!" He jumped up clapping his hands and almost losing his phone in the process. "This is going to be awesies." He was still clapping so wildly that Francoise, Annie, and I felt compelled to join in, even though we had no idea to what we owed the enthusiastic clapping and jumping up and down to.

"We're going to be going on an elephant ride through the jungle and then canoeing...yay!" He shrieked even louder.

"Yay!" I joined in, too, because that really did sound exciting. I mentally chuckled as I tried to imagine what my reaction to those two things would have been this past year.

Surprisingly Francoise seemed to be quite the organizer, and in under two minutes he had hailed a taxi (a proper one, one with four wheels and real doors that opened and closed), loaded our luggage into the trunk, bought snacks and ice-cold beers, and was ushering us into the backseat while talking loudly in French.

And then we were off.

The drive out of Phuket went by in a flash of excitement, and we soon came to the great Sarasin Bridge at the northernmost tip of the island, an impressive long bridge that joined the island to the mainland. Some hours later and we arrived at our final destination, the Phang Nga province. Even though it was morning, the humidity and heat were already unbearable and we felt it the second we climbed out of the air-conditioned taxi.

"Oohhh, this is amazing," Mark said while looking around. And it was all pretty amazing. We were surrounded by an enormous lush green tropical jungle. The jungle was so dense and thick that in between the massive green foliage, everything was pitch black. Every so often the green was punctuated by a splash of red, where a large alien-looking flower peeped out from behind the thick green curtain. Huge vines hung from the branches above us and also wound themselves around and over the trees in an intricate weblike structure that seemed to cover the entire jungle.

"Your man is somewhere in there." Mark was suddenly behind me pointing into the dense bush. "Oh em gee, maybe he'll come swinging down for you from a vine, hopefully with his shirt off like Tarzan." He nudged me in the ribs. "No, I have a better idea. You should go swinging down from the tree without your top on!"

Annie laughed at this. I wasn't convinced. "Um…" I gave Mark a stern look. "There will be no swinging from vines!"

"Fine." He sighed dramatically, seemingly genuinely disappointed that I wouldn't consider some form of vine swinging. "But I hope you've planned something—some kind of big, grand gesture?"

I glanced over at Annie—she was very aware that I still hadn't come up with a plan. "Not yet," I admitted.

Mark looked at me with wide blue eyes. "Please tell me you at least know what you're going to say to him. I mean…you've come all this way, what are you going to do?"

He suddenly put his hand on his hip and flicked his hair back, I assume in an attempt to imitate me, although I don't think I've ever done that before. "Surprise, Damien, it's me!" His imitation of me was horrible, and he made me sound a little like a drunken Cher.

"I don't know what I'm going to say yet, but I'm sure it will come to me." At least I hoped to hell it would.

I think Mark must have seen the worried look on my face, because he was suddenly by my side taking my hand. "Don't worry. I'm sure it will be fine."

"Don't they say love conquers everything?" Annie said as we all started walking through the dense jungle.

"Yes it does," I said faintly, hoping with all my heart that it would be the case this time round. Love *had* to be enough this time. It had to be, because I needed Damien in my life as much as I needed air to breathe.

Being inside the jungle felt like being inside a hot, suffocating greenhouse, and I instantly broke into a sweat. We continued carefully down a small path, following some small red arrows as we went. Although I couldn't see any animals, any giant hairy spiders or whale-sized snakes, I got the distinct feeling that the jungle was alive with all sorts of creatures: hidden under the moss, disguised on the leafy floor, and concealed suspiciously behind the large leaves. I tried not to think about the TV show I suddenly remembered watching a week ago about the king cobra, which was indigenous to Thailand and had a venom that could kill a person in minutes. Instead, I focused on what I was going to say to Damien. Was I prepared to leave my life behind and travel with him? This time, a year down the line, the answer was definitely *yes!*

We soon came to a large clearing in the bush where we found a small village, made up of only a few bamboo houses. They were all very quaint and well built; some of them even balanced elegantly on stilts and one or two were actually built into the trees like a child's dream tree house, complete with rickety rope ladders. A few local village children ran around outside playing, while others busied themselves with the morning duties of washing clothes and cooking. Our arrival caught their attention, and they started calling out to us in greeting, waving and smiling as we approached, prompting a young man to appear and gesture for us to follow him. He ushered us to the back end of the buildings, where about ten other people had already gathered. My eyes immediately scanned the crowd for Damien, but he wasn't there. Some of the other people looked vaguely familiar but that didn't seem to matter at all, because within a matter of moments everyone was hugging and greeting one another like long lost friends. You really couldn't help but get caught up in the party spirit. I had felt that contagious feeling the year before, and this year was no different.

We were still talking and laughing when another man came around the corner pulling two elephants behind him. I'd never been this close to an elephant before and I was momentarily taken aback. They were incredible to behold, imposing and intimidating with their strange gray leathery skin and long trunks. But despite all this, and despite my steadily growing misgivings about riding one of these beasts through the jungle, they were, in fact, remarkably calm and surprisingly affectionate—especially after we'd fed them some lettuce.

Each elephant had a kind of box strapped onto its back, which allowed for five people to climb in quite comfortably. So my BFFs and I hopped in, together with a gorgeous—and I mean simply stunning—German woman named Friederike, whose profession could only be model or actress or Miss Universe (if that counts as a profession?). Although I've never been attracted to a woman, have never "kissed a girl and liked it," I simply couldn't help but stare at her. Women like this always make me feel self-conscious and at least two sizes bigger than I really am. But I had other things to think about right now, like holding on to the sides of this little box for dear life as the elephant stood up.

Riding an elephant is an amazing experience; you move through the world in a kind of slow, rhythmic sway. None of us said a word, and the only sound we could hear was the cracking and snapping of the jungle under the elephant's huge, deliberate feet. Our journey took us deeper and deeper still into the rainforest, crossing green rivers as we went and climbing up steep rocky slopes, until we finally stopped at a large green pool of water.

A soft, delicate mist hung over it, giving it an ethereal quality. It looked like something plucked directly from the mystical Middle-earth depicted in *Lord of the Rings*. Once we'd disembarked, we made our way to the shoreline, where a few canoes patiently waited for us.

The water was a deep emerald color, surrounded by a brilliant palette of deep greens and blacks created by huge rocky overhangs. As we rowed across the water a gentle tide softly pushed us forward, making it much easier to navigate down the winding river. But some parts of the river became so narrow, framed on both sides by large rocky cliffs, that you had to use your oar to push yourself along.

"We're almost there," Mark shouted, his voice echoing around us.

Although the last stretch was short, it felt like it took hours to get through, as we carefully wove our way through a series of dark caves and tiny tunnels carved out of the enormous limestone rocks. As we got farther into the cave's rambling maze and closer to the party, we could feel the deep bass reverberating and echoing around us.

We finally popped out on the other side of the cave and straight into a lush green paradise—a small green lagoon that was surrounded by pebbly beaches and thick jungle. Directly across from us a waterfall cascaded down into the pool, whipping the water up into a white, foamy frenzy. My eyes followed the sheet of water all the way up, but I couldn't see the source with all of that thick misty-white foam shrouding the top of the hill. On the other side of the lagoon, the music drew my eyes to the familiar sights of Burning Moon. The dance floor—a large wooden platform that seemed to be floating on the water—was already filled with gyrating bodies, all swaying together to the loud beats that were reverberating all around us. There were the usual tents that had been erected on the shoreline, and beautiful floating candles had been released into the water.

"It's amazing." Annie gasped. "It's…it's more than you described."

I smiled to myself, remembering how I'd felt last year when I'd seen the party for the first time.

But it felt completely different this year, and it wasn't just the setting.

The loud, exuberant fun of the previous year had been replaced by a slower, smoldering sexuality that could already be seen in the bodies moving together on the dance floor, driving a deep thrill up along my spine.

The closer I got to it all, the more my heart thumped, my breath quickened, and my pulse raced in anticipation of seeing Damien. I methodically scanned the surroundings as far as my eyes could see, wondering where he would have decided to settle. I skimmed straight past all the blurry faces around me and landed my gaze on a large limestone cliff dotted by some rickety-looking wooden stairs, trailing the path of a rope bridge that joined it to another, even higher cliff. My bets were that Damien was there, at the highest possible place—the best vantage point from which to admire the eclipse that attracted him to this party every year. I didn't even wait to ask anyone. My instincts just told me that I was supposed to go that way and without a second of hesitation I pulled my canoe onto the shore and ran in the direction of the cliff.

"Here." I tossed my bag over to Annie. "Please keep this for me."

"You probably won't be needing clothes anyway," Mark said with a wink.

Annie ran up and pulled me into a hug. "I love you. Go get him."

And then Francoise's mouth opened again, and it was enough to stop me dead in my tracks. "*Bonne chance*," he said. I smiled at him, feeling so touched that he'd actually spoken to me.

"Thanks everyone!" I shouted over my shoulder as I started making my way up the rickety, and in places very rotten, wooden steps. I had no idea when I set off on my journey up the cliff that it would take over an hour of steep, sweaty climbing to get to the top. God, if my instincts about this were wrong, then I would have a long, angry walk back down. By the time I reached the top, it was already early evening. The journey to get to this point from that strip club had taken almost a full day. Luckily we had all managed to get some sleep in the car or I probably wouldn't be standing. I took the last step, somewhat exhausted and stiff-legged, I immediately walked onto a road. A short distance away I could see a large SUV parked in front of an enormous Balinese-style home, perched at the top of the hill that looked over the entire bay area. The home was beautiful, a wooden deck with an infinity pool stretched out toward the edge of the cliff, and it seemed to strangely fit perfectly in this remote setting.

At this stage, I had two thoughts: The first was if there was a road and a car, why the hell had we all not just driven here? Although I guess the adventure is part of the Burning Moon experience. But driving would have brought me to Damien a whole lot faster! And

thought number two: I had just walked into the front yard of someone's private, exotic villa. Clearly I was in the wrong place and now
I was going to have to walk all that way back down in search of
Damien. This was a complete disaster, and I made a mental note
to never trust my gut again as I felt pretty close to collapsing at the
thought of the long journey ahead, and I was positively dehydrated.

To my relief, I spotted a tap next to the deck of the villa and crept
a bit closer. The deck itself was lit up with what seemed like hundreds of candles, and it was scattered with bright-pink flowers. A
makeshift bed had been made on the floor with large blankets and
pillows; next to it a bottle of champagne and two glasses were chill-
ing in an ice bucket. Someone was obviously planning on getting a
little *somethin' somethin'* tonight, and I was going to take this as my
cue to leave. But as I was about to turn around, I saw someone walk
onto the deck.

Damien.

It was Damien.

In the flesh.

Standing no more than thirty feet away from me.

Damien. Damien Bishop—*and what the hell was he doing here in
this house?*

For some reason I immediately ducked and hid behind a large
palm tree. I wasn't thinking very clearly right now. I hid and I
gawked because he was…

Gorgeous.

Amazing.

Beautiful.

More beautiful than I had pictured him over the past 350-odd
days or so. And he was shirtless. Someone should pass a law that

required him to be shirtless all the time. I also thought I spotted a few more tattoos, but at this distance I couldn't quite make them out. His hair was cut into a strange style—half of it seemed to be shaved and the other side was longer and hung in messy wisps. He was wearing a pair of black skinny jeans, which he was still buckling up as he walked out…which meant that he had been pantsless just a few moments ago, a thought that almost made me stop breathing.

By now my mouth had gone dry and my heart was thumping violently inside my skull. The anticipation and excitement I was feeling in that moment was indescribable as I watched him pick up a shirt and slip it on, his stomach muscles rippling as he pulled it over his head. He then ran his hand through his black messy hair and slid his hands into his pockets.

God, he was so fucking cool.

And hot.

But then he did something that made everything change…he bent down and started straightening the cushions and moving the flowers around.

And then it hit me—excruciatingly:

candles + flowers + bed + champagne with two glasses = Romance and Sex.

With a capital *R* and a capital *S*.

He was expecting someone. A woman. A woman that wasn't me.

CHAPTER TWENTY-SIX

I was totally, utterly, wholly, and completely embarrassed. The feeling was so intense that it made my cheeks sting and my skin crawl.

I had come all this way. I had ridden an elephant, canoed through snake-infested waters, and spent a fortune on a plane ticket to travel halfway across the world—only to find out that my feelings were clearly not reciprocated. Jess obviously didn't know Damien as well as she thought she did! Or maybe she didn't know he was seeing anyone. She hadn't seen him in four months. Maybe he'd met someone and hadn't told her yet? Whatever the reason, though, it was pretty damn obvious that Damien was with someone else. There was no other possible explanation for all this.

But embarrassment soon gave way to anger. Burning, blazing anger that could definitely kill. I was furious with Damien, with myself, with the world, and not to mention the flickering romantic candles and stupid scattered petals that seemed to be taunting me.

And finally…cue hatred. I hated him! I hated this stupid party, the fucking moon and the rotten steps that I'd just climbed, practically dislocating my gluteus maximus as I went, and I certainly hated elephants and airplanes and anything else associated with this total disaster.

Every synapse in my brain was firing on full steam, creating a horrible whirlwind of thoughts that I knew were absolutely irrational, but I just couldn't help it.

I bet he was planning a big, hot night of sex with some gorgeous, cool chick…maybe it was that German girl. Yes, she looked suspicious and positively slutty. No one can be that beautiful, it's not right, it's not natural, and it's not fair. But it looked like it was more than just sex. In fact, on closer inspection, all this romance could only have meant one thing, surely? Guys don't go to the effort of lighting hundreds of candles and laying flowers if they aren't planning something big like a…

A proposal!?

Oh my God! I'm so stupid. They're getting married and their kids will probably be supermodels. Clever, astrophysicist, supermodel children born with six-packs and great hair.

Of course he didn't love me. Of course he hadn't been curled up in the fetal position pining for me all year. He's probably been having the time of his life, shagging up a storm.

I hate him.

No, I love him.

Bastard.

God, my mind was a mess.

I needed to get away. Make a quick escape before he saw me. I didn't think I'd be able to bear the humiliation of a face-to-face confrontation, so I started inching backward—my trembling legs barely able to support my body. I'd almost made my way to the steps when something suddenly stopped me.

A thought.

I'd come all this way. I'd taken a risk, I'd been totally prepared to wear my heart on my sleeve and put myself out there in the most vulnerable way possible. And that is nothing to be embarrassed about. To walk away from this now without saying something to him...I would regret that for the rest of my life.

So, despite my screaming sinews, my churning stomach, and the loud, visceral cracking of my heart, I turned around and started walking back.

Damien was still standing on the deck fiddling with the candles in preparation for his shagathon. I had no idea what I was going to say to him. What does one say in a situation like this? It's not like there's a guidebook, a how-to manual, or *The Idiot's Guide to Confronting the Man You Just Flew Halfway Across the World to Confess Your Undying Love for When the Feelings Are Not Reciprocated*.

"Surprise, surprise, Damien." My tone was acerbic to say the least, and perhaps it wasn't the most hard-hitting opening line, but it was all I could think of.

He looked up at me.

Surprised.

God, he was gorgeous. God, I wanted to smoosh his face into something.

"Lilly...I wasn't expecting you—"

I cut him off quickly. "Of course you weren't expecting me." Sarcastic as hell. "But the question is...who were you expecting...*huh*?" The *huh* was probably a bit loud and overemphasized, and even more so when I put my hands on my hips in an aggressive and dramatic stance.

Suddenly I felt like I was channeling my mother. If I could be big and bold and dramatic right now, perhaps he wouldn't see that my heart was breaking.

I stepped up onto the deck and looked around with melodramatic disdain; I even picked up a flower for added drama before tossing it to the ground with a flurry of petals. I almost expected to hear the swell of dramatic music. I was the star of my own soap opera now.

Damien stepped forward and opened his mouth to speak. "I was actually expecting—"

But I cut him off again. "I know who you were expecting. I know all about you and your German hussy. You and your little…" I rapidly searched for an insult. "Your strudel!" (Probably not the best choice of insult, but this was no time to second-guess myself.)

"I know you're probably going to propose and get married and have gorgeous children with cute German accents and…" But as soon as those words were out of my mouth, my bravado melted away. The mere thought seemed to deplete me of the reserves needed to keep up the cool, calm, confrontational manner. The hard, sarcastic exterior had cracked…

"I can't believe how stupid I've been, Damien. I mean…" I started to pace now and my voice was probably two octaves higher than it had been before. "I mean…I flew all the way here, to the middle of the jungle, to find you and tell you, well, to tell you…" I could feel the tears starting to well up and the words get caught in my throat. "To tell you…um…to fucking tell you that I'm fucking in love with you, okay? I've been in love with you this whole time and when I saw Jess and she told me all this stuff, about you and feelings and…stuff.

I thought that there might be a chance for us, but now I can see there isn't—"

"Lilly, just wait—" Damien tried to cut me off, but I wasn't having it.

"No, you wait!" I could feel the warm tears starting to escape. "I came all this way because I thought that maybe, maybe, just maybe you were 'the one.' My soul mate or whatever you want to call it. Because even though it's been a year, I haven't been able to stop thinking about you and—"

"Lilly, stop—"

"I'm still not finished." The more he tried to cut me off, the more worked up I was getting. I think I was also half-mad and delirious from dehydration and exertion. "But it's okay, Damien. It's okay. In fact, I'm glad I've seen this. Because now I know for definite, beyond a reasonable doubt, that it's over."

"Lilly!"

"Now I can move on with my life. And maybe I'll also find someone special and get married and have kids and a dog and a house in the suburbs with roses and—"

"Lilly, for God's sake—"

"So, I wish you and your girlfriend all the best, but I'm going to—"

Damien almost jumped across the deck and then…

He kissed me.

I froze.

The kiss was firm and forceful as he gripped my face between his hands tightly. It almost hurt.

And then he pulled away and looked at me, inches away from my face.

"Lilly. Shut up. Please, please, *pretty please* zip it for just one second so that I can explain." For some reason he said that with a smile on his face, which I wasn't sure how to interpret. Was he mocking me?

"Hey." I pushed him back. "Don't you dare tell me to shut up. And how dare you kiss me like that? It's not—"

And then he did it again!

He kissed me.

But this time the kiss felt tender. His lips were soft, softer than I'd remembered them. His fingers gently stroked the side of my face, while his other hand made its way around to the small of my back. He pulled me closer and despite myself, despite everything that my brain was screaming at me, I kissed him back.

It was a kiss over three hundred days in the making and it was amazing. Soft and slow and gentle and sexy. So, so sexy.

"Lilly." His voice was breathy as he pulled away and looked me straight in the eye.

Melt.

"Lilly, this is all for you. Everything. I knew you were coming, I just wasn't expecting you to find me. I was about to come down and look for you."

"What?" I was gobsmacked. "How is that possible?"

"Do you really think Jess can keep a secret?"

"Jess told you I was coming?"

Damien smiled. "Jess is incapable of keeping anything to herself."

I still felt a little confused. Mainly due to the roller coaster of emotions I'd just endured. And then, as the shroud of confusion started to lift, I started to feel the familiar sting of embarrassment all over again. The things I'd just said. The deranged ramblings!

"So this…" I looked around the deck. "The flowers, candles, are…for me? There's no one else."

Damien nodded. "It's only you, Lilly."

"Oh crap! I'm so sorry. I didn't mean to say that stuff. Shit! I don't know what got into me, I—"

This time I allowed Damien to cut me off midsentence. "I'm in love with you. I've been in love with you from the moment I laid eyes on you with those stupid pink bunny-rabbit slippers. Lilly, you're the first thing I think about when I open my eyes in the morning and the last thing on my mind when I go to sleep."

My breath quickened and I was overwhelmed by a strange sensation. My heart was swelling to dizzying proportions inside my chest. It was like that feeling you get when you're about to cry tears of joy—that strange happy ache right where your heart is. It was just like that—only multiplied by a thousand.

"You're my one, Lilly. And I'm not, *not* going to make the mistake of letting you go again. I've booked a plane ticket back to South Africa. I'm coming home."

The sun was dipping below the horizon once again and the bright moon was starting its steady climb into the indigo sky. The purple twilight around us was tinged with a warm gold, which made Damien look softer and gentler than I'd ever seen him.

"I love you."

"I…" I tried to say it back to him, but I'd officially been reduced to a puddle of speechless emotions. So I nodded and managed a "Ditto."

Damien smiled at me, clearly amused. "Fuck, I've missed you and your silliness."

"What silliness?"

"Come on…who's this German woman I'm proposing to and having kids with?"

"Oh that." I laughed. "She's this crazy-hot woman I shared an elephant with."

"Mmm." A boyish look glinted in his eyes and the mood suddenly changed. "But definitely not as hot as you. Especially with your new hair…what color would you call it?"

I ran my fingers through my hair. "Mmm, the stylist called it rose-copper-gold, I called it a total fuckup."

Damien laughed. I had missed that laugh. I had missed the fact that someone found me so damn funny. Someone got me, 110 percent.

And then Damien's eyes darkened and his mouth curled into that crooked, mischievous smile that I'd fantasized about for a whole year.

"I think it's very cute." He let go of my face and his hands found their way under my shirt and up to my bra strap. His voice was low and dripped with the promise of sex. There was absolutely no misinterpreting the situation now. I knew what was about to happen.

I felt my bra straps loosen and then Damien pulled my shirt off.

"I've thought about this every night for the past year," he said, as my bra and shirt fell to the ground. I could feel his eyes moving over my naked breasts.

"Me too." My voice was nothing more than a tiny whisper now.

"Come." He took me by the hand and led me across the deck to the bed he'd made where he laid me down.

I looked up at the sky. It was a deep, inky purple and the stars were starting to come out in all their glory, while the moon crept higher still.

This was the perfect night.

The perfect moment.

Damien was perfect.

And I was never going to let him go again.

This was meant to be.

This was syzygy.

And those were my last thoughts as Damien pulled his shirt off and kissed me...

Turn the page to read an
excerpt from Annie's story,

ALMOST A BRIDE

Available now from Headline Eternal

PROLOGUE

D-day—A year ago

I knew something was wrong the second I walked up to my front door.

Call it intuition. Call it a sixth sense. But I just knew.

I blame the shoes. The shoes were undoubtedly the cause of all the problems that day. It was the shoes' fault that I came home early, and the shoes' fault I was fired.

I suppose I can't blame the shoes for making me late, though—that was the alarm clock's fault for rudely deciding *not* to do its job.

And when I finally realized, through the thick haze of sleepiness, that it hadn't gone off, it was too late. I was already late for work. And when I say *work*, I mean my brand-new job—job of my dreams—as a fashion assistant at *Glamorous Girl* mag. The quintessential magazine for the "fun, fierce, and fabulously stylish South African girl™."

I'd just made a total career change, leaving behind a successful job as a stylist in advertising to pursue a job in the magazine industry. It was early days, so I was still desperately trying to impress by being perfect, polite, and oh so obliging. Whether it was the request for the latte to be served at 97.7 degrees with no sugar, soy milk froth, and a sprinkling of organic cocoa powder flown in directly from the foothills of the Andes. Or whether it was for the jasmine-and-lavender-scented candles to be burned in the office for exactly ten minutes before my boss arrived—*that was me*.

Little Miss Annie Obliging.

Because let's face it, the word *assistant* is just a glammed-up euphemism for *slave*. But I was ambitious and determined, so when I realized I wouldn't be able to attend to the scented candles, or fetch the latte, I panicked. So much so, that I left the house without the said *troublemaking, life-ruining, world-annihilating* shoes.

Let's take a moment to talk about the shoes. They weren't ordinary shoes, *oh no*, they were none other than the just-off-the-Paris-catwalk-and-not-for-sale-to-mere-mortals-yet Christian Louboutins. They also happened to be the centerpieces for that day's shoot.

The same rushed panic that had caused me to forget the shoes in the first place had also left me with barely enough time to scrape my hair back into a casual bun and slip on a creased T-shirt and pair of jeans from my floor.

The latter is a bigger sin than you think. Because where I work, wearing anything other than the most fashionable apparel is sacrilege. People practically throw holy water at you and start wailing in Latin for fear that you've been possessed by the demon of bad fashion. *In fact*, a real demon possession, complete with a backward-rolling head and the ability to speak in tongues, would be preferable to the demon of last season's handbag and Crocs sandals.

So when I finally got to work, underdressed, out of breath, without the shoes, and over an hour late, I was in serious trouble.

My boss was throwing a hissy fit, due to lack of flowery scents in her office, and her personal assistant Cedric was in the throes of an overly dramatic caffeine withdrawal, due to lack of latte.

And it kept getting worse.

Two hours later the panicky fashion director summoned the Louboutins. Those shoes had been troublemakers from the start. It had been an absolute trauma getting them in the first place. They'd been flown into South Africa late the previous night, and I'd been tasked with collecting them. Everyone was holding their collective breath for the grand arrival. So when I was forced to confess to their absence…*well*, you can only imagine.

When lunch finally arrived, I jumped into my car and sped home. I had exactly one hour to get in and out before the photo shoot, more than enough time.

I pulled into my driveway at breakneck speed, ran for the front door, slipped my house keys into the lock, and turned—

But…

Something made me stop.

Something told me *not* to go inside.

Something was *very* wrong.

I looked around nervously. Everything seemed normal. Peter across the road was blasting his TV as usual, the ratbag Chihuahua from number 45 was running up and down the garden perimeter yapping at an unseen force, and Mildred, my neighbor, was outside watering her hydrangeas.

So why was I hesitating?

I took a deep breath and inched the door open.

Nothing looked out of place.

Everything was exactly the way I'd left it.

Yet *everything* felt wrong.

I slunk down the hallway toward the kitchen, where I knew I'd find the shoes perched next to the coffeepot. But once inside, I was hit by a terribly eerie sensation…*someone was in the house*. A shiver licked the length of my spine when my suspicions were confirmed.

Creeeeaaakkk…A noise was coming from my bedroom directly above me.

Shit, shit, shit, there was an intruder in the house!

I launched myself at the cutlery drawer, grabbing the largest knife I could find while simultaneously dialing the police and still managing to hold on to the shoes for dear life.

"Police! Help, there's an intruder in my house. Forty-Seven Mendelssohn Road, Oaklands. Quick."

Now what? I'd never been in a situation like this before. What was the correct protocol? Should I hide, evacuate the house, attack the intruder, scream loudly? Or perhaps a combination of the above?

I thought for a second before deciding to get the *fuck* out of there! But just as I had one foot safely installed outside the front door, I heard another noise. This time it was different. It was…

It sounded like…

My blood ran cold.

But it couldn't be. Trevv was at work. Trevv had a *very* important day in court, he told me. His client's final hearing was today. Right now, in fact. I'd called him from my office about an hour ago and he'd told me he was in court.

He was in court, dammit!

I started climbing the stairs.

More noises.

Two voices?

But that was impossible…wasn't it?

The noises grew louder and louder the farther up the stairs I went. I'm not really sure at what point I knew what the noises were or knew what I was going to see when I opened the door. But I just knew.

It's one thing walking in on your boyfriend having sex with another woman, but it's another thing entirely walking in on him the second the other woman is coming. She was facing the door but was bouncing up and down so vigorously that her face was a blur. And then suddenly her body stiffened, she threw her head back, opened her mouth, and let out a high-pitched wail. As if that wasn't self-explanatory enough, she decided to toss in a few words for good measure.

"Yes, Trevvy, yes. Oh my God, oh my God, oh Trevvy. Harder! Ah, ah, ah." *Pant, pant, pant* "I'm coming!" *Long high-pitched scream*

Now…there were several things wrong with this picture, aside from the obvious. *Firstly*, who the hell screams like that in bed? No one does! Sex is not *so* good that you have to break the sound barrier with your squealing dolphin sounds. *Secondly*, what the hell was she wearing? She was clad in some kind of leathery studded number that looked like it had been worn by one of the Village People. And to make matters worse, Trevv was blindfolded with the tie that I had bought him two Christmases ago and…*OH MY GOD*…were those, were those…*nipple clamps?*

I felt sick to my stomach.

And thirdly, who was this mystery woman without an ounce of cellulite, without the slightest smidge of fat, and with boobs that seemed to defy all known natural laws of gravity and motion? Which woman can be that damn perfect...

...and then her features came into focus and the answer dawned on me.

Tess.

Tess Blackman.

My boyfriend's work "coworker." The woman I'd invited into my home on several occasions for dinner. The woman that I always phoned when I couldn't get hold of Trevv, because I knew they were probably together working on a case, tired and exhausted and burning the midnight oil when they'd rather be at home with their significant others. She had a fiancé after all.

Poor overworked Trevv and Tess.

God, I was naive.

But the show didn't end there. Tess's eyes were still closed when Trevv started making some delightful grunting-moaning-squeaking sounds. *He'd never made sounds like that with me before.* His sweaty hands reached up and grabbed at her hungrily.

Faster.

Harder.

Loud, long moan.

I was frozen. It's hard to know what to do when you watch your partner of two years with his penis somewhere you wouldn't even like to imagine, let alone witness in full blinding daylight.

Once all their postcoital panting had tapered off, Tess opened her eyes and saw me standing in the doorway. The look on her face was indescribable. Shock and horror and fear all at the same time. And then she opened her mouth and screamed.

Trevv then turned his head toward the door and whipped off his blindfold. Our eyes locked and then he did something truly bizarre. Unexpected. He grabbed Tess by the hand and dragged her to the other side of the bed.

"Anne, please…you don't want to do this." Trevv threw his hands in the air defensively. He looked terrified. She was bleating hysterically by this stage.

What was going on? Wasn't *I* the jilted one? Wasn't *I* the one that was supposed to be upset? I started walking toward them, which seemed to only make matters worse.

"Anne, please. Please." He seemed to be begging now. "Think about what you're doing. I know this is bad, but this isn't the way to handle it. Please don't do this."

Things happened pretty quickly after that. Suddenly, the room was filled with armed police officers. I was about to tell them they could all go home, when Trevv cut me off.

"She has a knife. She's going to kill us!" he shouted, pointing at me.

What knife? I glanced at my hands, and that's when I realized I was still holding the large knife, and it was pointed in their direction.

I quickly turned to explain. "I wasn't going to—"

"Ma'am…" One of the police officers cut me off and started creeping toward me as if I was a feral pit bull that hadn't eaten in a week. "Put down your weapon."

"I swear, this isn't what you think, I was just trying to—"

BAM! Face on floor, handcuffs around wrists.

Three really painful things happened at that point: One, the knife slipped and cut the entire length of my palm. Two, some of my newly acquired, gorgeous nails broke off. And three, the crystal-encrusted, six-inch heel of the priceless Louboutin snapped off, rolled across the floor lifelessly, and disappeared under the bed. As I was being dragged out, I glanced up and saw that Trevv was clutching Tess in his arms. He gently planted a kiss on her forehead.

"It's going to be okay, baby, it's going to be okay."

ACKNOWLEDGMENTS

Firstly, to my amazing husband, Gareth, who is a creative genius and helps me come up with all my book ideas. He spent hours and HOURS helping me with this story and is just super-awesome. Without him, his input, encouragement, and endless babysitting help, Lilly and Damien would never have come to life, so thank you!

A big thanks to Jessica Smit, who was instrumental in getting *Burning Moon* going. Thanks to my cheerleaders Owen and Lance, who have been there since the beginning of *Burning Moon* and have celebrated all my achievements along the way.

I would also like to thank my agent, Erica Spellman Silverman, who took a chance on an unknown author from the other side of the world with a bad cell phone signal. I'm super-thrilled to be a part of the Forever family. Thanks to Amy Pierpont, my editor, and everyone else there for believing in the book, taking me on, and making this happen.

And lastly, to my fellow authors, regular sounding boards, rant listeners, and friends Sarah White, Avril Tremayne, Melinda di

Lorenzo, Claire Chilton, and Amber Lindley. We all started this journey together, and will hopefully continue it together for years to come.

Newly single.

Holiday of a lifetime.

Bumping into 'the ex'.

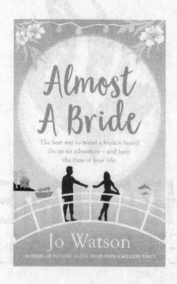

For more laugh-out-loud, swoon-worthy hijinks,
look out for Jo's next unmissable rom-com.

Available now from

HEADLINE
ETERNAL

HEADLINE
ETERNAL

FIND YOUR HEART'S DESIRE...

VISIT OUR WEBSITE: www.headlineeternal.com

FIND US ON FACEBOOK: facebook.com/eternalromance

FOLLOW US ON TWITTER: @eternal_books

EMAIL US: eternalromance@headline.co.uk